Vieques

Brian Grimm

 www.trafford.com

Chapter 1

In a rickety old guard shack outside what used to be the Vieques bombing area, a lone Puerto Rican man sat sipping his hot cup of strong coffee that he carefully prepared for himself before starting his watch. He was listening to a familiar Puerto Rican beat playing over a radio, which he had craftily secured to the counter with a wire hanger. He was drifting into a familiar daze, and was prepared to sit for hours without anything to do. His name was Hector and he had been a guard working for the Navy as a civilian contractor for the last five years.

Hector leaned over and grabbed a clip board with the day's activity and remembered that two Navy F-14's were scheduled for a live missile target run any time. He was relieved that the President of the United States cancelled his visit to this bombing range two days ago. The VIP seating to witness the live F-14 missile run would have been in Hector's area, and he was happy to get rid of the annoying Secret Service agents that had been poking around everywhere. Hector always hated when big wigs came to visit because of the disruption and extra work that was involved.

From past experience he knew that it might get awfully loud, so he reached down for his hearing protection. On his way back up, he saw what appeared to be the sun reflecting off a shiny projectile heading his way. He quickly dismissed it, thinking his eyes were playing tricks on him due to the sun's glare. He reached for his mug of coffee and took another sip. As his eyes came back up he realized that the object he saw was no mirage and was in fact heading his way.

Before he could even think to react, the missile hit his guard shack with a force greater than a freight train and then detonated, creating a fireball that rose one hundred feet into the air. Hector was killed instantly.

In the distance, an F-14 pilot nervously called in a missed firing.

"Air Hawk to base ops, the missile missed the target" the F-14 pilot announced over the radio to an operator at the Naval Station Roosevelt Roads Puerto Rico situated on the east side of the main island.

"Air Hawk repeat, did you say the missile missed the target?" questioned the operator.

"I repeat, the missile missed and landed grossly off target" announced Reaper. Reaper was the pilot's call sign, given to him by others because he was like the Grim Reaper, taking his enemies to the beyond.

"Do you have the coordinates of where it hit?" barked the operator.

"I believe it hit toward the perimeter," responded Reaper.

The Commander on watch came over and grabbed the radio from the operator and bellowed out "base ops to Air Hawk, you and your accompaniment return to base immediately!"

Reaper knew he was in for a long night of debriefing and hoped that his rogue missile did not hurt anyone on the ground. Reaper, whose real name was Jim Warden, was a family man and even though he did his job without flinching, he would never want an innocent bystander hurt or killed. He could only hope for the best as he returned to base to face the inquisition.

Chapter 2

Lying on his worn out leather couch at the Office for Domestic Readiness (ODR), a component of the U.S. Department of Homeland Security, Eric Hunter massaged his aching temples. His beating head was just a reminder of a hard night of sailing and celebrating, which was his usual Wednesday night event when in town. He was starting his Thursday morning with its customary roughness. He reached to his right and fixed what he calls a breakfast of champions: two Extra Strength Tylenol and a multivitamin.

Eric Allen Hunter was one of six Operation Specialists in charge of traveling around the globe in search of threats to the United States national security. He and his partner, Brad Spencer, are one of three two-man teams formed shortly after the Department of Homeland Security, which were created to investigate suspicious activity and neutralize any such activity before it becomes a problem. Hunter was in his early thirties, stood five foot nine inches tall and weighed around one hundred seventy five pounds, most of which was muscle. His boyish good looks proved to be a hit with women, and his adventurous stories and positive outlook made him a welcome guest at most social events.

Hunter's partner Brad Spencer was a bit shorter, topping off at 5' 6" with a stocky but not overweight build. Although Spencer had never had a problem with the ladies, he did not quite measure up to the Hunter's swaggering ease of conquest.

Spencer and Hunter first met at The Ohio State University in Columbus, OH. They entered in 1992, spent four years having a good time, and graduated in the spring of 1996. Throughout college they became close friends, and with some prodding from Hunter they both decided to apply to the U.S. Coast Guard's Officer Candidate School. After seventeen weeks of training, during the fall of 1996, they received their commissions. Since Hunter's father was a big business man in Washington and had influence, he managed, at Hunter's request, to keep the two of them stationed together.

Throughout their seven years in the Coast Guard, they shared many adventures and experiences, but saw an opportunity to get out three years ago to join the ODR. Their time together has taught them to trust each other without doubt. They often seem to know what the other will do next, which has proven to be handy on more than one occasion when one or the other has taken his exploits a little too far. They grew up on the water, shared a love of the ocean, and were avid scuba divers.

Hunter, deep in thought about one of their adventures, was startled by the ring of a telephone.

"ODR Operations Specialist Hunter speaking," he groaned over the phone.

"Hunter this is Chief of Operations Adam Reinquest."

"Hey Chief what can I do for you?"

"Gather up Spencer and meet me in my office in twenty minutes," Reinquest demanded.

"Will do Chief ... if I can find where he is hiding." replied Hunter.

"Well you better. I need the two of you in here right away." Reinquest stated then hung up the phone.

Adam Reinquest was a hard-nosed boss who did not take scuff from anyone. He retired his commission as a Coast Guard Captain to take the position as the Chief of the Office for Domestic Readiness. Hunter and Spencer both served under him during their last tour as Lieutenants aboard the USCGC Gallatin (WHEC 721) stationed in Charleston, South Carolina. Reinquest instantly saw what kind of team they would make and recruited the two of them to work for him at the ODR. If you ask him, he jokingly says it is a decision he has regretted for the last three years.

Twenty minutes later, Hunter and Spencer stumbled into Reinquest's office. The room resembled a museum. Reinquest loved to collect anything nautical; from a large wheel off an ancient sailing vessel to a 300-year-old ship's bell he keeps in the corner behind his desk. Along the walls were model sailboats and artifacts he collected during his twenty-five years of traveling the world's great oceans. It was all eloquently displayed and seemed to put newcomers in a state of awe.

"You both look and smell like crap," Reinquest said without hesitation.

"We both feel like crap," Spencer said in a smart-ass tone.

"It was sailing night last night I presume. I am sure you two have a grand story to tell about it but right now we have to get down to business."

"What do either of you know about the Vieques Island?" Reinquest asked.

"I know the Navy used half of it for bombing practice," said Hunter.

"You are correct and it has been under attack by local politicians for some time," Reinquest added. "They shut it down because they said it was polluting the environment and locals complained about the noise and long term effects on the island."

"Wasn't it being bombed when most of the people that inhabit the island decided to move there?" Spencer asked more as a comment.

"I am sure it was but you know how politics are. Some big time land developer probably wants to buy the land cheap and sell off parts to make a fortune. They get locals mad about the bombing and have a social outcry," Hunter said.

"Enough about its politics. A rogue missile went astray yesterday and I want the two of you on the next plane down there and check it out," ordered Reinquest.

"Why are we concerned with a faulty missile?" asked Spencer. "And why are they bombing on it anyway? I thought they closed it down."

"They did, but the President is trying to get it re-opened and he was suppose to be down there for the show. He would have been sitting in the blast range of the missile." Reinquest replied.

"Do you think it is foul play?" asked Hunter.

"I am not sure, but the pilot is a veteran and swears he was on target and thinks someone may have altered his missile. The plane had a full system check when it arrived home and everything seemed in order. The recorder also showed that the pilot had a lock on the right target so it has to be a problem with the missile, which is obviously in pieces and not easily examined," explained Reinquest. "I want you two to interview the pilot, check out the impact sight, and do some snooping around the hanger, asking questions and seeing what you find."

"You can count on us Chief! Two days in Puerto Rico sounds like our kind of job," Hunter said with a smile.

"Just remember you two are down there to work," Reinquest reminded them.

"Yes and we will also check out the place above and below the water to be as methodical as possible, Chief," Spencer added as he walked out.

"Remember, you two are professionals," Reinquest called after them. For some reason, he felt he had to remind them of that fact before each of their missions.

They gave him a friendly nod of compliance and continued out of the room. Hunter was already calculating their next move.

"Lets go talk to Marty and see what he has for us," Hunter said to Spencer as they walked from Reinquest's office.

Marty Landover was the main logistical force behind the whole operation. The agents often said, "Marty can get you anything from a rental car to a space shuttle ride to get you where you need to go." He was recruited after he took an early retirement from the CIA. No one really knew why Marty left the CIA. He doesn't like to talk about it. When asked directly, he just says he's a lot happier now.

Hunter and Spencer entered Marty's office to find him eating a McDonald's breakfast sandwich. Marty was a stout fellow to say the least, weighing 250 pounds at 5 foot seven inches. He barely fit into his chair.

"What do you have for us, Marty?" Hunter asked as soon as he saw him.

"Eric and Brad -- good to see you two!" Marty said as they walked in. "I have two first class tickets on American Airlines flight 1054 leaving out of Dulles Airport in two hours." He handed them the tickets with a smile.

"How did you get the old man to go for first class?" Hunter asked, referring to Reinquest.

"I have my methods."

"Can I bring you back some rum for you efforts?" asked Hunter.

"You know I don't drink rum. But how about a hat?" asked Marty.

"A hat it is. I could bring you a hat and some Don Q." Hunter replied.

"The hat will be fine." Marty remarked.

Eric Hunter was an avid rum and Coke drinker and his favorite brand of rum was Don Q Gold. To his way of thinking, the best way to live is to drink rum and listen to Jimmy Buffet. If you let him, he will try to push his way of life on you any chance he can get.

The two took the tickets and itinerary from Marty and walked out, waving good-by. They proceeded to their own offices to gather up the required clothing and supplies for the trip.

Having been with the organization since it started three years ago, they were both used to the idea that they may have to leave at a moments notice. For this reason, they keep a supply of clothes at the office. They also keep an ample amount of equipment, including their precious scuba gear. They gathered up items needed for the trip and met down in the lobby. Marty had already located a cab, which was waiting at the building's entrance.

"Good old Marty." Spencer said when he saw the cab idling outside.

"Brad, Let's get this show on the road." Hunter shouted as he handed the cab driver his bags.

Chapter 3

Due to the lower amount of traffic in the middle of the day, they arrived at the airport in record time. Spencer thanked the cab driver and threw him an extra ten dollars as Hunter grabbed the bags and lined them up on the sidewalk. Each of them picked up their bags and rolled them toward the entrance of Dulles Airport. The airport, located on the west side of Washington DC, is a little over ten miles outside of the beltway. It is not the most ideal airport for them but it contains the most direct flights in the District.

After the usual adventure through airport security they arrived at their intended gate. Brad looked down at his pass and noticed they would be traveling to Puerto Rico in style aboard a Boeing 757.

"We are really going to have to get Marty a great gift for these seats." Brad commented to Hunter.

"You can always trust Marty to send us away in style." Hunter replied.

After a short wait, the airline announced the boarding of First Class passengers.

"I do believe they mean us." Brad said as if mocking the other travelers.

They boarded the plane and took their seats. Within minutes, a flight attendant approached them.

"Can I get either of you anything before we take off," she asked.

"Do you have Don Q rum on board?" asked Hunter.

"Sorry, Sir, we only have Bacardi."

"We will take two Bacardi and Cokes," Hunter responded before Brad could say anything.

She returned with their order.

"Here are your rum and Cokes sir," the flight attendant stated while she handed them their drinks. "Is their any thing else I can get you?"

"Not right now but after take off I am sure we could use another round." Brad Spencer stated.

"Do you think we should drink on the clock?" Spencer joked as he took his first sip.

"Did you book a dive with the Fajardo dive shop for tomorrow morning?" Hunter asked.

"It's all taken care of. We meet the dive company at 8:30 in front of the dive boat. They will have tanks and weights on board," said Brad with a smile.

Just then a woman in her mid to late twenties entered the plane.

"You almost missed the flight," stated the flight attendant.

She was lugging around a lot of equipment and it was clear to all but her that there was not going to be enough room in the overhead bins.

"Ma'am, I am going to have to check your largest bag before you go back to your seat," suggested the flight attendant hoping not to have conflict about the item.

"That will be fine just do it and let's getting going," replied the young woman obviously having a rough day.

As the flight attendant checked her bags, Hunter noticed she was agitated and not at ease.

"Don't like flying?" he asked.

"No, I am just flustered from almost missing this flight."

"Well you are here now and I am sure the rest of your journey will go much better," offered Hunter.

"Yes, I believe it will, thank you," she replied.

As she finished her words, the pilot announced over the intercom that flight attendants should prepare for departure. The young woman turned and headed for her seat, breaking off their conversation.

"I am going to have to catch up with her later," Hunter said, turning to Brad.

"I don't know Eric, she seems like a handful," he replied.

"Aw, don't be so judgmental, she's just having a bad day." Hunter responded.

He turned and focused on the flight attendant while she gave the standard pre flight debriefing and checked the seat back for the card that displays the exits and checked for the nearest one. After putting the card back into the seat back pocket he leaned back to relax.

The rest of the flight went as usual and they arrived in San Juan around noon. They were the first to get off the plane and head to baggage claim. Hunter had hoped to catch up with the young lady, but in the confusion he lost track of her. He was intrigued by this mysterious young woman and would of liked to get to know her better but in his true fashion he would shake off the encounter soon.

After a brief delay at baggage claim, Hunter and Spencer gathered their belongings and headed toward the exit. They stopped briefly while the exit attendant checked their baggage slips and then exited toward the bus pick up area. Spencer spotted the Charlie's Rental pick up van and motioned for Hunter to head in that direction.

They boarded the bus and put their bags on the baggage shelf.

"You are renting a car, Senors?" the driver asked, making sure they were on the right bus.

"Yes, we already have a reservation," Hunter replied.

"Gracias senor. I am waiting on one more customer and then we can leave."

They gave him a nod and took their seats. Before long the other customer showed and they were off. After a short ride they arrived on the lot. When the doors opened they gathered their belongings and headed for the main desk.

"What is your name sir?" The attendant asked.

"I believe the reservation is under Office of Domestic Readiness. But if not try Eric Hunter or Brad Spencer," Hunter replied.

After a few minutes of checking the attendant found the reservation.

"Si, it is under your name, Mr. Hunter," he replied.

They finished the paper work, gathered their bags, and headed toward the rental car. The attendant did a brief inspection, noting the imperfections, and then handed Hunter a slip to sign verifying that it was accurate.

"Thank you, sir," he said as he handed them the keys and headed back toward the office.

"I am not totally impressed with the car," Brad said about the average looking mid size. "I thought Marty would have hooked us up with a Ferrari after the streak he has been on."

"Brad, all I know is it will get us there. And best of all it has enough room for all our gear. You can't do that in a Ferrari," Hunter pointed out.

"That's true but I am sure we would of found a way to make it work." he replied.

They loaded up the car and headed east for the Roosevelt Roads Naval Base.

Chapter 4

It was not yet rush hour so the drive from the airport took a little over two hours. Driving in Puerto Rico is not as easy as driving in the states and the amount of red lights on the road to Roosevelt Roads can drive a person crazy. Despite the conditions they arrived safely at the base's front gate.

"How can I help you two gentleman?" asked the gate guard.

"We are from the Office for Domestic Readiness a branch of the Homeland Security Department," answered Spencer.

"Oh, you guys. I have been told to expect you. Can I see your identification and your rental car agreement so I can give you a car pass and security badges?"

"Here you go sir," Spencer said handing him the information.

The guard briefly went into his shack and returned with the proper passes. "You two need to go straight until this loops around and look for the airport. Go to Hanger Four and I will let them know you are coming."

"Thank you Petty Officer Barns and have a great day," Spencer said as they pulled away. Since the Navy used the same ranks as the Coast Guard, Spencer had no problem using the proper greetings.

After following the guard's directions they arrived at the hanger. As they were getting out of the car, a navy Lieutenant approached to greet them.

"Welcome Mr. Hunter and Mr. Spencer. My name is Lieutenant Don Hernandez and I will be your liaison," he said.

"Sir, how was your trip?" the Lieutenant asked Hunter.

"Pretty good but we are both ex-Lieutenants from the Coast Guard so please call me Hunter and this is Brad Spencer," replied Hunter.

"No problem and feel free to call me Don."

"Will do, Don." Hunter replied.

"Right this way please. They are all waiting for us."

The two of them followed Don into the hanger, where Captain John Harkin, the commanding officer of the air station, greeted them. "How were your travels?" asked Harkin.

"Fine just enjoying this fine Puerto Rican humidity," Spencer stated with a sarcastic grin.

Harkin ignored the comment and continued, "There is a helicopter standing by to take the two of you straight to the crash site. I am sending Lieutenant Hernandez with you and he will assist you any way he can. Also you are going to be joined by Doctor Amy Evans, who is a forensic expert sent down by the FBI to assist you with this investigation."

Just as Harkin was finishing his speech Amy peered from the women's restroom located at the end of the hanger. Amy Evans, a half Puerto Rican half German beauty, has been working for the FBI in forensics for about five years. Standing at five foot four inches tall, she strutted a body that drives men crazy. Because of her looks she has never had a problem getting dates, but because she prefers work to any thing else she rarely goes on them. This was to be her first solo mission. She was partly chosen for this mission because of her Spanish speaking skills but if you ask any of her superiors she has definitely earned this assignment. She was born in Puerto Rico but her parents moved to Orlando Florida when she was three.

Hunter recognized her right away as the young woman from the plane and was glad he had another chance to make her acquaintance.

"My name is Eric Hunter and this is my partner Brad Spencer," he stated as she approached.

"My name is Amy Evans and didn't I see you on the flight over here?" Amy asked.

"Yes ma'am. We talked briefly but as I recall you where not very receptive to conversation."

"Sorry about that. I needed rest," responded Amy.

"That's OK you can make it up by joining me for dinner tonight after this event," Hunter said as he glanced into her eyes.

"If we have time," she replied.

"OK everyone this way. The Helicopter is warming up to take you to the site," interjected Captain Harkin.

Hunter, Spencer, Amy, and Lieutenant Hernandez all boarded the helicopter. Lieutenant Hernandez grabbed the closest headset and gave the command for the pilot to take off. Hunter and Spencer noticed right away that the helicopter was a modified Black Hawk that had missile-launching capabilities. They thought this was fascinating because neither had seen one modified in this fashion.

Hunter, being a fixed wing pilot himself, always loved the opportunity to fly. He holds the experience as high as his love of scuba diving and sailing.

As they left the main land not many words were spoken. Instead they all looked out toward the beauty and the wide variety of images the east coast of Puerto Rico had to offer. Hunter thought that from the air the Puerto Rican coast looked like the Caribbean paradise that is shown in brochures. The island of Vieques was just a few miles away and its outline became visible shortly after take off. Within minutes they approached the island. Lieutenant Hernandez gave the pilot a signal to circle the island before landing so they could assess the situation and so everyone could have a full view of its beauty.

As they circled, Hunter noticed a small recreation boat at the military dock close to the missile crash site. He pointed it out to Spencer who in turn gave the thumbs up signaling they would check it out later.

"It is probably just a pleasure boater in the wrong place but we'll still check it out," he said loud enough for only Brad to hear.

"They probably docked up to ask for directions from the security gate, or it may be one of the off-duty guards boat tied up to talk to one of his buddies," he thought to himself.

"We are going to set down on the helo pad and a Jeep will take us to the crash site," yelled Hernandez over the sound of the rotors.

The helicopter set down and Hernandez told the pilot to return in three hours. The helicopter was diverted from a practice operation that it was supposed to perform with a nearby Coast Guard Cutter. This helicopter was scheduled to practice raising and lowering its basket containing a mannequin to simulate rescuing survivors off a sinking boat. This training was part of many joint operations between the Coast Guard and Navy to ensure a better response time and increase the likelihood of being rescued in this area.

The Helicopter set down as promised and the guests disembarked. As soon as everyone was clear the helicopter pilot took off, heading toward the rendezvous point with the Coast Guard Cutter.

"That is odd," the Lieutenant, said, "I wonder where the Jeep and driver are?"

"What's the problem?" Hunter asked, as he approached Hernandez.

"Not a major deal, but before we left the Captain had called for a Jeep and driver to be standing by," stated Hernandez. "It is not like the Marines to be late, given the serious trouble they could get into for disobeying the Captain's orders."

"How far is the site from here?" asked Spencer.

"Just under a mile," answered Hernandez.

"Well if no one is opposed I say we hike to the site. Mrs. Evans, what gear would you like me to carry?" asked Spencer.

"It is Miss Evans, and if you are so eager to go for a walk you can carry those two cases over there." She said pointing to a couple of large pieces.

"Hunter, how about some help over here?" asked Spencer.

"Sorry my friend you are on your own. I will have my hands full carrying our supplies." he responded.

The four of them hiked for about 20 minutes on the main dirt road until they came to a crossing that veered off to the right.

"We go right here for a quarter of a mile," said Hernandez.

"If you look through those trees you can see the guard shack." He continued, pointing to its location.

"I don't like how this looks, let's stop here for a moment while I get out some supplies," whispered Hunter.

He set down his backpack and pulled out two shoulder harnesses with nine-millimeter Beretta handguns. He quietly loaded the first, put it in its holster and handed it to Spencer along with two additional fifteen round magazines. Next he slowly loaded the other gun trying not to make excess noise, put it in its holster, and put his shoulder holster on. He took out two more magazines and put them in his pocket. Finally he grabbed a third nine-millimeter handgun already in an ankle harness and offered it to Hernandez.

"Would you like to arm yourself Lieutenant? I have a feeling it may get rough up there," he softly asked.

"Sorry but I don't have anymore shoulder harnesses." He stated as he handed him the gun.

"The weapon will do fine. You're right -- things don't seem to be in order," Hernandez whispered back.

Hunter handed Hernandez the weapon and their last two magazines, got up, and put on his backpack.

"Do you really think all this is necessary?" Amy quietly whispered in Hunter's ear.

"Well here are the facts. I don't see any gate guards, we were not picked up by the Jeep, and I saw a mysterious boat docked at the pier when we circled the island. I would say something is not right," Hunter said, speaking as quietly as possible.

"Ok, Lieutenant I want you and Miss Evans to go over there and wait. If you hear the signal I want you to go for help," Hunter ordered as he pointed to the right of the path.

"What will be the signal?" Hernandez asked.

"When you hear a lot of shouting and guns being fired," replied Brad.

Hernandez and Amy did as they were told and waited in the trees just outside the guard shack while Hunter and Spencer went in for a closer look. As they approached the guard shack they did not notice any movement. They crept in through the woods keeping a low profile and moved in on the shack. When they arrived, they saw what appeared to be a foot to the right of the guard shack.

Hunter motioned for Spencer to head toward it and that he would cover him. Spencer moved closer, trying not to make a sound. He had his pistol ready, awaiting anything that might jump out at him. He nervously approached and noticed that there was a man laying face down in the mud beside a barrier of sand bags. He motioned for Hunter to move up and join his position. He then proceeded to peer over the sandbag wall. He slowly put his head over the wall with his gun ready. He saw something jump his way. He pulled the trigger and got off a shot at the approaching attacker. Just then Hunter came from behind and grabbed the weapon.

"Hold on there Wyatt Earp, it's just an iguana," he said to a rattled Spencer.

"I think they are already gone and from the looks of it they took whatever evidence they could find in regards to the missile. These guys weren't as lucky as us. Most likely they got ambushed," Hunter said as he looked down at what appeared to be the four dead Marines that had been assigned to guard the area.

"Who do you think did this?" asked Spencer.

"I don't know but I am bound to find out," Hunter said, as he motioned for the other two to join them.

"Spencer and I are going to go to the docks and see what we can find. I want the two of you to stay here and call for back up. Miss Evans, will you please start a forensic examination of the area? Look for anything they have not taken," requested Hunter. "Hernandez did you bring a radio with you?"

"No, I didn't think it would be necessary. But I could try and call base on my cell phone."

"Good luck, but I already tried and mine does not have service. I knew when I forgot to bring my satellite phone it would bite me in the ass," said Hunter.

Before leaving Hunter turned toward Amy and as he looked into her eyes he said, "I am sorry Miss Evans we may have to postpone our date for this evening."

"I will forgive you this one time," she responded, mesmerized by his gaze.

Without another word he turned around to join Spencer, who was already heading toward the docks. The two ran at a quick pace and since it was only a half-mile away they made it there in less than five minutes. Spencer pointed toward the dock, signaling that the pleasure craft they saw earlier was missing.

"Quick – let's check the small Navy assault craft at the dock and see if it is operational," Spencer said as he headed toward the boat.

"It looks like they where in too big a hurry and did not get a chance to scuttle it. I think I can hot wire it and get it started."

Spencer jumped on the boat and went directly for the starter wires. Hunter decided to take a look around before he lent his friend a hand. He started opening compartments, looking for anything that could help them.

"Hey Brad why don't we just use the keys?" he said as he opened a small compartment next to the steering wheel.

"Keys! That's a new concept. Ok let's go. Not a moment to waste," Spencer stated, trying to cover up his blunder.

A turn of the key later and the engines roared to life. For a brief second Spencer thought how he enjoyed the military's love for power. As soon as Hunter threw off the lines he pushed down the throttles. The two 225 HP engines took off like a rocket and they were soon accelerating to an alarming speed.

Hunter saw a boat nearby that appeared to be racing away from them. He picked up the binoculars to get a better look. "I think that is the boat we are looking for, Brad. I don't think they got much of a head start so we may be able to catch them. Start heading toward them so we can get a better look."

The military boat with its twin 225 HP engines was faster than the single engine pleasure craft it was pursuing. As they got closer, Hunter could see four men dressed in black, all brandishing AK-47's and some kind of side arm.

"They are pretty well armed. It appears there are four of them with AK-47's and side arms," yelled Hunter over the engines. "I am going to look around for weapons aboard this boat, why don't you call the Coast Guard and see if anyone is in our vicinity that can help."

"Will do," stated Spencer and then turned on the VHF radio to the Coast Guard working channel of 22A.

Hunter went into the small cuddy cabin to check for weapons. He didn't see anything they could use, so they'd have to rely on the side arms they had brought. Their weapons were no match for the enemy's but Hunter hoped they could hold off the opposition long enough for the Coast Guard and Navy to arrive.

As soon as Spencer finished giving his location to the Coast Guard, he looked up and noticed something stirring on the other boat. "Hunter get up here!" he yelled with all his strength. "I think we are in for a rough ride."

Hunter poked his head up to check what all the excitement was about. As he looked up he saw one of the men on the other boat pull out a rocket launcher and prepare to fire it.

"Evasive maneuvers," spouted out Hunter.

"I thought I would just stay in the rocket's way," Spencer said, more than slightly shaken from this development.

"This is just like when we were in the Coast Guard on that drug operation outside of Haiti when you almost got us killed," said Hunter.

"You are going to bring that up in a time like this," Spencer bantered back.

"Turn now!" Hunter shouted.

Spencer turned just as a rocket flew by, missing the two of them by a matter of inches. Spencer knew they would not survive another launch, so he gunned the accelerators and went straight for the other boat. Hunter knew exactly what he meant to do without even asking. They have been on so many adventures together that their combined instincts were taking over.

Spencer rammed into the side of the other boat, knocking the assailants off their feet and rattling the crew for a few seconds, just long enough for Spencer to turn a hard left and attempt an escape.

"Down!" Hunter screamed as he pulled Spencer to the deck

trying to avoid the on coming bullet barrage. All four of the men opened fire.

"Maybe this was not such a good idea after all," Spencer said as the bullets riddled their boat.

"I agree, buddy, but I don't think we had another choice," said Hunter.

"I am hit!" Spencer cried as a bullet stuck him.

"Let me see were it got you," Hunter ordered.

Hunter did a quick inspection and saw the bullet had grazed the right side of Brad's rear end.

"It just nicked your ass. Don't be so dramatic, you Nancy," Hunter said, trying to lessen the situation.

"It hurts, it really hurts," screamed Spencer.

"It will hurt a lot more if we don't get out of this mess," screamed Hunter.

"I've had enough of this, it is time for us to fight back," Hunter said as he grabbed his firearm.

He waited for the men in the boat to reload and then took aim. He knew he had only a couple of seconds while they reloaded. He got off two shots and then took cover. They were still close enough for his aim to be semi accurate. The first shot hit one of the men in the leg, knocking him to the ground. The second shot hit another in the shoulder. Unfortunately they would soon regroup and at best this was just enough to slow them down.

It did give Spencer a window of opportunity to reach up and throw the throttles forward to full speed. He wanted to make the most of Hunter's efforts.

The engines started to drive forward as the other boat began to fire. Before they could get far, machine gun bullets hit their engines with deadly accuracy, taking out one engine and leaving the other smoking and barely holding on.

"I think my plan to out run them might have just fallen apart," Spencer screamed over the sound of bullets.

To make matters worse, the men on the other boat were positioning the rocket launcher for another attempt. Hunter, noticing that they had stopped firing, peered his head up to get a better look. At the same time the second engine began to sputter and then died, leaving them floating like sitting ducks.

"I don't want to be the bearer of bad news but they are getting ready to fire another rocket," he yelled.

"We need to jump for it!" he continued.

Even though they both knew that jumping at this point would probably only give them a slim chance of survival they rose up and prepared for disembarking. This plan became futile quickly. The other boat began to fire and pinned them down making escape impossible.

"It looks like this may be the end. Sorry about making fun of your ass wound," Hunter apologized.

"Don't worry. Soon that will be the least of our worries," replied Brad, trying to make light of the situation.

The other boat got into position and prepared to fire the rocket. Spencer and Hunter looked at each other for the last time as they heard the sound of the rocket being launched.

This time the rocket hit its target. Killing everyone onboard the vessel. The impact split the boat in two quickly sinking it to the bottom.

After the blast everything went silent and for a moment only a distant sound of a helicopter could be heard.

"Are we dead?" Spencer asked.

"No but we should be," replied Hunter.

"What happened?" Spencer asked.

"I don't know. Maybe their rocket exploded before it launched," Hunter replied.

He got up to look around while Brad laid back trying to gather his thoughts. Still dazed, it took a few minutes for him to assess the situation.

"Well the radio is out, both engines are caput, and I think we may be taking on water," Hunter stated.

"The good news is the other boat must have sunk to the bottom because all I see is some floating debris," he continued

The sound of the helicopter was getting louder, so he turned to see if it was heading their way. "I think the same helicopter that dropped us off is heading toward us!" he said.

"We may get out of this one yet," Brad said, getting up to check for himself.

Within minutes, the helicopter was overhead. Hunter pointed at the radio and tried to signal to pilot that they had no means of communication.

After a few minutes the pilot picked up on his signal and decided to use another method to communicate. "Are you OK?" The helicopter pilot broadcasted over the crafts external speaker.

Spencer and Hunter waved with rather large smiles on their faces.

"I guess it was not our time after all," Brad said as they continue waving.

"The Coast Guard Cutter Cushing is on its way to assist you and should be here in about 20 minutes. Continue to wave your arms if you can hold out that long," announced the pilot.

They both waved back, just happy to be alive.

Chapter 5

Sitting in the Oval Office, President John Bushard contemplated the news of the rogue missile incident. He realized that he might not be here right now if his visit had not been cancelled. Originally, he had been quite upset that talks about re-opening the bombing site had broken down. Under the circumstances, he now felt very fortunate to be alive.

The President, being a religious man, had vowed to put an end to stem cell research. It was one of the hot ticket items that helped him to get elected and since he wanted another four years, he was not about to change his mind. President Bushard also had a strict policy on terrorism and went after any country he believed harbored the activity.

On the other side of the spectrum was his Vice President, Mike Rivers. The rumor around Washington was that he believed in the research and would allow it to continue if he were President. He had a live and let live policy about the dealings in the Middle East and many believed if he where President he would pull the troops out of the entire region.

It was believed by some that the missile was no accident and was in fact a failed attempt on the President's life. To many it proved that some people were more than willing to find out what the White House would be like with the Vice President in charge.

As the President was contemplating all this, Bob Renousky, his Chief of Staff, entered the room.

"Mr. President there has been an incident off of the Island of Vieques. The crew that was sent down to investigate the missile crash was attacked by what they believe to be a terrorist faction. The terrorists had recovered the missile fragments and were making their escape. Two men from the ODR gave chase and were almost destroyed by the terrorists when at the last minute one of our Navy helicopters fired a missile and took the terrorist boat down."

"Did we experience any further losses?" asked the President.

"Four Marines standing guard on the crash site, sir. From the looks of things they were ambushed by the terrorists," Renousky stated gravely.

"How about the two Homeland Security guys from the ODR?" The President asked.

"One received a flesh wound from a stray bullet and the other only minor scrapes and bruises," Renousky continued. "They plan on diving the wreckage within the hour. I will keep you posted on everything I find out.

"I want you to take charge of this incident personally, Bob. Someone or group made an attempt to end my life and we must find out who and why before they try again."

"Sir I will make this my top priority," Renousky vowed.

"I know I can count on you," replied the President.

As Bob was leaving the President's office, it struck him how important his new mission was to the United States. If he failed and the President was killed it would be a major blow to the confidence of this great country. He was determined to find out who was behind this and bring them to justice.

Chapter 6

As promised, The Coast Guard Cutter Cushing arrived within the next twenty minutes to assist them. Hunter and Spencer gave a big wave to assure them they were still all right.

The Cutter had to distance themselves from the wounded vessel in order to launch Cush 1 and retrieve them. Cush 1 was a twenty-eight foot boat with inflatable sides and a hard bottom. It was predominately used by the Cutter Cushing for rescues and to board other vessels during law enforcement operations.

As Hunter and Spencer watched the boat being lowered, it brought back fond memories of their time in the Coast Guard. They had seen this evolution many times but this was their first time seeing it through the eyes of the person being rescued.

The launch process did not take long. Within minutes, a group of Coast Guardsmen were heading their way. Cush 1 pulled alongside the wounded boat to render assistance.

"Good of you guys to come over and give us a lift," Hunter stated with a smile.

"No problem sir. I'm just glad we found you in one piece," said Boatswain Mate First Class Carpenter. BM1 Carpenter was a veteran Coast Guardsman with twenty years in the Guard. He lived for action and loved his work.

"Thank you Petty Officer Carpenter, please come aboard. My name is Eric Hunter and this is my partner Brad Spencer."

"Nice to meet you sir," replied Carpenter.

"I brought our EMT to check out the two of you before we transport you to the main ship." he said.

"You can check out the ass wound on my friend here, but watch yourself, he is very sensitive." Hunter said, trying to get a rise out of Spencer.

"Very funny. Don't listen to him. I am fine. We just need a lift back to the Navy base so we can get our dive gear," replied Spencer.

"You guys plan on diving the wreckage?" asked Carpenter.

"Of course. We want to know who was behind all this and look for other information that may help. Plus we would never miss a chance to be the first to dive a new wreck," said Hunter.

"I am sure that is something you need to discuss with the Captain," said Carpenter, not playing along with his game.

"Is your boat stable enough to be towed back to Vieques?" he asked.

"I believe so. They shot mostly above the water line so she looks bad but she will float," said Spencer.

"All right sirs, if you will get on our boat I will leave two of my guys on yours and prepare her to be taken in tow," Carpenter said, with a part asking and part ordering tone in his voice.

"Sounds like a good idea to me," Brad replied as he hopped aboard.

Hunter and Spencer boarded the small Coast Guard boat and headed for the main ship. Once they arrived, Petty Officer Carpenter motioned for them to climb up the Jacobs's ladder and board the vessel. Upon reaching the main deck, they were greeted by Lieutenant Harry Norman, the Captain of the Cushing.

The Coast Guard Cutter Cushing was one of six Island Class Coast Guard Cutters stationed in San Juan, Puerto Rico. It was originally stationed in Mobile Alabama but was moved in 1996 because the President at the time wanted to crack down on drugs. It was 110 feet long and it had a crew of seventeen. Its main jobs were drug interdiction, migrant interception, and search and rescue. It was a fast ship that could reach speeds of thirty-two knots in many sea conditions.

"Welcome aboard, gentlemen. My name it Lieutenant Harry Norman and I'm the Captain of this vessel."

"My name is Brad Spencer and this is my partner in crime Eric Hunter."

"You are the two from the ODR?" Norman asked.

"I didn't know we were famous, but yes that is us," Hunter said.

"I read an inter Coast Guard message about the missile event and remember your names being mentioned. It stuck out in my head because I did not expect them to send anyone from your department to investigate something as simple as a missile accident. It didn't appear to be a matter of National Security but it looks like maybe I was wrong," Norman continued.

"Well Captain, I didn't think much of it either but I must tell you I have changed my opinion," Hunter said, looking at his bloody hand and some scrapes on his arm.

"I am sorry. Where are my manners? Let's get the two of you inside and get you cleaned up. I have some clean coveralls and a nice warm shower awaiting each of you." Norman pointed them in the direction of the main hatch.

"Captain, do you have a list of phone numbers to the Navy Base?" Hunter asked. "I need to call Captain Harkin and discuss our situation."

"I am sure I can round up something, what do you have in mind?" the Captain asked.

"I want to dive this wreck before anyone else gets to it. I think there is a lot we can find out about these men and their mission," replied Hunter.

"All right, I will call one of my petty officers down to escort you to the bridge and get you what you need. I will join you shortly after I get your friend here situated with a warm shower and a dressing for his wound."

Captain Harkin proceeded to do as he said and called the bridge upon arriving inside. Within a few minutes a young petty officer appeared to escort Hunter.

"He is to have full access to our facilities. Is that clear?" Ordered the Captain.

"Aye, aye, sir," came the response.

"Right this way, sir." The young man said pointing to the direction of the bridge.

"Brad, let me get you situated in my stateroom so you can take a shower and tend to that wound. Has our EMT had a chance to take a look at it?" asked the Captain.

"No, but I think the bullet only grazed me and it stopped bleeding a while ago. It's nothing a nice warm shower and a bottle of rum can't fix," Spencer said with a large smile.

The Captain set out all the needed items, and left for the bridge. Once he reached the bridge, he noticed Hunter had already started calling the base, trying to reach Captain Harkin's office.

"No, I need to talk to Captain Harkin now. This is an emergency," Hunter said, practically screaming into the phone at some hapless secretary.

"Hold on and let me see where he is, sir," she said as she hit the hold button. "Captain, I have an Eric Hunter on line one. He says he needs to speak with you immediately."

"Yes, I will take it!" he replied.

"Hunter, I'm glad you made it alive. Are you on the Coast Guard Cutter right now?" asked Captain Harkin.

"Yes, sir, they are taking very good care of us. Sir, is it possible for us to dive the wreckage and see if we can find out the reason for all this?" asked Hunter.

"I tell you what, I have a four-man salvage dive team getting ready to launch as we speak. I will let you go join them as long as you don't interfere with their investigation." replied Captain Harkin.

"Sir, they won't even know we are there. One more favor. Could you have them grab our dive gear from our rental car?" asked Hunter. "Two black bags contain all of our equipment, we just need them to throw a couple of extra tanks on board."

"I think I can manage that. My guys will be on station in thirty minutes. Can I speak with the ship's Captain and coordinate all this?" asked Captain Harkin.

"He is standing next to me, sir. I will put him on. Thanks again for your help." Hunter handed the phone to the Cushing's Captain Lieutenant Norman.

After a brief conversation, Norman hung up the phone and turned to his men on the bridge. "Men, we are going to stay on station for a few hours to assist a navy dive team with their investigation on this wreck. Petty officer Johnson, I need you to call GANSEC and notify them of our situation. Chief James, what is the status of our small boat towing the disabled Navy craft?"

"Sir, Cush 1 is almost at the dock and the crew should have the vessel secured within the next fifteen minutes," answered the Chief.

"Very well, Petty Officer Johnson call Cush 1 and have them remain with the vessel until the Navy guys can get over there to investigate," ordered the Captain.

"Aye, aye, sir" came the response.

"Everything is a go Mr. Hunter, would you like to lay below and wash up?" Asked the Captain.

"I'll be all right. I would just like to make one more phone call and let my office know of the updated situation," said Hunter.

"Go right ahead. My bridge is at your disposal."

Hunter called his boss, Adam Reinquest, and filled him in. He let him know that he and Spencer were going to dive the wreck and find out what they could. It was clear that the missile was no accident.

Hunter hung up the phone and turned to the ship's Captain.

"Sir, I want to thank you again for all your help," he said.

"Don't mention it. It's just one Coastie helping another."

"How did you know I used to be in the Coast Guard?" Hunter asked.

"You probably don't remember me, but I arrived on board the Gallatin one month before you and Mr. Spencer left for the ODR," he replied.

"I think I remember. You were a Lieutenant JG and that was your first sea assignment."

"Yes, but I have come along way in the last four years and now they let me skipper this vessel," he replied with a chuckle.

"Well it looks like you are doing a fine job," Hunter said.

"Why thank you," replied the Captain.

"I think I'll take you up on your offer and clean up before the divers arrive said Hunter.

After being excused, Hunter went below to wash up. Upon finishing he re-joined Brad, who was already on the bridge, and awaited the Navy divers. It felt good to be back on a Coast Guard vessel and both wanted to take a moment to savor this experience.

They did not have long because shortly after they arrived on the bridge, the Navy men appeared. As they approached, Hunter and Spencer excused themselves and went to the stern of the ship to meet them.

The smaller Navy craft pulled up alongside the larger Coast Guard Vessel and threw over a line, which Hunter grabbed and made fast to a cleat. With the help of the Coast Guard petty officers, they secured the vessel and prepared to embark the crew. By this time the Captain had joined them on the stern and Hunter, Spencer, and the Captain greeted the men as they came aboard.

After about fifteen minutes of discussion, all parties ratified the dive plan. Since they wanted to complete the dive before nightfall, they had to get the show on the road.

Along with the navy divers Hunter and Brad boarded the small boat, which would take them to the wreck site. As soon as lines were cast, Hunter and Brad grabbed their dive bags and started to suit up. The two of them dove with a full mask system, which allowed them to talk while underwater. As Hunter expected, the Navy divers also had these systems, so all six men would be able to communicate during the dive.

The crystal clear waters of the Caribbean meant that the visibility on this dive would be about a hundred feet. This made the wreck easy to spot from the surface.

It sat in forty feet of the most beautiful blue water imaginable. At that depth they would not have to worry about the amount of time they spent at the bottom. Their air would run out before they had to worry about the nitrogen buildup in their blood.

During diving, excess nitrogen builds up in a person's body. The deeper you go the more quickly it enters. If a diver stays down too long, the buildup can harm the body. This condition is commonly referred to as the bends.

Hunter and Spencer took a moment to enjoy the scenery before the dive. They were situated in the calm waters between the islands of Culebra and Vieques and with the clearness of the day; they could see the splendor of both islands. Since the sun would be setting in an hour and a half, they would only have time for one daylight dive. The decision to do a night dive would be made once they finished and determined whether they had collected enough information.

Spencer and Hunter finished suiting up and were eager to dive. They waited patiently for the last Navy diver to submerge, and with one look Spencer jumped off the side of the boat, submerging himself in the warm waters of the Caribbean. Hunter soon joined him and together they headed toward the bottom. Because the waters of the Caribbean stay around eighty degrees, they had decided to dive without wet suits.

"Systems check. Can everyone hear me OK?" asked Spencer.

"I have you loud and clear buddy. How do you read me?" Hunter asked, giving Spencer the OK sign that divers often use to signal all is well.

The other four Navy divers also answered back to check their hearing systems. As soon as this task was completed, they split off from the group. Hunter and Spencer started by circling the boat and assessing the damage. The missile had impacted the boat almost dead center and split the boat in two pieces, or more like chunks because not a lot of the boat remained intact.

The Navy divers were pointing at some fragments still attached to a missile part. They could tell right away that should not have been on the missile. Hunter and Spencer went in for a closer look.

"What do you think about this?" asked Hunter, pointing to the missile parts.

"I don't know, but they are not suppose to be attached to this type of missile," replied one of the Navy divers.

"Do you think this is why the missile went astray and these guys were trying to cover it up?" Spencer asked, looking at Hunter.

"I don't know, but I think it would be a hell of a coincidence if it were not the case. What do you guys think?" asked Hunter.

"We will have to bring it back to base and get it analyzed before we can say anything definite," replied the same Navy diver.

"We are going to check out our friends and see what we can find out," Hunter said over the intercom system as he started to swim away.

They headed for the area where they had spotted one of the bodies. They found the body face down on the bottom a few feet away from the boat. Spencer slowly turned the guy around and they examined his facial features.

"Are you thinking what I am thinking?" Hunter asked Spencer.

"If you are thinking these guys look a lot like mercenaries, than yes I am," replied Spencer. "I would say they might be from Libya."

"I also think these guys could easily be discounted as terrorist, which would be a great escape story if the operation went bad, like it did. Whoever is behind this wants us to believe this cover," Hunter continued.

Part of their training before being indoctrinated in the ODC had been a grueling six months of classes that had taught them how to identify different factions and organizations around the world. This included friend and foe, and in this case there was no mistaking that the guys who attacked them where hired professionals.

"Do you see that?" Hunter asked noticing a chain with a unique emblem hanging around the man's neck. He pulled off the chain and put it in his dive vest.

"I want to find out what this symbolizes. It may give us a clue as to where he came from."

Spencer gave him a nod of approval and they continued toward what remained of the bow. Once they arrived, they saw that one of the rocket launchers was still intact.

After further examination they determined it was, along with the

AK-47's, Russian made. Since the break up of the Soviet Union, these types of weapons could be easily purchased on the black market. It probably would not give them any specific clues to who was behind all this, but it was still something they would check out later.

After another trip around the area and a temporary distraction, where Spencer chased a sea turtle, they started their ascent. They had been down for over an hour and even though it was not entirely necessary, they leveled off at fifteen feet and did a three-minute safety stop.

"What do you make of this?" Spencer asked Brad as they hovered.

"I am not sure, but I can tell you this has become a lot more interesting than I thought it would be," he replied.

Since the Navy divers all had taken two tanks with them, they could stay down for a longer time. They were tasked with retrieving the bodies and collecting any items that they deemed noteworthy to be analyzed later.

Hunter and Spencer reached the surface to find Cush 1 awaiting their arrival.

"The Captain asked us to come over and check on the operation. Is everything going all right?" the petty officer driving the craft asked as they floated on the surface.

"Everything is fine," Brad replied. "The Navy divers have to finish collecting items but we are through for the day."

"Do you two want a lift back to the Cushing?"

"That sounds like a great idea." Replied Hunter.

The idea of a warm shower and a change of clothes sure beat sitting on the boat soaking wet for the next half hour. With the help of the Coast Guardsmen, they climbed aboard.

Chapter 7

About forty miles away from the salvage operation, sitting just off the shores of Spanish Town, located on the island of Virgin Gorda in the British Virgin Islands, the mother ship of the mercenaries sat. The captain realized something was amiss because his orders were to meet a boat and four men at this location and they were more than four hours overdue. It was getting dark and he feared telling his boss about the failed mission because his boss was not a man who took failure lightly. He decided to remain at anchor for another hour and see what happened. He was on a 140-foot pleasure yacht, and in this area he would not be viewed with suspicion. If the authorities started snooping around, his cover as a captain waiting for his boss to arrive for vacation should suffice.

Captain Jose Gevalia was Spanish born and had moved to the United States with his parents when he was ten. He received his citizenship when he was sixteen and joined the United States Navy at eighteen. He'd had a successful career as an enlisted man, making the rank of a First Class Quartermaster. But decided he wanted more and applied for the Navy's officer training program.

Because of his high marks and strong will to succeed, he finished at the top of his class. He spent the next fifteen years as an officer and retired his commission at the rank of commander.

He had been divorced years ago and had no immediate family to take care of, so he decided to head south. After acquiring his commercial captain's license he applied for jobs throughout the Caribbean. He landed this job, which based him out of Charlotte Amalie in Saint Thomas.

He had pictured a fun and carefree lifestyle, but the reality was quite different. He had been hired to captain a pleasure yacht throughout the Caribbean and southern Florida but he soon found that was only the beginning of his responsibilities.

To this day, he still had no idea what his boss was into, but he was constantly sent on shady missions that required him to do things that go against his better judgment. He had tried to quit once a couple of years ago, and was greeted at the pier by four thugs who had roughed him up and made it perfectly clear that if he were to leave he would be hunted down and anyone he cared about would be killed.

"Regrettably, it's time to call the boss," Gevalia thought to himself. "He is not going to be happy, but when is he?"

He nervously picked up the phone and dialed.

"Sir," Jose said into the ship's cell phone. "I think there has been a problem with the guests."

"What is it?" a sinister voice bellowed on the other end.

"Well, sir, I have not heard from them since they left the dock and that was five hours ago," Jose said, trying to stay calm.

"Do you know anything else about the situation?"

"No sir, what would you like me to do next?" Jose asked.

"Just stay on station. I am sending you a couple of guys to assess the situation. They will be there by tomorrow afternoon."

"I will make the arrangements, sir." he replied.

Jose hung up the phone and could not believe how deep of a mess he has gotten himself into with this job. He knew he needed to get out, but so far could not find a way. For now, he would just have to deal with things and have the crew prepare for the new guests that would arrive tomorrow.

* * *

David Bruner hung up the phone with Jose and contemplated what could have gone wrong and how it was going to get fixed. Bruner was the head of the Oasis Company, which was comprised of many sub companies under the umbrella of this mother company. He was a ruthless man whose main driving force was more power and money. His company had always been shrouded by mystery. The U.S. government had been investigating him for years and so far had not been able to turn up any wrong doings. He changed his name 20 years ago when he started this empire and his original identity was not known. He had no family left and no close friends that anyone knew about. Since he started his empire, he has kept his social life very guarded. If you added up all of his net worth from his businesses, including the legal and illegal ones, it would be in the billions.

Bruner picked up the phone. "Hello," said the voice on the other end.

"I need you and your companion to go on a trip tomorrow. I will send all the briefing materials to you within the hour," he said as the man answered.

"You have something interesting for us to take care of?" the man asked.

"You'll see, just start packing for the islands," Bruner responded and hung up. He usually said as little as possible on the phone due to the fact that someone might be listening.

Chapter 8

Sitting on the mess deck of the Coast Guard Cutter, Hunter sipped a fresh cup of coffee and stared at the necklace he had recovered.

"Do you recognize it?" asked Spencer.

"I can't seem to place it, but it definitely looks familiar. We will have to take a picture of it and send it back to headquarters and have Clyde take a look at it."

Clyde Forman was the research guru at the organization. He has access to all of the government databases and was said to know every useful site on the Internet. If anyone could come up with its origins it would be him.

"We will be pulling into Roosevelt Roads Navy base in about fifteen minutes gentlemen," the Captain yelled from the top of the ladder. "If you would like to join me on the bridge, I would be honored."

"Thank you, Captain. We will be up shortly. I am just going to finish my coffee," said Hunter, not in any hurry to move after the day's events.

Hunter took the last sip of his coffee and put it in the galley sink. He was still looking at the emblem on the end of the necklace and was upset he could not place it. The emblem was round and had two palm trees curved around the circle, with the sun in the middle. He knew he had seen it before. But where?

Hunter followed Spencer up the ladder, down the passageway,

and up another ladder that led to the bridge. They were used to a larger Coast Guard Cutter and found it humorous that it took such little time to get from below decks to the bridge.

"Permission to come on deck?" Spencer asked as he reached the top of the ladder before entering the bridge. It was standard Coast Guard procedure to ask the Captain or officer of the deck permission before stepping onto the bridge.

"Please join us. You two can forego Coast Guard courtesies," the captain said, smiling. Once a sailor always a sailor definitely applied to these gentlemen. "Please, follow me to the open bridge. We usually moor the boat from there because it gives a better view of things."

"Sir we are on the range, we will turn left to a new course of 288 in five minutes," yelled the quartermaster from the lower bridge.

"Very well QM1," the captain acknowledged.

"After we make our turn it is only five more minutes until we moor up," he explained.

The docking of the ship went like clockwork and Hunter and Spencer went below to gather their gear and disembark.

"Thank you for all your assistance, Captain," Spencer said as he walked toward the gangway.

"My pleasure, gentlemen. It is always good to help out a couple of ex-Coasties. Here is my card. Give me a call if I can be of any further assistance. I put the ship's cell number on the back of the card," the Captain said as he handed Spencer the card and shook his hand.

"Thank you again, Captain," Hunter said. "I owe you a beer next time we are both in San Juan."

"I look forward to it," the Captain said, shaking Hunter's hand in a good-bye salute.

Hunter and Spencer walked to the end of the fuel pier where, to their amazement, a car was awaiting them.

"The Captain must have arranged this," Spencer suggested.

"He definitely has our back," agreed Hunter.

"I am here to escort you anywhere you would like to go, sirs," stated the petty officer as he helped them with their bags.

"Please take us to Captain Harkin's office," Hunter said.

"You want to get a picture of this to Clyde before we go to our hotel room, don't you?" Spencer asked, already knowing the answer. "It is 10 p.m. What can he do with it tonight?"

"You know he lives at work," replied Hunter. "Plus, I already asked the Captain on the Cushing to take a picture of it and send it an hour ago."

"They have underway e-mail now that is strong enough to send pictures?" asked Spencer.

"Yes, and they can even surf the Internet in certain areas," said Hunter.

They arrived in front of the hangar where their car and Captain Harkin's office resided. Both men grabbed their gear, thanked the driver, and proceeded toward their rental car.

After a brief stop to unload their stuff, they headed inside to the Captain's office. They were surprised to still see him at his desk.

"Don't you ever go home sir?" Hunter asked as he and Spencer walked in.

"I don't rest until my men are home safe." he replied.

"I think you will be interested in what your friend Clyde sent," he continued. "He is standing by in Washington for your call."

"Thank you, sir. What phone can I use?" asked Hunter.

"Here, sit at my desk. All you have to do is click this icon and you will be linked up via video conferencing with your man." Hunter did as he was told and Spencer joined him from the other side of the desk. He clicked the icon and within a couple of seconds Clyde appeared on the screen.

"Eric Hunter and Brad Spencer, the two who never let me rest. How are we both this fine evening?" Clyde asked with a hint of sarcasm.

"We are doing great. What do you have for us?" Hunter asked, getting down to business.

"If you open the folder that I sent, you will see that the symbol has many matches but the one that is most useful would be from the Oasis Company," Clyde said.

"They have been under investigation for shady practices for years but no evidence has ever been found to show any wrong doing. I have sent you a list and description of all their known factories and offices but other than that I don't have a lot. This company likes to keep its operations close to the vest. I will do more digging tomorrow but I am going home for the night."

"Thanks for everything Clyde, I owe you one," Hunter said as he looked through the paper work.

"Yeah, I've heard that one before. Maybe someday I may actually collect. Have a good night." Clyde closed the computer connection after he finished his sentence.

"You should get to your hotel room and get some sleep. We are scheduled to debrief back here at 0800 tomorrow," Captain Harkin said with a tone that could be construed as an order.

"Yes sir, but what about the Lieutenant and Miss Evans?" asked Hunter.

"Oh, yes, Miss Evans. Don't worry. She will be at tomorrow's debriefing. You will have plenty of time to lay on your charm during the meeting."

"We'll be there," Spencer said as he motioned for them to leave.

"Yes, sir, bright and early," Hunter said as they walked off.

*　　*　　*

At 6:00 AM, Captain Gevalia stood on the bridge with coffee cup in hand, awaiting the arrival of his mystery guests. Everything was prepared for their arrival and two of Gevalia's crew were standing by to tie down the helicopter when it landed. Gevalia knew this was not going to lead to anything positive, but could not think of a way out of it. The sound of the rotor blades from the helicopter awoke him from his thought.

"Look alive gentlemen here comes the helo," shouted Gevalia into the radio.

The helicopter landed successfully and his men securely tied it to the landing pad. When this was completed, one of the men gave the pilot thumbs up and opened the door on the passenger side.

A very large man emerged from the aircraft. He stood about six foot four inches tall and had a scar over his left eye. The intense look in his eyes gave the impression of someone who was capable of almost anything. Gevalia was sure this man was not sent to just look for clues about what happened, but to do what whatever was necessary to cover them up.

The pilot soon joined him. He looked a little more refined, obviously the brains of the operation. At five foot eight, he was a significant size smaller than his counterpart but Gevalia was sure he was along to execute the plan and would leave the muscle duties to his companion.

"My name is Mr. Smith and my friend's name is not important," the pilot said. "I need you to pull up anchor and move this boat in the vicinity north of Vieques. Please inform me when we are twenty minutes from our destination. Now will you please show us to our quarters? We intend to rest before we arrive."

"Mr. Edwards, will you escort these men to their quarters?" Captain Gevalia asked a crewmember who was standing by. He was sure that the mans name was not Mr. Smith, but he figured the less he knew the better.

After his guests went below to their cabins, Captain Gevalia headed for the bridge and gave the order to raise anchor. After twenty minutes they were under way, en route to their destination. The trip to the island of Vieques would take around five hours, placing them on the scene by lunchtime.

Chapter 9

The morning came too quickly for Hunter and Spencer, which was evident by the large black coffees they had purchased before arriving at the meeting. As they walked into Captain Harkin's office, they saw they were the last ones to arrive.

"You're late!" exclaimed Harkin.

"Are we late? Brad, my watch does not say we are late. Does yours?"

"No, my watch says 8:15, which for us is right on time," Spencer replied.

"All right you two, stop your banter and take a seat," ordered Harkin, realizing that he was dealing with civilians and not his normal military personnel.

"We have a key issue here. The Oasis Company is a major power that is said to have many politicians in its back pocket. They donate a substantial amount of money to senators' campaign funds and rumor has it they have been bribing the Governor of Puerto Rico and many members of his executive council. It is hard to touch them on the island, and with all their pharmaceutical plants here, which is sixty percent of their legitimate operations, we will have to keep our investigations low key. Their biggest and most secretive plant is located just south of Mayaquez on the west side of the island. Miss Evans will now brief us all on her findings and forensic tests," Harkin said.

"Gentlemen I have analyzed the bomb fragments and discovered that the missile was altered, as we previously thought. We believe the missile was intended to hit this area and kill whoever was in the vicinity."

"What most of you know is that the President of the United States was scheduled to witness the live missile demonstration, along with other local representatives. He was coming down here in support of re-opening the bombing area that was shut down due to protesters and political pressure a few years ago," she continued.

"The event was cancelled when the talks about re-opening the range broke down. Since the targets were already set up and the mission was approved, they allowed the aircraft demonstration to continue as planned. We believe that the gentlemen that Mr. Hunter and Mr. Spencer intercepted wanted to retrieve the missile parts and thus eliminate any evidence of what happened."

"Wouldn't four dead Marines and a missing missile alarm us to foul play?" asked Spencer.

"Yes, but at least they would have covered their tracks and we would have no idea who or what did this. We still don't know if the necklace was from the Oasis Company or not. We came up with ten matches for the necklace and four of them are just necklaces you can buy for decorative sake. The official word from Washington is that the Oasis Company is not a suspect and it should not be pursued in this case," said Harkin.

"So you're saying we can't investigate our prime suspect?" asked Spencer, almost in a rage.

"Mr. Spencer calm yourself," continued Harkin. "I said the official word was they are not to be investigated. I have a Top Secret memo from the White House Chief of Staff that says we shall use all means necessary to get to the bottom of this but to be as discrete as possible. This means that only the members of this room, the President, his Chief of Staff, and the head of the ODR know about this side order. As I said, this company has a lot of power in Washington, so we can't expose our hand until we have solid proof. The President does not consider the necklace solid enough to make this public."

"Captain Harkin, may we call our boss and get authorization to check out the plant and research center south of Mayaguez?" inquired Hunter.

"I think your boss must know how you think because he already granted permission for that operation. Let me know what supplies you need and I will make sure you get them with no questions asked," replied Harkin.

"I have a few more tests on the bomb I would like to conduct and Captain Harkin, with your permission, I would like to witness the autopsies of the four men the Navy divers brought back last night," Evans said.

"Very well Miss Evans," he replied. "Men, start putting together a list of things you need."

They all got up and started to walk out the door, leaving Captain Harkin alone in his office. On the way out, Hunter caught the attention of Miss Evans.

"So we missed our date last night due to all the commotion. Do you think I can make it up and take you out tomorrow night?" Hunter asked.

"I think that can be arranged. Besides, after two days with dead guys and missile fragments, a girl could use the break," Amy said with a small smile.

"Then it's settled. I know a great restaurant in Isle Verde that you will love."

Hunter turned to catch up with Spencer, who was already spouting off items needed for their journey to a supply clerk in the next room. Captain Harkin had a man waiting to meet the two of them outside his office.

Hunter arrived as Spencer was finishing the list of items.

"We also we need two Romeo and Juliet Corona style cigars, a bottle of Don Q Gold, and a six pack of Coke," Spencer said, concluding his list.

"Why are you asking for those things, Brad?" asked Hunter.

"Because we have no time to pick them up ourselves and last night we had to do without because we arrived home too late. The least Uncle Sam could do is make sure we are having a good time."

"All right, buddy, but you get to explain that to the boss when he asks," commented Hunter.

"It should take him an hour or so to get the supplies. Meanwhile, we need to study the layout of this factory and find its weak points," suggested Hunter.

They took the next hour to smooth out their game plan. They had only limited knowledge of the plant, so the plan had to leave room to maneuver. Their best weapon was stealth, with their main goal getting in and out of the complex without being noticed. This was merely a reconnaissance mission to get additional information and neither wanted to let their opposition know what they were up to.

After about an hour, as they were finishing their rough plan, the supply clerk arrived with the equipment they had requested. As Spencer checked the supplies off the list, Hunter loaded them into their rental car.

"Thanks for all your assistance. Everything is accounted for. I am impressed that you could get all the items in such a short notice," Brad remarked.

"Thank you sir." he replied.

"I'll let Captain Harkin know about your performance," Spencer said as he shook the man's hand.

"All right, Brad, let's get on the road. We want to make it there before dark." Hunter interrupted as he grabbed the last box.

Although the distance was only about 140 miles, the trip was going to take between four and five hours, depending on traffic. The roads in Puerto Rico were not as easy to maneuver as the roads in the States.

Hunter looked at his watch, which read ten thirty; he was hoping to make it by three thirty so they would have at least three hours of daylight to stake out the factory. The pharmaceutical plant was surrounded by hills, dense trees, and brush, which would supply them with plenty of hiding places while they studied the area.

As Hunter put the car in drive and pulled away, Spencer turned on the CD player and immediately pressed track two on Jimmy Buffet's album License to Chill.

The song Boats to Build rang out over the car's system and they both found themselves drifting away to the music. It was plain to see that the theme for this trip was going to be Jimmy Buffet songs.

To the unsuspecting person, it would appear that the two of them where just a couple of tourists driving Route 3 toward San Juan. This was precisely the cover they wanted, and since they enjoyed this lifestyle they had no problem making it work.

The trip took them across the northern part of Puerto Rico. They would have plenty of time to go over the plan during the stakeout, so for now they both sat back and enjoyed the ride.

Five hours, two pit stops, and a driver switch later, they found themselves outside the great pharmaceutical factory of the Oasis Company. They drove by slowly to see which area would be best for them to set up their base camp. No matter how they looked at the situation, it was not going to be an easy mission.

At Spencer's suggestion, they parked about two miles away, down what appeared to be an abandoned road. They were going to hike through the thick forest toward the factory to limit the chance of being detected. It would also give them a safe place to run to and escape if things went wrong, which so often happened.

Hunter dropped Brad and their packs a short distance away from the main road next to the tree line. He was going to take the car further down the road so as not to be detected by cars passing by. It only took Spencer a few moments to disappear amongst the foliage and await Hunter's arrival.

After leaving the car, he climbed a nearby hill and took a lookout position pulling out his binoculars and scanning the area to see if anyone was watching. After a few moments he was sure they had made a clean entrance and decided to take a drink of water while he waited.

After about fifteen minutes, Hunter entered the forest heading for Brad's position. He approached on Brad's blind spot as not to be detected.

"Are you waiting for someone?" Hunter said in a sharp loud voice right at the point when he was directly behind Spencer.

Spencer jumped to his feet and turned around quickly. "You son of a bitch! You scared the shit out of me. You're lucky I didn't shoot you," he said as he was placing his pistol back in the holster.

"Your reflexes are getting better. I am going to have to keep you on your toes more often," Hunter said as he picked up the spare pack and put on his gun belt.

"Very funny. Next time I think I may shoot first and ask questions later," Spencer replied.

"I think we should put on our face paint before heading out. No telling what kind of surveillance cameras they may have in the woods," Hunter suggested.

The men covered their faces in a thin layer of camouflage paint designed by the Navy Seals to disguise their identity and limit glare.

The area was rough but manageable and they made it to a good vantage point within thirty minutes. They started to unpack and set up equipment to begin their investigation. Hunter looked at the time. It was nearly four o'clock. This would give them roughly two and a half hours of light to finalize their entry plan.

Chapter 10

As night began to fall, they gathered up their equipment and prepared for entry. They determined that the weakest point in the security was a service door located on the backside of the complex. It was still not going to be easy, but it looked to be the best bet.

They silently approached the door, keeping in the shadows as much as possible. Hunter stood lookout as Spencer slid a code-breaking card into the slot next to the security door.

"We have thirty seconds to break in. After that, they'll know we're here," whispered Spencer.

"Let's hope this works," Hunter replied.

They both stood barely breathing as they waited to see if the card would work fast enough. Every security system is unique and no method of cracking a code is fool proof.

"Twenty three, twenty four, twenty five, come on, come on," Spencer whispered.

"Lets abort and run for it!" Hunter said under his breath.

"No, no, just a second!" Spencer replied.

"A second is all we have." Hunter remarked.

"I got it," Spencer said with a sigh of relief. "Do you hear any alarms?"

"No, let's just hope they don't have the silent type." Hunter replied.

They waited for a few more seconds to make sure the coast was clear.

"Let's jerry rig the door so we can get out without having to go through this again," Hunter suggested.

"I can make it look like normal from a distance but if anyone comes close enough to inspect this door, the gig is up," Spencer informed him.

"That's fine. I want to be in and out in twenty minutes." Hunter said.

"Let's set our watches starting, now!" replied Brad.

"We witnessed a guard come by every thirty minutes. This should give us some time to spare," Hunter commented.

They entered and did a quick jog through the complex passing the factory floor and heading toward the offices on the other side. So far, it looked like a typical factory.

As of yet they had not come in contact with any of the factory's security force. According to the plans they were given, the research area was up one more corridor and to the left. They had no idea what kind of security would be there, but they were sure they could count on some resistance.

They arrived at the research area and saw that the door leading in had more security than they expected.

"It looks like a card swipe and a finger print to get in. I'm afraid this is the end of the line because fingerprint scans are impossible to duplicate," Spencer stated with regret.

"Can't you powder the area and lift off a print with tape or something?" asked Hunter in a joking tone.

"What do you think this is? The movies? You know that doesn't work in real life," Spencer said, laughing.

Hunter could hear the sound of footsteps coming from the other end of the hallway.

"Quick, duck around the corner. I think I hear something," he said as he headed for a dark spot.

A guard appeared and walked toward the door. They watched as the guard swiped his card and put his thumb on the scanner.

He reached for the door, hesitated, and then turned toward their direction.

The guard cautiously started heading toward them. Hunter looked back to warn Spencer but he was nowhere to be found. As the guard approached, Hunter pulled out a long knife and readied it for use.

"Four more steps and I have to take him out quietly," Hunter thought to himself.

Three. Two. One. Hunter readied for the attack.

From behind, Spencer appeared. With one swing of his flashlight, he dropped the guard to the ground. All that was heard was a soft thud as his body hit the concrete, unconscious.

Hunter, still in shock but relieved, stood frozen for a moment.

"Eric, are you going to help me carry him to the door or just stand there with a stupid look on your face?" Spencer asked, which snapped Hunter out of his trance.

"Good job, Brad. How in the hell did you get behind him?"

"When he was facing the door, I slipped to the rear of him. I was going to knock him out at the door but he turned toward you and I figured it would be easier to give him a rap on the head when he was focusing your way."

"We still need to get in, download all the material we can, and get out."

"My sentiments exactly!" Spencer said as he raised the guard's hand toward the thumb scanner.

"I figure we have about ten minutes to get in and out before they notice something is wrong," Hunter said.

They entered the room, which appeared to be a very large laboratory with chemicals and computers at many stations. It was seven thirty at night, so most of the scientists had gone home for the evening. There was one exception, and he was working behind a glass wall through even more security.

"Do you think our guard has access to that room?" Hunter asked.

"Only one way to find out," replied Spencer.

They dragged the unconscious guard toward the door and put the card and thumb print to the test.

"OK, on the count of three we enter. Do you think you can subdue the scientist behind the desk?" asked Hunter.

"I think I maybe able to manage the task," replied Spencer as he reached into his bag and pulled out a bottle of sodium chloride that he had packed for such an occasion. He pulled a rag out of his backpack, twisted off the bottle's cap, and soaked the rag with the chemical.

They placed the card in the slot and then scanned the thumbprint. To their relief it worked, and as the door opened Spencer leapt at the scientist and put his handkerchief over the man's mouth and nose before he could react. The scientist struggled but the sodium chloride worked fast. Within a few seconds he was on the ground out cold.

As planned, the scientist had not had time to lock his computer. This left it vulnerable and gave Spencer the opportunity to download some information.

"What files do you think I should download?" asked Spencer.

"I don't know. What was he working on? Start with that and go from there," replied Hunter.

Spencer started downloading as Hunter stood watch.

"Hurry! We're going to be exposed any second now," Hunter said as he looked at his watch and noticed five minutes had already passed.

"Just a couple more minutes and I'll have the whole file," Spencer said.

Hunter did a visual sweep around the room and turned to Spencer once again to tell him to hurry. Before he could get the words out, the factory's alarm sounded.

"They're on to us!" Hunter screamed over the alarm. "We need to get the hell out of here."

"I got the last of it!" Spencer exclaimed. "Let's go before it is too late!"

The two headed for the door, dragging the unconscious security guard. Sets of security doors were beginning to close and if they did not get out soon they would be sealed in the lab, unable to escape.

During the transport, the guard started to come around. Without hesitation, Spencer delivered a blow to the back of his head, knocking him out instantly.

"Nice hit!" Hunter exclaimed.

"Thanks. Now put his finger on the pad as I swipe the card," replied Spencer.

Hunter did as he was told and the door opened. The gates were closing in fast. They had only a few more seconds before it would be too late.

Spencer pulled on the door and it would not open.

"Eric, we have a problem!" Spencer yelled out.

"Stand back!" replied Hunter. "I hope this works."

Hunter raised his M-16 and as soon as Spencer was clear opened fire. If the glass panels in the door were bulletproof, the ricocheting bullets could fatally wound them both.

Luckily they were not, and as the door was shattering into a million pieces Hunter grabbed Brad and jumped through the opening, landing outside just moments before the outer doors closed.

"That was a close one," Brad said as they took a second to regroup.

"How did you know the glass wasn't bullet proof?" He asked.

"I didn't," Hunter replied as if it were no big deal. "It was the only shot we had to escape."

"So you're saying you could have killed us if you were wrong?" asked Brad.

"Pretty much."

"Well, that's good to know," Brad replied.

"I think we should get out of here before any more surprises show up," Brad suggested

"I could not agree with you more." Hunter replied. "Let's double time it out of here."

They grabbed their gear and started a quick jogging pace retracing their steps toward the back door they had come in through.

They headed over the factory floor and to the other set of hallways without encountering any of the security force. But as they rounded the last hallway, two guards appeared, pointing their weapons and preparing to fire.

"Run for it and cover your eyes!" Hunter yelled as he pulled out a hockey-puck-like object and hurled it toward the guards.

The puck exploded with a large flash, temporarily blinding the guards. The blast was only the first stage in the process. The puck also emitted a smoke cloud containing a form of knockout gas that within seconds rendered the guards unconscious.

"Hold your breath as you run through the cloud of smoke," Hunter yelled as he headed toward where the guards were standing.

Brad did as he was told and they both held their breath as they ran through the smoke cloud.

They only had to go down one more hallway and then out to freedom. With only a few more yards to go, it appeared they would make it out of this debacle yet.

As they rounded the corner, they picked up the pace. Spencer approached the door and reached for the handle. But as he grabbed it, a sharp pain went threw his nose, into his brain, knocking him unconscious.

Appearing from the shadows of the exit was the biggest man Hunter had ever seen. His fists were like giant rocks. He was the only man Hunter knew of who could have dropped Spencer with just one punch.

Without breaking stride, Hunter attacked, thrusting his elbow into the big guard's face. It did not have the result he hoped for. In fact, it hurt Hunter worse than the guard.

As Hunter was holding his arm in pain, the guard hit him with a closed backhand. This dropped Hunter instantly, but did not render him unconscious. The guard picked him up and put him in a bear hug. Hunter hit the guard in the face with all his might, but it did little to slow him down. The guard just laughed at Hunter for fighting back in vain.

Hunter started to feel tunnel vision and knew he was close to blacking out. As his eyes closed, he tried to think of a way out.

Just before Hunter blacked out, he felt the guard loosen his grip. But thought it was probably just his imagination.

Hunter slowly opened his eyes to find Brad standing overhead with a bloody nose and empty bottle of sodium chloride.

"Did you think it was the end?" Brad asked as he came around.

"Yes. I didn't think I was going to wake up from this one," Hunter replied.

"I don't mean to rush you, but you need to get up. We still need to get out of here," Spencer said, offering Hunter a hand.

Hunter got up and followed Spencer out the door. He was still unstable from the fight, but knew he had to keep moving or they were going to be in big trouble. They ran as hard as they could for about a half mile, and then slowed to a brisk hike to catch their breath.

"You look like hell," Brad said, looking at Hunter.

"You don't look so great yourself."

"Do you think we're ever going to hear the end of this travesty?" asked Spencer.

"I'm sure the boss will forget it in time, like he does all the rest." replied Hunter. He was more worried about keeping conscious than what the boss was going to do to them if they made it home.

It took them another twenty minutes to reach the car. Once inside, they took off without hesitation. The guards were close behind and they had no time to lose.

As they drove away, they could see many lights in the distance and hear the sounds of men trampling through the woods.

"I think we may just get out of this yet," Hunter said as they left the dirt road and headed south on the main drag. They had an alternate route chosen for just this type of emergency. It would take them south of the factory and wind through the western hills of Puerto Rico, giving them adequate coverage in case the guards gave further chase.

For the next fifteen minutes, neither said a word. They were both in shock and for the first time were able to think about the mission.

"We need to take care of our injuries," Hunter said breaking the silence.

54

"I agree," Spencer replied. "If you look in the back seat, you'll see that I have taken care of it."

Hunter did as instructed and pulled a bag from behind his seat. In it, he found two towels, a first aid kit, soap and bottles of water.

"You really planned for this operation didn't you?" asked Hunter.

"I know our track record. We have never been known for clean getaways, so I figured we might need to mend our wounds after our adventure," Spencer said with a big grin.

Chapter 11

"What do you mean someone has broken into one of my factories?" David Bruner screamed into the phone to the head of security at his plant. "What the hell am I paying you for?"

"Sir, it is not as bad as you think. All the information they downloaded is encrypted and can only be viewed on our system. That program has more encryption than any other in our database. It will be impossible for them to view the information they stole unless they return here to read it," Kyle London replied, trying to calm Bruner down.

"Do you have any idea who is behind all of this?" Bruner asked in a calmer tone.

"We do not, sir, but we caught a glimpse of one of them. He took off his mask after one of our guards hit him in the face and we may have enough of a picture to make out his identity. I am having one of my government connections check it out as we speak," replied London.

"Call me when you know something more," Bruner demanded.

"Wait a minute, sir, I just received an e-mail from my contact." London said. He opened an attachment and read through the information before replying. "The man in the picture is Brad Spencer. He is an operations specialist with the Office of Domestic Readiness. This is part of the Department of Homeland Security. The department was formed shortly after the September 11th attacks to combat threats to national security. I am going to check all the intelligence traffic I have received in the last couple of days and let you know what I find out. I will call you back in one hour with the results."

"I'll be standing by," Bruner said, and then hung up the phone. He sat back in his office chair and sipped from the glass of Scotch he had poured before receiving the call. He thought if anyone could get to the bottom of what was going on, it would be London.

Kyle London was an American born man who had lived a unique life. He had grown up on the streets of New York, never knowing his parents. He was sent to a Catholic orphanage shortly after he was born and was raised there until he was seventeen. After a year of traveling from place to place with no direction, he joined the Army and spent the next twenty years as an Army ranger.

London was known for his brutality and at the age of thirty-seven was forced into retirement. No one but the men he served with really knew the depth of his evil, but the rumors were enough to turn one's stomach.

Shortly after he was released from active duty, an ex-Army sergeant he had been stationed with recruited him to work for the Oasis Company. He was hired and placed on a detail that guarded the most secretive research the company conducted.

After working for the company for five years, he was promoted to Head of Security. His quick promotion was mostly due to the fact that two of his superiors had died in mysterious accidents. No one knew exactly what happened, but for some reason Mr. Bruner trusted him and no one in the organization would dare questioned why. London was the only one that could stand up to Bruner without fear of reprisal.

London was just thinking about his past when one of his men walked in, carrying a CD and a stack of papers.

"Sir, here are the items you requested," the man said, handing London the information.

"Thank you. That will be all," London said, motioning for the man to leave his office.

London's intelligence department had learned how to decipher the security codes of the local military vessels and would intercept encrypted radio and data traffic that flowed from the ships around Puerto Rico. They had someone monitoring and recording the transmissions around the clock. Most of the time it was useless babble about possible drugs in the area or illegal migrant activity, but every once in awhile there was something useful. In this case, the information put together pieces of the puzzle that they desperately needed.

The phone rang, and David Bruner picked up.

"Tell me what you have and it better be good!" he said before London could utter a word.

"I think you will be more than satisfied, sir," London stated. "I was looking through the intelligence we intercept from the Coast Guard and found some interesting facts. Our friend Brad Spencer and another gentlemen named Eric Hunter were down here on a mission to check out the missile incident. A report sent from the Coast Guard Cutter Cushing stated that they intercepted the men I hired as they were leaving the missile wreckage scene and gave chase. During the chase, a rocket that was launched from a nearby Navy helicopter destroyed my guys."

"The report also stated that Eric Hunter and Brad Spencer were taken back to port that evening and that the Coast Guard Cutter would return to the site and await further tasking." He finished and waited for a response.

"It appears they are still investigating the case and it has led them to your back door," Bruner said.

"I don't know how they put us together with the missile strike. I used men from the Middle East so if anything went wrong they would not trace them to us and at the least suspect terrorism. It appears our two young adversaries are more clever than suspected," London continued.

"Would you like me to send a crew to intercept them?" London asked.

"No!" Bruner replied. "Send me all the information you have, and I will take care of Mr. Spencer and Mr. Hunter." Bruner had already thought up a plan to get rid of the two troublemakers.

"Very well sir I will keep looking for more clues and be standing by if you need anything," London said as he hung up the phone.

Bruner sat silent for a moment and then called Captain Jose Gevalia.

"Captain Gevalia," Jose said as he answered the phone.

"Gevalia, Bruner speaking. I need to talk to Mr. Smith."

"Yes, sir, I will send for him right away." Jose replied.

"Gevalia when you get him, have him call me back on the secure phone in your office," he ordered.

"Yes, sir, right away," Jose said and then hung up, relieved that the conversation was short and over.

Fifteen minutes later the phone rang in Mr. Bruner's office.

"Bruner speaking."

"Mr. Bruner, this is Mr. Smith returning your call. I am secure, sir." Mr. Smith said making sure the security feature was enabled.

"Mr. Smith, I need you and your associate to get to San Juan and take care of some business for me," Bruner stated.

"I am sending you the information as we speak. I want you to eliminate both targets by tomorrow evening. Take the helicopter to San Juan and intercept them before they can get back to the Naval Station at Roosevelt Roads. The file I just sent you will have all the information you need. Your usual fee will be deposited into your account."

"I will take care of your problem sir." Mr. Smith said, then ended the call.

Mr. Smith took out his laptop, logged onto a secured satellite link, and downloaded the file. After the download was complete, he headed to his associate's cabin to form a game plan.

Hoping that the last of the excitement was done for the evening, Captain Gevalia headed for his cabin to get some rest. He entered his stateroom, turned on his television, and sat on his bed to take off his shoes. Before he could get the first one off, the phone rang.

"What now?" He thought to himself.

He let out a big sigh, then answered. "Captain Gevalia speaking."

"Captain Gevalia, this is Mr. Smith."

"What can I do for you, sir?" asked Gevalia.

"I need you to have your men ready my helicopter for departure," Smith ordered.

"How soon will you be leaving?" asked Gevalia.

"Within the next thirty minutes." He replied

"Then I will get on it right away." Gevalia stated. He hung up, then called the bridge and made the proper arrangements.

Thirty minutes later, Mr. Smith and his companion emerged from below decks and climbed into the front seats of the helicopter. Mr. Smith gave a wave to Captain Gevalia, who was standing on the bridge wing, signaling him to ready his men. Smith powered up the electronic systems, yelled for all to be clear, and then started the helicopter.

The rotor blades started to rotate and then slowly gained momentum until they were humming away at takeoff speed.

"After takeoff we should arrive in San Juan in less than an hour," Mr. Smith said through the intercom system to his associate's headset.

"Did you double check our equipment?" Mr. Smith asked.

His associate pointed to the back seat and shook his head, affirming all the items were present.

Mr. Smith gave one last signal to have the tie-downs removed. As soon as everyone was clear, he pulled back on the altitude lever and raised the helicopter, hovering for a moment over the ship's deck before making his turn toward San Juan.

As the helicopter wandered out of sight, Captain Gevalia breathed a sigh of relief. He was glad that his role in this endeavor was over for now. He hoped that it would be his last, but knew there was a good chance he would be called upon again.

Chapter 12

After a three-hour drive, Hunter and Spencer arrived in Condado, a suburb of San Juan, shortly after midnight and checked into the Condado Plaza Hotel & Casino. They had made the reservations earlier that day and secured them for a late arrival.

Spencer checked in at the main desk while Hunter unloaded their bags and handed them to the attendant.

"Here are your keys, Mr. Spencer. Enjoy your stay with us," the lady at the front counter said as she handed him the room cards.

Spencer, not wanting to wait another minute for a cocktail, headed out to see what was keeping Hunter.

"We are good to go. I definitely need a drink after that mission," Spencer said, as Hunter was finishing.

"What room are we in?" asked Hunter.

"Room 420," Spencer replied.

Hunter took out a ten-dollar bill and handed it to the baggage attendant.

"Will you please take these bags to room 420 for us?" Hunter asked the attendant.

"Thank you, sir, no problem," replied the attendant as he took the money.

"I need a drink in the bar before we go up to our room. Spencer would you like to join me?" Hunter asked, already knowing the answer.

They were both beat up and exhausted, but wanted a relaxer before heading to their room. They walked into the bar and scanned the room for a couple of empty seats.

Hunter noticed a stocky man with a scar over his eye and shorter skinny man sitting at the far end of the bar. Both were wearing casual business attire, but something just seemed out of place. Hunter decided his mind was playing tricks on him and that they were probably just tourists.

Since the bar was full, Hunter and Spencer settled on a table on the main deck overlooking the ocean. A cocktail waitress showed up a within a few minutes, and they both ordered Don Q and Coke – double and in a tall glass.

"I think the adrenalin is wearing off. I'm starting to really feel the pain," Brad remarked after the waitress delivered the drinks.

Hunter saw that Brad's nose was pretty swelled and beginning to turn black and blue. "You really took a hit on that one," Hunter replied.

"Yes I can feel it in the back of my head." He said holding his rum and coke glass against his nose.

"I tell you what. Let's drink these, go to our room, and crack into the stash you had them get for us. That way you can ice your face and we can smoke those cigars, toasting another mission accomplished," Hunter said as finished his drink.

"I like that plan. Let's pay and go," Brad replied as he downed his drink. Brad flagged down the waitress and handed her his credit card. A few minutes later, she returned with the receipt. He added a generous tip and they adjourned to their room.

As they entered the room, Spencer asked Hunter to make a couple of drinks and get the cigars ready as he headed to the bathroom to take a quick shower. Hunter did as requested, taking all the supplies to the patio and setting up a makeshift bar, with ashtrays for the cigars.

He sat back on one of the patio chairs, took a sip of rum and Coke, and reached for his cell phone. He flipped it open, and observed that it was around one o'clock in the morning. He wondered if Amy was still up and if she would be upset if he called this late. Deciding to take the chance, he reached into his pocket for the business card she had given him earlier. He typed in her number and pressed send.

Amy, startled by the ringing of her cell phone, put down her scalpel and checked her caller ID to see who was calling this late.

"Mr. Hunter, I presume you made it back to your hotel safely," she said as she answered.

"Yes, thank you for asking. The mission went well. I will download what we got first thing in the morning and send it to the guys back in Washington," he replied. "Did I wake you?"

"No. Unfortunately, I am just finishing the examination of our friends and I am looking forward to a good night's sleep," she replied. "What are you up to?"

"I am having a glass of Don Q and Coke and waiting for Brad to get out of the shower so we can light up a couple of cigars."

"I'm am jealous. After sixteen hours with dead guys, I could use something like that."

"Well how about we have lunch and cocktails tomorrow?" Hunter asked.

"Well, I am wrapping up my work here and I'm supposed to fly back tomorrow. I could postpone my departure a day and tell them I want to confer with you on the subject matter. So that's a yes." She answered.

"Great. Where would you like me to pick you up?" asked Hunter.

"I rented a car and need to return it. Do you know Charlie's Car Rental in Islaverda?"

"Yes of course. Would you like me to meet you there around eleven?" Hunter asked.

"That would be great. See you then."

Shortly after the conversation, Spencer walked out to the patio wearing an old pair of shorts and a worn out t-shirt with Ohio State written across the chest.

"I think it's time we toast another adventure where neither of us got killed," Spencer said, raising his glass.

"To another day of living," Hunter said and clicked Spencer's glass.

After lighting their cigars, they both sat back to enjoy the sound of the ocean.

*   *   *

The next morning, Amy pulled into Charlie's parking lot and saw that Hunter was already there standing by a Mustang convertible. She parked and handed the attendant her keys.

Have you been waiting long?" she asked as she approached Hunter.

"Not long at all," he responded.

"Did you rent that car you're leaning against, cowboy?" she asked, a devilish grin on her face.

"This is a great ragtop day and I definitely didn't want to miss out. Why don't you finish your checkout while I load your bags?" He replied.

"Sounds like a plan," Amy said, turning slowly so he could get a good look, before walking toward the main office.

When she emerged ten minutes later, Hunter was waiting by the passenger side and opened the door to let her in.

"My, what a gentleman you are," she remarked as she climbed in.

"I do my best to prove that chivalry is not dead," he replied as he shut the door.

"Do you like Mexican Food?" he asked as he climbed into the drivers seat.

"Because, I know a great local place called Lopez, just down the street," he continued.

"Sounds good to me. I am starving!" she answered.

They turned right onto the main road drove a few blocks before turning left into the parking lot at Lopez.

"That was quick." Amy remarked.

"I told you it wasn't far," Hunter replied.

They got out and Hunter led Amy toward the outside deck. He

picked out a table and as they approached, he stepped ahead and pulled out her chair.

"Thank you, kind sir," she said as she sat down.

He took the seat next to her and they sat for a moment just looking into each other's eyes. He could tell she was enjoying herself and so was he. She had the most beautiful light green eyes he had ever seen.

"Can I get you some drinks," a waitress asked in English breaking their trance.

In the resort areas of Puerto Rico servers will often start in English if they think they have American customers.

"I will have a Cubra Libra," replied Amy.

"I'll have the same, but make mine with Don Q," added Hunter.

"Don Q for mine as well," Amy interjected.

As the waitress left, Hunter noticed the two suspicious men from the bar the previous evening walked in and sat at a corner table.

"This can't be a coincidence," he thought. Since there was not much he could do until he was sure they were up to no good, he decided not to alarm Amy and continue with their lunch date.

"So, Mister Hunter, what do you do for a good time?" Amy asked, snapping him out of his thoughts about the men.

"Well, I love having lunch with beautiful women." He replied.

Amy's face lit up, and she was having a hard time hiding it.

"I'm also an avid scuba diver and sailor," Hunter continued.

"A sailor!" she said with enthusiasm. "What kind of boats do you sail?"

"Anything with a mast and sails, but mostly a sloop-type rig," Hunter replied.

"You'll have to come sailing with me when we both get back up north."

"I'd like that. I haven't sailed since high school. My dad loves to sail and I would go with him any chance I could get," she stated.

"Why did you give it up?" He asked.

"Life just seemed to get in the way. You know, you work toward getting a degree, then a career, and before you know it, ten years have gone by," she replied.

"We'll just have to rectify that when we get back." He said with a big smile on his face.

The rest of lunch went by like a blur. They discussed their careers and many other details of their lives. After an hour, which seemed like only a few minutes, the waitress cleared their plates and asked them if they would like anything else. They decided on the check, not wanting to delay their convertible ride on this beautiful day. Hunter quickly paid before Amy could offer.

"Thank you so much for lunch," she said.

"You're welcome. Now, let's go and enjoy this day," Hunter responded.

As they were leaving, Hunter noticed that the two gentlemen were already gone. He was surprised that he had not seen them go. He had been so focused on Amy during lunch that they must have slipped by.

Within a few minutes, they were driving down Highway 187 with the top down and Jimmy Buffet playing in the background. Both were lost in the moment and it seemed that life couldn't get any better.

As they were casually driving along Hunter noticed a car approaching fast from behind. He knew Puerto Rican drivers could be pretty aggressive, but this guy was approaching fast even for a local and he did not appear to be slowing down. The other car closed the gap between them in seconds. He kept getting closer and closer. Not wanting to have this guy on his tail the whole drive, Hunter slowed down and motioned for the car to pass.

The car did not slow down and the driver seemed to have no intention of passing. Before Hunter could react, the mystery car slammed into the back of the Mustang. It threw him off guard and made Amy almost jump out of her skin.

Hunter quickly pushed the gas peddle to the floor and the Mustang was off. The convertible was faster than the black Lincoln Continental that pursued them, but with all the curves and traffic on the highway, outrunning the Lincoln would be a challenge. Hunter glanced in the rearview mirror and noticed the same two men he had seen last night and then again at lunch. He knew there was something amiss with these two, but was still surprised to see them attacking him in broad daylight on a busy street.

"Brad and I must have hit a nerve when we checked out the factory," he thought. He didn't have long to contemplate his dilemma before the stocky man in the passenger seat of the pursuing car brandished a small automatic weapon and shoved it out the window in their direction.

"Get down!" Hunter screamed as he pushed Amy's head down and jerked the wheel back and forth.

The little machine gun spurted out its deadly projectiles. The oncoming bullets hit the trunk and parts of the windshield, which continued until the magazine was expired. After the last bullet flew, Hunter took the chance to slam on the gas trying to out run his predator.

It was a wasted effort because the Lincoln slammed into the back of his car once again and then proceeded to come alongside. Hunter swerved to the left toward his attacker trying to run them off the road. To avoid the collision the Lincoln moved back into position behind the Mustang.

Again and again the Lincoln tried to come alongside, but Hunter held off the advance, knowing that if they managed to come along side it would certainly be the end of them.

Slam! The Lincoln hit the Mustang again and again. Hunter wondered how much his little car could take. He also was amazed but relieved that the pursuers had not tried to fire on them again.

Back in the Lincoln, the two men continued their pursuit. They were both trained professionals and patient. They both had side arms to fall back on, but preferred to get the job done with their machine gun, so they were saving their bullets for a better shot.

"This is taking longer than expected," Mr. Smith said to his companion.

"Nonetheless they will be dead soon and we will be off to collect the money for another completed job," he replied in a very confident tone.

The two approach Hunter's car again and managed to catch the left corner, which caught Hunter off guard. The Mustang began to spin out of control. All Hunter could hear was a swooshing sound as they barely avoided an oncoming car.

They completed two full 360-degree turns and somehow managed to get the car under control, coming to a complete stop facing sideways in the traffic lane. The front half of the car was in the lane while the back half protruded out toward the median.

Hunter looked up to see the Lincoln baring down on them fast. He floored the accelerator, but it was too late. Just as the Mustang began its forward motion, it was struck hard in the driver's side.

Hunter's head snapped to the left and hit his door, leaving him dazed and almost unconscious. Amy, who had been hiding on the floor to avoid the oncoming bullets, did not have on a seatbelt and with no restraint hit her head on the center console. The impact left her unconscious, with blood streaming down the side of her face.

Even after the impact, both cars where still traveling around 25 miles per hour with the Mustang facing sideways. Thinking he had the situation in hand, the passenger of the Lincoln reached down for his automatic weapon in order to finish the job.

As the man was coming up with the weapon, he heard two shots fired. He looked quickly to his left and saw that the driver was slumped over and did not appear to be conscious. He pulled the driver's head back and attempted to grab the wheel but it was two late.

The Lincoln missed the oncoming turn and ran off the road. Without the Mustang in front to slow them down, they accelerated to about 55 miles an hour before hitting a cinder block shack head-on. The passenger, who was not wearing his seatbelt, flew through the windshield and landed on the hood. He died instantly.

Still sitting in the middle of the road, Hunter, amazed to be alive, tried to gather his thoughts. Just seconds before the Lincoln hit Hunter's Mustang; he had reached down and retrieved a 9mm pistol out his ankle harness. The impact left him temporarily dazed, but he had regained enough consciousness to raise his weapon and get off two shots. Lucky for him they both hit the intended target, striking the driver in the shoulder and through the head.

He knew he had only one chance to get his car off the Lincoln so he had turned the wheel all the way to the left and pushed the accelerator to the floor. This combination presented enough force to dislodge the Mustang from the Lincoln. He accomplished this just in time to avoid being pinned between the Lincoln and the building, which would have led to most certain death.

He turned to Amy and see how she was doing. She had regained consciousness and looked up with a bloody face and a dazed look in her eyes. She was glad to be alive but couldn't grasp what had happened.

"Are you all right?" Hunter asked with a concerned look.

"Is this how you treat all your first dates?" she asked, trying to smile through the pain.

"No, just the ones I really like," Hunter replied. "That wound looks bad."

"I think I'll live, but I may need medical assistance," Amy remarked.

"I'll arrange it," Hunter said as he climbed over the wreckage that was the driver's side door and then onto the street.

"Do you feel well enough to be moved?" Hunter asked as he opened her door.

"I think so, with your help," she replied.

As Hunter helped Amy out of the car, he heard the sound of rescue sirens.

"Someone must have seen the wreck and called the authorities." He thought to himself.

Glad that help was on the way, he gently guided Amy toward the median. He laid her down on a small patch of grass on the side of the road and pulled out a handkerchief to blot the blood away from her face.

"This cut looks really deep," he said, trying to be gentle.

"Then it looks as bad as it feels," she replied. "Should we call this in and let those in charge know what happened?"

"When help arrives and I know you are all right, I will do just that," Hunter replied.

Two police cars arrived, followed by an ambulance and a fire truck. The ambulance driver and EMT jumped out and proceeded in their direction.

"Where are you hurt, ma'am?" the EMT asked as he approached.

"She has a gash on her head and may be suffering from a concussion," Hunter replied.

"How about yourself, sir?"

"I'm fine. Just a few scrapes and bruises." Replied Hunter.

"I would like to take a look at both of you," the EMT said.

"Just take care of her first. Then you can worry about me," Hunter replied.

Knowing that he would get nowhere by pushing the issue, the EMT began to assess Amy's vitals. Within a few moments, the driver appeared with the gear and stretcher.

"She is stable enough to be moved, but we need to get her to the hospital," the EMT said.

They put a board under Amy and immobilized her neck. With the help of Hunter, they placed her on the stretcher and then wheeled the stretcher toward the ambulance. The driver opened the back doors and with the EMT's assistance placed the stretcher in the back of the ambulance.

"I'll meet you at the hospital," Hunter said as she was placed in the ambulance.

"Take your time. I could use some rest before our next date," she said with a slight chuckle as the back doors were closed.

Hunter waited until the ambulance was out of sight before grabbing his cell phone. He made two calls, one to Spencer asking for a pickup and one to his boss back in headquarters.

"Sir, this is Eric Hunter," he said.

"Hunter, I thought you would be on a plane heading home by now," Reinquest said.

"Soon, sir. I ran into a problem that I thought you should know about. I'll give you more details later, but it seems we hit a nerve with the Oasis Company. I think they sent assassins to kill me."

"Are you OK?" Reinquest asked with concern.

"I'm just a little scraped up, but they took Amy to the hospital for further evaluation."

"Let me get this straight. You had Amy Evans with you in the car?" Reinquest asked.

"Yes, sir. I took her out to lunch to discuss her findings on the project." Hunter Replied.

"So where was Brad during this event?"

"The hotel, I assume. The fact remains he was not apart of this incident," said Hunter.

"So these guys interrupted your date with Miss Evans and tried to kill you."

"As a matter of speaking, yes, but I think they were after just me and Brad. After finishing me off, I'm sure they would have gone after him. I saw them in the hotel bar last night and then at the place I was having lunch today with Miss Evans. They looked out of place, but at that point they had done nothing wrong so I did not pursue the issue."

"Where are they now?" asked Reinquest.

"Their car with them in it ran through a cinder block shack a few hundred yards from where I am standing," explained Hunter.

"So it's safe to say they are both dead."

"Yes, sir, I believe so," said Hunter. "Sir, another ambulance is here to check me out and I think the police want some answers. I will call you back in a few hours after Brad arrives and once we have more time to assess the situation."

"That's fine. Just let them make sure you are all right. No more cowboy stuff," ordered Reinquest.

"No problem sir. You know me -- Mr. Careful," Hunter said and then hung up the phone before his boss could respond.

Other than a few scrapes and bruises, Hunter turned out to be in good condition. As he waited for Brad, he decided to check on the status on his pursuers.

The wounds on his head and arm began to ache as he walked

toward the wreckage. He did not tell the paramedics about the pain because he knew they would want to take him to the hospital with Amy. These were not the first injuries he had incurred on the job and he knew they weren't serious.

Spencer arrived, flashing his credentials so the police would clear him to enter the crash area. He caught up with Hunter as he was walking to the Lincoln.

"So you can't seem to have a normal date can you?" Spencer said as he approached his friend.

"No, it seems someone did not like our little visit to their factory and wanted us dead." Hunter replied.

"Don't lump me into all this," Spencer retorted. "How do you know it was about the mission and not some jealous husband exacting his revenge?"

"Well, lets check out these guys and find out," Hunter said.

Hunter and Spencer headed toward the car and saw that the paramedics were already examining the bodies. Spencer walked up to the heavier of the two dead men and asked the paramedic his status.

"The big guy expired on impact and the driver died from two gunshot wounds," the paramedic replied. "I think the cops want to talk to whichever of you were driving the Mustang."

"I was," Hunter said as he pulled out his credentials and showed them to the paramedic. "My partner and I are going to look over this area. Please let the authorities know who we are if you are asked."

Spencer crouched in front of the heavy man and pulled off his necklace.

"Remind you of anything?" he asked, showing it to Hunter.

The necklace was exactly like the one they found earlier on the other group that tried to kill them.

"I think you can count out the jealous husband theory," Hunter said with a smile.

Chapter 13

After looking around for more clues, Hunter and Spencer gave up and went to the hospital to see how Amy was faring.

Unfortunately, they were going to have to make the visit a short one because they were due at the Coast Guard base in Old San Juan within the hour to have a secure close conference meeting with Adam Reinquest and other decision makers. It was evident that the situation was getting out of hand and this operation could no longer stay under wraps.

Hunter entered the hospital and headed for the front desk.

"May I help you sir?" The receptionist asked.

"Yes ma'am I was in the car with Amy Evans and I would like to visit her if possible." He replied.

"Yes sir Miss Evans is in room 201 just go down the hall to the elevator and up one floor." She replied.

"Gracias," Hunter said as he walked away.

By this time Spencer, had parked the car and caught up with Hunter in the hospital hallway. When they arrived they were both taken back to see so many Puerto Rican Police officers guarding the door.

"Can I help you sir?" one of the guards asked in English.

"We are friends of Amy Evans and would like to pay her a visit," Hunter replied.

"Sorry, sir, this room is off limits to visitors," the guard informed them.

"We are with the ODR and I was in the accident with Miss Evans," Hunter said as he presented his identification.

The guard grabbed their IDs and studied each of them intently before responding.

"Sorry sir, you may proceed inside," he said, handing back their identification.

Hunter entered the room first and Amy's eyes lit up instantly when she saw him.

"I was wondering when you were going to come and visit," she said.

"I came as soon as they let me leave the scene," He replied. "So how is my favorite patient doing?"

"They say I'll make a full recovery. I just need a couple days of rest. I had a mild concussion and as you can see some cuts and bruises," she replied. "And how about you Mr. Hunter? I saw you take a couple of good hits. How are you feeling today?"

"Nothing I can't handle. Just a little sore."

"Men," Amy said, shaking her head. "You just can't admit when you are hurt. Nonetheless, I'm glad to see you."

As they continued their conversation, Brad's cell phone rang.

"Yes sir, we can be there in twenty minutes." Brad replied before hanging up.

"Sorry you two, but that was our boss and he wants us in a meeting at the Coast Guard Base ASAP." Brad said.

"I understand. If the tables were turned I would do the same." Amy replied before Hunter could say anything.

"I may not be able to make it back to see you here, but don't forget, we still have a sailing date when I get back to Baltimore." Hunter said.

"I would like that very much. Now you better get to work," Amy replied, smiling.

Before he left Hunter leaned over and gave her a hug and a small kiss on the lips. Brad followed Hunter out both turning back to wave good-bye as they departed.

Thirty minutes later, they entered the conference room at the Base. They noticed that there were only two others, the captain of the Coast Guard Base James Duke and the captain of the Cushing, Lieutenant Norman.

"My name is Captain Duke, and I think you have already met Lieutenant Norman," Duke said, rising to shake hands with the two men. "I have asked Lieutenant Norman to join us because his boat will be standing by to assist you if needed."

"Thank you, Captain. All your help is appreciated," replied Hunter.

"We should be connected momentarily to the others. Please have a seat and I will see if they are ready," said the Captain.

Moments later, the computer was turned on and the meeting began. The screen was split in two, with the head of the ODR on the right and White House Chief of Staff Bob Renousky to the left.

"Gentlemen, thank you all for joining this meeting today," Renousky said. "We have a serious problem that needs to be addressed. Let me remind all of you that this is a Top Secret meeting. None of this information can be discussed with anyone outside this conference."

"As some of you may know, we believe that the missile incident was not an accident but an attempt to take the life of the President of the United States. Thanks to the work of Mr. Hunter and Mr. Spencer, we believe the main entity behind this is the Oasis Company. What we don't know is why and when they will try again. Because of the company's political pull and financial power, this investigation will have to be kept very discrete."

"Did we get useful information on the data we recovered from their factory?" asked Hunter.

"Unfortunately we could not, Mr. Hunter. The data was so well encrypted it might take months to get anything we can use," said Renousky.

"What's our next step?" asked Spencer.

"Well, Mr. Spencer, it's funny you asked. You and Mr. Hunter are to head to the airport immediately after this meeting and board a flight for the Austrian Alps."

"What is in Austria?" asked Hunter.

"Our intelligence tells us that Mr. Bruner, the head of the Oasis Company, has a ski house there where he spends a great deal of time. We want the two of you to see what you can find out. It's an extremely cold October and they already had a large amount of snow, so you will need to buy some winter attire for your trip. I have a private jet standing by awaiting your arrival. You will receive your briefing package once you board the jet."

"We've never been to Austria, but it sounds like fun," Spencer said to Hunter. "Hopefully we can get a little skiing in during our visit."

"We will try to get this file decrypted as soon as possible, but any other information you can find will be helpful," said their boss, Adam Reinquest, ignoring Spencer's comment.

"Is there anything we can do in the meantime Mr. Renousky?" asked Captain Duke.

"Just keep an eye on the factory in Puerto Rico and let us know of any odd behavior. But please be discrete. We don't want them to know we are on to them." Renousky continued. "Gentlemen, you have your orders. Good luck."

After the connection was severed, Hunter and Spencer shook hands with the two Coastguardsmen and headed out. After a quick stop at the hotel and then a not-so-quick drop-off of their rental car, they arrived at the airport security gate to find a man waiting to escort them to their private charter. Within fifteen minutes of boarding the aircraft, they were in the air and climbing to an altitude of 30,000 feet. They were both impressed with the swankiness of the aircraft and astonished when they realized it was a Gulf V charter. They had lucked into this aircraft because the Gulf V was the only plane in the area that Renousky could get on such short notice that could travel the distance without refueling.

Spencer kicked back to enjoy the ride; it was not every day he got to experience one of the most luxurious private jets on the market. It was even equipped with Champagne and fine caviar, no doubt intended for some bigwig senator or congressman. Hunter opened the packet they had been given and started to read through the information.

"It does not look good," he said to Spencer. "This guy has more security at this place than most buildings in Washington."

"Does it look like something we can handle?" Spencer asked.

"We will find a way," Hunter said, but a look of doubt washed over his face.

Chapter 14

They arrived in Austria to find a car waiting for them as they disembarked the aircraft. It was reserved to take them to a room that had been arranged on the side of the mountain where David Bruner's house resided.

As they drove through the Austrian Alps, Hunter and Spencer lost themselves in the beauty of the landscape. The drive gave them time to drift off and enjoy their fascinating surroundings.

Even though it took an hour it seemed like only a few minutes before they arrived at the hotel. The driver parked the car, got out, and headed to the trunk to unload its cargo. Spencer followed to collect the bags and then reached into his wallet and handed the driver a $20 Euro bill. The driver accepted the gratuity with a nod of thanks and they headed to the main desk to check in.

"Where did you get a twenty Euro bill?" Hunter asked.

"Remember the last time we were in Europe? I had forty Euros left and I tried to cash them in but it was going to cost $15 in fees to do so. The two twenty Euro bills have been in my wallet ever since." Brad replied.

Although they came in handy Hunter just shook his head at the fact that his friend had kept the two bills all this time.

The hotel had a wonderfully large main entrance filled with the heads of many animals. From the looks of things, it probably doubled as a hunting lodge during the summer months.

Hunter checked in while Brad looked around. He was amazed at the beautiful carvings that adorned the ceilings and most corners throughout the main hall. He could have studied them all day, but before long Hunter approached.

"We're all checked in and our bags are on their way to our room as we speak," Hunter stated.

"Great. That means we have time to buy some warm clothes on the company tab," commented Brad.

They headed to the hotel's gift store and found it to be very limited so they only purchased jackets and hats. Later they would have to go into town and buy all the remaining attire they would need for their mission.

*   *   *

"Mr. Bruner, this is London. I am secure on this end," Kyle London said as he picked up the phone on their private line.

"My phone reads secure also. What's the news?" Bruner asked.

"It seems our luck is not improving. This Hunter fellow managed to kill the men you sent." London said.

"Those men were no amateurs." Bruner replied, a hint of anger in his voice. "It appears our adversary is more clever than expected."

"Do you know where they are right now?" he asked.

"Our sources said that Mr. Hunter and Mr. Spencer boarded a private jet this morning and headed to Austria. It appears they are coming your way." London paused before continuing. "I don't think we can write this off as a coincidence."

"I agree. I think I will have to invite the two over for dinner," Bruner said before ending the call.

*   *   *

After a short nap, Hunter and Spencer awoke to a knock at the door. A drowsy Brad Spencer answered in his boxers.

"What do you want?" he said in a grouchy tone as he swung

open the door. Standing there was a beautiful young woman with an envelope in hand.

"I'm sorry to bother you, sir, but this was dropped off at the front desk with direction to deliver it to you at ten o'clock this morning," she said, a little embarrassed about waking him.

"Sorry ma'am. I am still on United States time, where it is 4 in the morning. I appreciate you delivering the letter. Wait a minute and I'll give you something for your effort."

"No thank you, sir. I have already been taken care of by the person who gave it to me."

"And who was that, by the way?" asked Brad.

"He did not say, sir. Have a nice day." As she walked away, he took a moment to admire the sight. He'd have to visit the front desk for more information, he thought.

"Who was at the door?" Hunter asked, with one eye open just enough to see.

"It was the front desk with a package for us. It appears to be an invitation to a party being held at David Bruner's ski lodge mansion tonight. It is a black tie event."

"How in the hell did he know we were here?" Hunter asked.

"This guy has his spies," Spencer replied. "The question is are we going?"

"You know I would never miss a party!" Hunter said, putting his head back on his pillow to get more sleep.

Chapter 15

Hunter awoke five hours later to find Brad already up and walking out of the bathroom.

"How long have you been up?" he asked.

"I got up an hour ago and took a nice long hotel shower," Brad replied.

"What time is it?" Hunter asked.

"It is nine o'clock in the morning our time, which makes it three in the afternoon Austrian time."

"Three o'clock!" Hunter exclaimed. "We need to get a move on before the stores close."

"Well then you get ready and meet me in the lobby in half an hour," replied Brad, heading out the door.

"Sounds like a plan. See you in thirty," Hunter said.

At first Hunter could not figure out why Brad was in such a hurry to leave but then it hit him. He remembered the attractive girl at the door and if he knew his buddy as well as he thought he did, he knew that Spencer wanted to get down to the front desk before she finished her shift.

He slowly got out of bed and walked over to the bar refrigerator area where a fresh pot of coffee sat. He poured himself a cup of life and walked to the patio window.

"It snowed last night," he noted. "This will be great for skiing tomorrow."

He took the entire thirty minutes to get ready. As he was putting on his shoes, Brad walked into the room.

"How did it go with the Austrian girl?" Hunter quickly asked before Spencer could utter a word.

"I will be seeing her later tonight at Max's bar after we finish our dinner party," Brad said, smiling ear to ear.

"Do you think it was wise to make two plans for the evening?" Hunter asked trying to prod Brad.

"Are you about ready? We need to get fitted for tuxes and we need to buy more clothes." He replied, blowing off the comment.

"Yes, I am," said Hunter. "The tux place is expecting us at quarter till four, so we have fifteen minutes to get there. I already called a cab, which should be waiting for us as we speak."

"You never cease to amaze me," Spencer replied in a joking manner. "You did all that yourself?"

As expected, the cab was waiting for them in front of the hotel. They hopped in and drove through freshly snow-covered streets to the store.

Hunter and Spencer walked in and found themselves in a place that time forgot. The store was well maintained but looked, as it must have a hundred years ago. Huge exposed timbers braced the ceiling, while a rather large fireplace lined the northern most wall. As they were taking it all in an old man emerged from the back room.

"Hello sir my name is Eric Hunter we spoke on the phone." Hunter said as he approached.

"Yes I remember you two need to be fitted for tuxedos," the man replied in a thick Austrian accent.

Before Hunter or Brad could mutter a word in response the old man continued.

"I saw you admiring the shop. This store has been in my family for four generations. This area of town was built in 1869. My great-grandfather opened the doors of this establishment in the summer of that year. It has come a long way since it started as a supply store that sold all sorts of goods. The only thing that still reflects the original store is it had a small section of clothing in the back. Now, as you can see, we are entirely a clothing store and sell designer clothing from around the world."

"Enough about that," he said when he realized he had gone on for long enough. "We need to get the two of you fitted for your evening."

"Can these be ready before you close today?" asked Spencer.

"I will have them ready by six. Come back and knock on the door at that time, and I'll be waiting for you." Replied the old man.

"Are you sure it is no trouble? We know you close at five," said Spencer.

"I can't have you going to your party in your undergarments can I?" He remarked as he reached for the measuring tape.

While he measured Hunter, Brad browsed the store. He returned fifteen minutes later, when it was his turn to be measured, with his arms full of clothing.

"Is that all for you?" asked Hunter.

"I picked out a few things for you, too," Brad replied, holding aloft a single pair of socks.

"Not to worry. I can shop for myself," Hunter replied.

The old man ignored their conversation and began work on Brad's measurements. He took a lot of care in what he did and always strived at getting the perfect measurements. He spent the same time acquiring Brad's measurements, which gave Hunter plenty of time to return with clothing of his own.

"Could you ring up and package all these clothes for us?" Hunter asked. "I'll pay you when we return for the tuxes."

"No problem. Mr. Spencer told me you still had to go to the ski shop today. I will see you at six." He replied as he waived them goodbye.

They walked out of the store to find that the cab driver was waiting for them. As they approached they heard the song "Tubthumping" by Chumbawamba.

Hunter smiled as the lyrics "I get knocked down but I get up again" blasted from the radio. "What a small world" he thought to himself.

"Are you waiting for us?" Spencer asked startling the cab driver.

"Yes please get in." He replied in his best English.

It took ten minutes to get to the ski shop. They asked the driver to wait out front and keep the meter running.

Twenty minutes and four hundred Euros later, the two emerged with bags full.

They had an hour before they had to pick up their tuxes so they had the cab driver drop them off at Max's pub.

"We will take two Hefeweizen's," Hunter said after getting the bartender's attention. Hefeweizen was a local beer served in Germany and Austria and starting to make its way to the United States

"Here's to your health!" Spencer said, lifting his glass.

"Yes, see you in the emergency room," Hunter replied and took a drink.

"We need to go over the plan for this evening." Hunter stated as he took another sip.

"How should we play this one?" Asked Spencer.

"I think we need to just show up, play it calm, and find out what kind of man we are dealing with. Remember, he's the one who invited us."

"At least we can get free food and drinks out of the situation," Brad replied.

Chapter 16

From an Internet café located next to the hotel's main entrance, Hunter was sending an e-mail to headquarters with an update on their status. He did not telephone because he knew that his boss, Adam Reinquest, would never go for anything this forward.

"I can't wait until Reinquest gets this e-mail," said Spencer. "He's going to be so pissed at you for not letting him know beforehand."

"My friend, if they have not fired us yet they will probably let this one go as well. That is," Hunter continued, "if we come up with some good information."

"Now, how do I look?" Hunter asked.

"Well, if this is our last party at least we will go out looking good," Spencer said as he admired his reflection in a hallway mirror.

"The old man did a great job on these tuxes. It was nice of him to stay so late," Hunter commented.

The Mercedes and driver they ordered were waiting outside to take them to David Bruner's gathering. They could only imagine what the evening held in store for them.

As they drove, the driver tried to make small talk by asking them where they were from and whether they were enjoying their stay in Austria. Spencer chatted while Hunter gazed out the window, dwelling on the fact that this night could get ugly.

After a forty-five minute drive, they arrived in the front of the David Bruner's palatial home. It was decorated with a Japanese theme and two lion statues guarded the entranceway. A couple of large men greeted them as they approached the door.

Hunter nudged Spencer to point out that both men had gun bulges under their tuxedoes. From the large outline of the weapon, he figured they both were packing at least 45's.

The guards asked politely for their invitation, which Spencer showed with a smile. After a quick glance, the guard placed it on a small table with the rest of the ones he had collected.

"Please enjoy your evening sirs," he said, motioning them inside.

As they entered they stopped to look around the room. The inside of the house was even more amazing then the outside. To the right of the main entrance stood a fifteen-foot rock waterfall that emptied into a basin. The basin fed a slow-flowing river that eventually circled the room and ended in a collection pool somewhere behind the rock structure. The glass floor of the entranceway was clear to provide a view of the river beneath it. Four exposed logs supported each corner of the massive room, some of the largest Hunter had ever seen.

They did not stand and admire long because others were beginning to enter. As they stepped down the main stairs a man offering them Champagne, which they both accepted, greeted them.

"I give this guy credit," said Hunter. "He really knows how to live."

"It just goes to show you what dirty money can buy," Spencer remarked. "Now let's go see what kind of trouble we can get into."

"I am with you my friend. Let's head to the bar."

The room was filled with what appeared to be very important people. No one the two of them knew, but most were well dressed and the party had a certain regal appearance about it. Hunter scanned the room as Spencer ordered the two of them a round of beers.

"I have not seen our host yet," Hunter commented.

"I am sure he will appear soon enough," Spencer said as he handed him a beer.

"This is a long way from the parties we used to attend at Ohio State," Hunter said as he raised his glass for Spencer to toast.

Just as they were taking their drink, Hunter spotted Bruner walk into the room. He motioned for Spencer to discreetly look over toward his vicinity.

"I thought he would be taller," Spencer whispered, taking another sip of beer.

"That's what you always say. Do you think all bad guys have to be six five?" asked Hunter.

"No, but this guy is no bigger than I am," Spencer replied.

David Bruner spotted the two men, recognizing them from the files of information his men had collected on them. He headed directly toward them, approaching Hunter first and holding out his hand.

"I don't think we have met. My name is..."

"David Bruner," Hunter interrupted. "Everyone here knows who you are. But let me introduce myself. My name is ... "

"Eric Hunter," Bruner interrupted. "And this is your partner Brad Spencer. I also do my homework before I invite my guests, Mr. Hunter."

"I didn't know we were even in the radar of a man of your status," Hunter said.

"I make it a point to know about all that goes on with my businesses. You and your partner have been busy lately, haven't you, Mr. Hunter?" asked Bruner.

"The same could be said about you Mr. Bruner. But please just call me Hunter. The mister is reserved for my father."

"Very well, Hunter. You can call me David. Tell me, Hunter, what brings you to Austria?"

"I think we both know the answer to that, David," Hunter said.

"I am not sure I do," replied Bruner.

"For the skiing of course."

"Of course. I could not agree more. Please excuse me I must attend to my other guests. Please make yourselves at home. It was a pleasure meeting you, Hunter and Mr. Spencer." He shook both their hands and walked away.

Neither spoke until he was across the room and out of earshot.

"Ok buddy, we need to put on our game faces. I want to look around before we bump back into our gracious host." Hunter said as he put down his beer. "I want you to stay out here and mingle. I'm going to go look for a bathroom."

"You mean that's what you want me to say if anyone asks," Spencer said.

"Of course, Sherlock. I hope I won't be long, but send me a text message if our host spots you and comes over to talk."

"I got it. But what should I do in the mean time?" Spencer asked.

"Just mingle with the other guests," Hunter said putting his hand on Spencer's shoulder and walking away.

"Just mingle," Spencer muttered under his breath.

"I look as out of place as a urinal in a ladies restroom," he thought to himself. "But I'll do my best to blend."

Hunter walked toward a far hallway and disappeared down a corridor. As he entered he saw four doors, two on the right and two on the left. He tried the first door on the right and opened it to find a bathroom. He shut the door and continued on to the next. He tried the remaining three doors, which all led to bedrooms.

There was one door left at the end of the hall. He tried it and found it to be locked. Giving a quick glance around to make sure no one was looking, he pulled out a small set of tools and made an attempt to gain entry. Within a few moments he accomplished his mission and unlocked the door. He slowly entered what appeared to be Bruner's office.

The office was as grand as the rest of the house, with two large saltwater aquariums set back into the wall on the left as he entered. He noticed a small nurse shark in the first tank and thought to himself that this fish was far from home.

He quickly moved behind the desk and proceeded to check out each drawer. He struck out in the side drawer and decided to attempt the one in the middle. It was locked, so he pulled out a Swiss Army pocketknife he had picked up earlier at the ski equipment store and after a quick jimmying of the lock he was in, sifting threw the paperwork.

He didn't find much -- only the ripped off top of a letter with the words "Stem Cell Research Project" written across it. It looked as though it had caught on the back of the drawer and ripped off as the rest was pulled away. It was probably nothing, but he was going to take it just in case.

As he was re-locking the drawer, he heard the handle of the office door begin to turn. Without hesitation he made a quick move toward a sliding glass door located on the other side of the room. He slid the door open just enough to squeeze out.

"I told you these tanks where worth seeing, didn't I, ambassador," David Bruner said as he pointed to the two fish tanks in his office. "You don't see many of these around here. I had the tanks shipped down from Munich and these fish were all captured just outside of Puerto Rico."

"Very impressive, Mr. Bruner, but I didn't want to speak to you alone to discuss fish. There has been a lot of talk about you being involved in some dirty pool and I wanted to discuss this with you," said the U.S. ambassador to Austria.

"I assure you, it is all rumors," Bruner said, hesitating before he continued. He turned and walked toward the outside door and noticed it was slightly open.

"I don't remember that door being open when I left," he thought.

Outside, Hunter was hiding and trying to listen to their conversation. He saw Bruner look in his direction. He didn't think he had been spotted, but he knew he had to make a quick escape. Since it was a twenty-five foot drop to the ground, jumping was out of the question.

"Mr. Ambassador, I have something I have to attend to. Let us continue this meeting over lunch tomorrow, and I will set your mind at ease and let you know everything is on the up and up," Bruner said as he guided the ambassador into the hallway, where a guard was patiently waiting.

"Please escort the ambassador back to the party," Bruner said to the guard.

Mr. Bruner went back into his office and locked the door behind him. He knew that there was no way off the deck, so he headed back to see who had paid him a visit. He pulled out a 45-caliber semi automatic pistol just in case. He slowly opened the door and maneuvered the pistol into position. He did a quick search of the right side of the deck, with his pistol out in front.

He then turned to his left and proceeded to scan the rest of the area. Knowing that the deck was too high to jump, he concluded that the person in question had to be either on the deck or hiding in his office.

Convinced that the person he was looking for was not outside, Mr. Bruner decided to head back into his office. As he turned around, something impelled him to look up.

As he did so, Eric Hunter jumped from the rooftop, landing on top of Bruner and knocking the gun out of his hand. Before Bruner could react, Hunter delivered a blow to his head, knocking him temporarily unconscious.

Hunter had climbed onto the snow-covered roof and was hiding, hoping to escape after the office was clear. In his desperation, he had made the only play he had. He and Spencer were going to have to make an immediate exit, so he quickly dragged the unconscious Bruner into his office, shook the snow off his tux, and headed toward the door.

Hunter tried the door, but it was locked. Realizing Bruner must have locked it when he entered, he knew that the only way out was to go back in and get the key.

As Hunter turned around, he saw that Bruner was not lying where he had left him. He scanned the room but before he could react, Bruner was on him. He punched Eric in the gut and then the head, knocking him off his feet.

Hunter rolled over on all fours, holding his stomach in pain as Bruner kicked him again in the stomach. This launched Hunter to his back almost rendering him unconscious from the pain.

Bruner lined up to give Hunter the knock out kick to the head. As he cocked back his foot, Hunter grabbed the planted foot, which knocked Bruner backward.

Hunter stumbled to his feet, trying to keep his balance. Bruner rose up and charged, ramming Hunter into the wall.

Hunter decided he had had enough of this and quickly looked around for any thing that would help his situation. He grabbed a trophy made of rock off the wall and crashed it down on Bruner's head with all his might. The smashing force not only broke the trophy but also knocked the unsuspecting Bruner unconscious once again.

After taking a moment to regain his composure, Hunter searched Bruner's pockets and found the key to the door. He stumbled to his freedom, unlocking the door and exiting into the hallway. As he walked down the hallway, he saw that the bathroom was unoccupied and entered it to straighten up.

He knew he didn't have much time, so after only a minute of readjustment he headed to the main floor to meet up with Brad, which he found talking to the daughters of the ambassador of Germany. He approached and kindly asked if his friend could be excused for a moment.

"What are you doing and why do you look so rough?" asked Spencer, visibly upset that he had to leave the lovely ladies.

"First off, you are supposed to be paying attention. And second, we have to leave. I just pulled a Russell."

"You just pulled a Russell? We need to get out of here. Now," Spencer said, almost racing Hunter to the door.

A Russell was a term they used for this situation because one night in college Hunter was messing around with the Ohio State quarterback's girlfriend at a team football party. Right before Russell, the quarterback, walked in on them, Hunter jumped into the closet. A suspicious Russell started to investigate and Hunter had to jump out and give him a good rap on the head. Before the other players knew what had happened, Spencer and Hunter had made it out of the party.

Those football players chased them at least ten blocks before they gave up. Spencer could only imagine what would happen this time.

They walked to the door as calmly as possible and were almost home free when a staggering David Bruner immerged and yelled to the guards to stop them.

Not giving up without a fight, Hunter and Spencer charged the guards, knocking them off balance and pushing their way through. The stars were definitely shining on them that night, because the valet had just pulled up a Rolls Royce for the ambassador of France.

"Thank you!" Spencer said as he grabbed the keys from the valet.

"I am sorry, Mr. Ambassador, but we need to use your car for a little while," Hunter said as he raced by the ambassador and his family and quickly took a seat on the passenger side.

"That was a close one!" Spencer said as the tires squealed and they made their getaway.

"Don't count your chickens before they are hatched. We have a couple of cars behind us," Hunter said.

"What should we do, buddy? This guy knows where we are staying," Spencer said, stating the obvious.

"First thing we need to do is lose these guys. We're about forty-five minutes from our hotel, and my guess is these guys don't know were we are staying. If we lose them, they'll have to regroup back at Bruner's before coming for us, which will cost them valuable time. We can then stop in town, call the hotel and have them check us out and bring our bags to the front desk. Looks like we will have to find another place to stay tonight." Hunter said.

"That all sounds good, but how do we lose them?" Spencer asked, as he tried to keep the car on the road while passing cars and whizzing around curves.

Instead of answering, Hunter cracked a big smile, and Spencer knew he was in for a rough night.

"Don't even think about it. We'll be killed," he yelled.

"Not if you can keep us on the groomed path of the snow cat," Hunter replied, as his smile grew larger. "Turn left behind that house around the next bend," ordered Hunter, pointing to the house.

"This is going to hurt. I just know it!" exclaimed Spencer.

"NOW!" Hunter shouted, and Spencer jerked the wheel sharply

to the left. The car made the turn and headed toward a three-foot snow bank at the end of the driveway.

"Were you expecting this?" Spencer asked frantically.

"No, but floor it!" Hunter screamed out.

Spencer did as he was told and they hit that snow bank at about fifty miles an hour and crashed right through.

"I hope the French ambassador was not in love with this car because it's going to need a lot of work after we get done with it," Hunter commented.

As the car sped down the ski slope, Spencer tried to regain control.

"Steer this pig!" Hunter shouted out.

"I am! This car was not exactly made for these conditions," Spencer spouted back. However, he did manage to get the car under control enough to keep it heading down the mountain.

"Have you thought of how we are going to stop this thing?" Spencer asked as they sped down the slope.

"I got us away from the chasing cars. Now it's your turn to come up with something," Hunter replied.

"You mean you don't have a plan to stop? Are you crazy?"

"Well we'll figure it out one way or the other soon enough because the end of the slope is coming up!" Hunter shouted back.

Spencer guided the car the best he could, but he was heading straight for a group of trees and there was nothing he could do about it.

"Hold on! This is going to be a rough landing!" shouted Spencer.

The car drifted toward the tree line and brushed the first tree, sending them into a spin. The back end hit another, which slowed their spin a little. Just when they thought it would go on forever, the right fender hit another sending them sideways into two other trees on the driver's side. They hit, stopping instantly, which deployed both front and side airbags.

They laid there for a few moments before either spoke.

"Spencer, are you still alive?" Hunter asked, desperately awaiting his response.

"I think so. But from now on I make the decisions." he replied.

"Anything, my friend. I'm just glad you're still with me."

"I think we need to hail a taxi and get to our hotel," Spencer said, attempting to dislodge himself from the driver's seat.

"Hold on, buddy. Your seat belt is stuck. I need to get to my knife and cut you free," Hunter said.

He pulled out his knife and cut the restraints that held Spencer. They both climbed out the passenger side.

They were a little bloodied and bruised, but did not have time to attend to their wounds. They practically crawled the twenty-yard distance to the road and managed to hail a cab.

The driver was kind enough to lend them his cell phone. Hunter called the hotel and let them know they were coming and asked them to have their baggage ready for pickup.

After a forty-minute cab ride, they arrived at the hotel. Hunter hastily checked them out and within ten minutes they were loading their bags in the waiting cab.

"Do you know of a place where we can stay the night?" Hunter asked the cab driver.

"Why not continue your stay here, sir?"

"They were full. Do you have any place in mind?"

"I have a friend that runs a bed and breakfast that may have a room left," responded the cab driver.

"That would be great. Could you take us there?" Hunter asked, handing the driver a hundred Euro bill.

The cab driver gave a nod of approval and drove away. On the way, the driver called his friend to check availability. "You're in luck," he said. "He has one room left but it only has one large bed. Do you want it?"

"That will be fine," Spencer said, looking up through a partially swollen eye.

At the bed and breakfast, the owner was waiting at the door to greet them. He was in his pajamas and robe and it was clear they had woken him.

They got out and Brad began to unload the bags. Hunter went to the driver and pulled out another hundred Euro bill.

"If anyone asks, you did not pick up two Americans this evening," he said as he handed the bill to the driver.

"What Americans are you talking about? Americans usually do not visit this part of Austria," he replied as he took the money. The taxi driver gave his friend a quick wave and pulled away.

As the two wounded men settled in to their room, the reality of the evening started to set in. They both knew they had a lot of explaining to do and neither wanted to make the call.

"You did what?" Adam Reinquest yelled into the phone.

"Now, sir. Let's put this into context. I did get a clue," Hunter said.

"You mean the letterhead that had Stem Cell Research Project printed on the top of it?" Reinquest shouted. "I don't call that a clue. I call that a piece of trash."

"Sir, listen to me for a moment. We both know that the President opposes stem cell research and that there was an attempt on his life. We also know we found two men wearing Oasis necklaces. I think there is a link that ties all of that together. Proof is what I am lacking at this time," Hunter said with a confidence that only he could display in a time like this.

"What's your next move?" Adam asked.

"We need to prove that all this is connected. Or at least find enough proof so that the President can act."

"Where am I sending you next?" Reinquest asked, a bit of worry in his voice.

"Home first would be a nice start," Hunter said. "I would like to do a little more research on this subject and talk with some people in the know."

"Let me see what Marty can do. Are you secure at your present location?" inquired Reinquest.

"We will be fine until morning, but the sooner we leave here the better!" Hunter replied.

"I will have your arrangements ready by tomorrow, just hang tight," Reinquest said as he hung up the phone.

He sat back in his chair and rubbed his temples. He had no idea what this would stir up in Washington, but he was sure he would have a lot of explaining to do.

*   *   *

Mr. Bruner received the news that Mr. Hunter and Mr. Spencer had eluded his security force a few hours before the end of the party. He had no choice but to continue as if everything was all right. When asked about the incident, he described it as a botched robbery.

His men had gone to their hotel to find that Hunter and Spencer had already checked out. No one knew where they had vanished.

After another painstaking three hours, the party started to wind down. "I'm going to retire to my office and handle some business," Bruner told a member of his staff.

He entered and locked the door behind him, then punched a command security code into a keypad next to the door. This turned off the security cameras in his office and set an alarm that would sound if anyone tried to enter. He headed toward his desk, pulled out a thick leather chair, and comfortably sat back.

His head was swimming with the events of the night. How he was going to get even for the disrespect Hunter and Spencer had shone him played heavy on his mind.

He sat for a minute in thought, then picked up the phone and dialed. There was only one man he could trust for a job like the one he had planned. The phone rang and Kyle London picked up.

"I am getting really sick of these two annoying gentlemen, Mr. London," Bruner said without giving London a chance to say hello.

"Are you referring to the men from the ODR?" he asked.

"Yes, of course."

"Would you like me to take care of them sir?" London asked.

"I believe it would attract too much attention if they were to die now," Bruner said. "We need to lure them away from all the politics. Somewhere we can take care of them, out of the public eye. Somewhere we can make it look like an accident."

"To do that, sir, we will need them to go on a trip in an area we control, where nobody knows they will be, and where we can make it look like an accident. I don't see how that can be accomplished," London replied.

"I am one step a head of you," Bruner continued. "All we need is something or someone to draw them to an area of our design."

"What do you have in mind?" asked London.

"It's simple. Amy Evans is a soft target. We kidnap her and force them to come after her. As far as she knows, no one is after her, so she shouldn't have her guard up," Bruner said as he leaned back in his chair. He had impressed himself with his brilliance and was not afraid to let it show.

"I will have some of our men in Washington pick her up and take her to the warehouse in California," London said in response to Bruner's orders.

The California warehouse was where they liked to take care of some of their less-than-reputable business. The main part was used to store legit items, but the secret rooms underneath had been used in the past for anything from the storage of illegal goods to a place to hide from authorities. This would be the first time they would be used to store a prisoner.

"Using local muscle to do the job is no good. I want you to personally take care of this one. Take four or five of your most trusted men. Remember, this is a top secret mission and only those involved need to know about it," Bruner ordered.

"I will charter a private jet under a fake name and leave as soon as I can," answered London.

"Very well, but remember there can be no mistakes on this one."

"I will see to it that nothing goes wrong sir," London said before hanging up.

Chapter 17

Amy Evans sat at her desk at FBI headquarters in Washington, DC, chewing the end of her pencil. Her mind, as it had been doing so often lately, drifted to thoughts of Eric Hunter. She imagined the two of them on some romantic beach in the Caribbean. She would be drinking a margarita while he would be snorkeling, catching the fish they would eat that evening.

She loved the idea of a self-sufficient man, one who could survive no matter what the conditions. Hunter was that kind of man, but she also knew that men like that tended not to stay around for long. She was willing to take the chance with Hunter. He had said he would call when he arrived back in Washington and she eagerly awaited another rendezvous with her hero.

"How is everything?" her boss, Mark Williams, asked as he entered her office.

Amy had been so engrossed in her daydream that she had not heard him enter the lab.

"Fine," she replied, a little embarrassed to be caught in a daydream. "I was just finishing the final research."

"Are you OK?" Williams asked with a concerned look. "Are you sure you don't need more time to recover?

"No, I'm fine." She replied.

"It must have been traumatic to be in a high-speed chase. I

don't know how I would feel if I had come so close to death," he continued.

"I never thought of it that way, sir, but I am fine," Evans said, realizing once again that her boss had no tact with conversation. He was a genius at forensics, but a moron at dealing with people. She always found forensic television shows humorous because in her experience, most of the forensic specialists were nerds with no people skills whatsoever.

Seeing Amy's look of dismay, his tone softened. "Have you found any more useful information from your research of the items recovered in Puerto Rico?" he asked.

"I think we're going to have to close this case on our end. I have turned over every stone I could find and haven't come up with any more evidence than we already had," She replied.

"Well, it's Friday and close to lunch. How long do you think it will take you to finish your report?" he asked.

"I could probably be done in an hour," she answered.

"I want you to finish this report and go home. I won't take no for an answer."

"Normally you would get some static from me on this, but I am tired and an early day does sound good. Thank you sir." she replied.

"I will see you on Monday," Williams said as he left.

She had been working a lot of hours and decided this would be a perfect time to go home, draw a warm bath, and relax with candles and light music. Amy couldn't remember the last time she had pampered herself so she finished her report in record time, gathered up her belongings, and headed out the door. With a gentle wave to the front desk security guard, she was out the door and headed toward freedom.

As she was leaving the FBI parking lot, she drove by an all-black van with no markings and windows only in front parked outside.

"It must be an FBI stakeout van," she thought. "But it should be in the garage not on the street."

She quickly dismissed the thought and went on her way, stopping for a sandwich at Panera Bread before heading home.

As she ate, she spotted the same black van in the mall parking lot that sat adjacent to the Panera Bread. A quick stab of panic rose in her.

"I am sure it is nothing, just my nerves," she thought. "I can't let that incident in Puerto Rico get the better of me." Besides, she was of no use to the bad guys. She knew nothing. Why would a forensic scientist with no evidence be a threat?

She went back to her lunch, her thoughts drifting to the warm bath she would soon be enjoying. Before getting back in her car, she walked next door to Pier One Imports to pick up some candles for her night of relaxation. In the store, she noticed two men that seemed out of place meandering about, but quickly dismissed them as men looking for gifts for their wives.

Walking toward her car, she saw the black van again. This time, it seemed to be heading her way.

Her heart started to beat about a thousand times per minute as she realized what was about to happen. "I should have paid more attention to my gut feeling and acted sooner," she thought. She dropped everything and attempted to make a run for her car. What she didn't notice was that the two gentlemen from Pier One were closing in fast from behind. Before she could take her first step the bigger of the two men grabbed her from behind and held her tight.

Administering a technique she had learned in self-defense class, she stepped hard on the man's foot while biting his arm. The blow surprised the big man and he let go of his hold. Not taking any chances, she turned and kicked the stunned man in the groin and watched him fall.

Her victory was short lived because the second man was not far behind the first. At the same moment she was dropping his friend, he threw a right hook that landed on the side of her face, knocking her to the pavement.

The stabbing pain of the hit almost knocked her unconscious. As she struggled to get back to her feet, the other man regained composure and the two grabbed her with all their might. Amy quickly discovered that overpowering them was impossible. Within seconds, the van arrived. Someone from inside the van slid the side door open and jumped out to help the other two force her inside. They shut the door and pulled the van away in a hurry.

A sharp pain shot up Amy's back as she was pushed down on the bare metal floor of the van. Her eyes went shut and she once again almost fell unconscious from her attackers blow.

When she opened her eyes, she saw the devilish grin of a sinister-looking man hovering over her. He was saying something that in all the confusion she could not make out. The last sounds she heard were of this man saying good night as the cold prick of a needle penetrated her arm. Within a few seconds her world started to go black. She wondered if she would ever wake up again.

Chapter 18

Hunter woke to the annoying sound of his cell phone ringing. "Hunter speaking," he barked.

"Good morning. It feels weird saying that because it is still 10 in the evening back here in Washington," Marty Landover said.

"Marty, my head is throbbing and I got about three hours of sleep. Quit with the small talk and let me know what you have for me," replied a grumpy Hunter.

"I have you and Spencer on a 7 a.m. flight leaving out of Munich direct to Washington Dulles. You will arrive approximately at 8 a.m. Eastern Standard Time. I booked you first class again so you can get some rest on the way home, but you'll have to leave within the next thirty minutes to make your flight. I scheduled a car that will pick you up and take you to the airport. It should be in front of your hotel at 4:30 a.m. your time."

"Thank you, Marty. I can't wait to wake up Spencer and let him know," said Hunter. "See you tomorrow."

He hung up, and then yelled into Spencer's ear. "Hey, Brad, get your ass up. We have to go."

"What? I don't want to go to school today, Mom," Spencer mumbled.

"We have a cab meeting us in a half hour, so get up and don't go back to sleep," Hunter ordered.

After a ten-minute shower, five-minute shave, and a once-over grooming, Hunter emerged from the restroom to find Spencer still asleep.

"Sorry buddy but you forced me to do this," he said as he poured a glass of freezing cold water on Spencer's head.

"I'm up. I'm up. What the hell was that?" Spencer sputtered, jumping to his feet.

"We have fifteen minutes before we leave," Hunter said.

"I'll leave some money and the key in front of the innkeeper's door and meet you out front in fifteen minutes. If you are late, my friend, I am going to be forced to leave you here."

Hunter grabbed his bag, paid the innkeeper, and went out to meet the four-wheel drive taxi van that would take them to the airport. After about five minutes, Spencer appeared, bags in hand.

"You know you are going to pay for the water incident, don't you?" Spencer said as he took his seat.

"I was aware of the consequences before I did it, and it was all worth it," Hunter replied.

They both slept in the cab on the way to the Munich airport and during most of the seven-hour flight.

As they walked through the terminal, they saw a familiar face, sent to greet them. "How was your flight?" Marty asked Hunter as he was leaving the restricted area of the airport.

"Marty, you didn't have to pick us up. We could have taken a cab," replied Hunter.

"I know, but I live over this way and I figured it would be a nice change for the two of you," Marty said. "Plus, I wanted to hear about your adventures."

"Well, you know, Marty just the same old boring thing. Brad almost got us killed a couple of times and I had to save the day," replied Hunter with a big smile.

"Oh yeah that's how it went down." Spencer interjected. "I almost got us killed. Marty, let me tell you -- this guy is notorious for getting into trouble. I'll fill you in on the real story, not Hunter's fabrications."

"All right, you two, let's get going before you break out into another one of your quarrels," Marty said as he walked away. They followed Marty to his car and loaded the bags.

"Do either of you need to go home first before going to the office?" asked Marty.

"No. We keep spare clothes at the office," replied Spencer.

"You guys need a life outside of work!" Marty said as he pulled out of his parking spot.

"We get all the fun and excitement we need at work. Why would we need a life outside of it?" asked Brad, laughing.

During the forty-five minute drive to headquarters, Spencer filled Marty in on as much information as he could. Since Marty spent most of his time behind a desk, he loved to hear about adventures in the field.

When Marty let them out at headquarters, they went straight to Clyde Forman's office to see if he had decrypted any of the information on the disk they had given him. They found him hard at work as usual, staring at three computer screens at one time.

"How do you do that?" Spencer asked.

"It is easy. You just have to do it twelve hours a day, six days a week to get good at it," replied Clyde.

A man in his early forties, Clyde's dedication to work had already cost him two marriages. It didn't seem to bother him. He had made a lot of money over the Internet and always had a new young girlfriend on the rare occasions he was seen outside the office.

Due to the fortune he had made freelancing, he pretty much considered his job a hobby. He got away with a lot because he was one of the best in the business and Reinquest knew he would quit if he were not happy.

He called himself a computer island bum because he came to work in Hawaiian shirts accented with board shorts and reef sandals, even in winter. Add this to his long hair and glasses and you had a unique individual.

"I like the outfit today, Clyde. Is this government standard office attire?" Hunter asked sarcastically.

"That's why they keep me down here and out of public view,"

Clyde responded. "I bet you guys came here to find out about the disk you sent me."

"You must be part psychic, Clyde," Hunter said.

"Well, I don't have good news. This disk is encrypted so well that it can only be read at the main computer. The program you downloaded is not a stand-alone program, which means it is only part of the puzzle. The main computer holds the only key that can unlock it. It would be like having only the first and last letter of every word in a sentence. The information in between could be so many combinations that it would take ten years just to decipher the first paragraph and even then there is no guarantee it would be correct," Clyde said, with a look of disappointment. "As you know, I am not one to give up easily. But this encryption is impossible."

"Thanks for the effort, Clyde. If you can't crack it, nobody can," said Hunter. "I don't want to leave you empty handed, so here is an envelope with some things I found out. Please don't let Reinquest know about this because I acquired the information through ... let's just say ... untraditional methods."

"Thanks Clyde," said Hunter.

"You're welcome, but I should be thanking you. The case file I just read about how the two of you went to that party without permission, stole the French ambassador's car, wrecked it, and almost died was awesome. I almost pissed my pants laughing when I read it." He said trying to contain his laughter.

"Thanks for rubbing it in." Replied Spencer. "Any way, how did you get your hands on that file? Reinquest hasn't even sent that out yet."

"Like I said I get my information from non traditional methods. Now excuse me, gentlemen. I have some work to do," he said as he placed a pair of headphones over his ears and loaded his favorite computer game.

"I am going to my office to check my e-mails. I say we meet up again in a couple of hours," Hunter said.

"Good. That will give me time to shower and clean up before we face the wrath of Reinquest," Spencer replied.

On the way to his office, Hunter stopped to say hello to some colleagues. Once there, he threw the package from Clyde on his desk and logged on to his computer. As always after a mission, he was amazed at how many e-mails he had received in such a short time.

He sat back in his chair, opened the envelope, and dumped the contents onto his desk. The information inside was about the Oasis Company and included a hand-written letter from Clyde.

"I don't know if all this makes sense but I do know a gentleman that may be able to sort this stuff out," it said. "You can reach him at the following number. Your friend, Clyde."

After reading the letter, Hunter set it aside and scanned over the other information in the package, which documented different ways stem cell research could be used to develop new pharmaceuticals.

He reached into his pocket and pulled out the torn piece of paper with the words stem cell research on them.

"This can't be a coincidence," he said aloud.

He picked up the phone and dialed the number Clyde had given him.

"Central Intelligence Agency Harold Silver speaking."

"Mr. Silver, my name is Eric Hunter. I am an Operations Agent for the ODR and got your number from Clyde Forman."

"I've been expecting your call. Can you meet me in the Mount Vernon parking lot in one hour?" asked Silver.

"How will I know who you are?" Hunter asked.

"Don't worry. I'll know you. And please come alone. The fewer people who know about our meeting the better. See you in an hour," Silver said and hung up.

Hunter knew he couldn't tell Spencer about this meeting because he would insist on tagging along. He grabbed his coat and headed toward the parking garage. Even though he could reach Mount Vernon in about thirty minutes he wanted to make time for the morning DC traffic, which could delay him as much as an hour if he caught it wrong.

In the parking garage, the friendly parking attendant greeted him. "Making it an early day, Mr. Hunter?"

"No George, I just need to take off for a few hours and run some errands. Do you think you could lend me one of the unmarked ODR vehicles?"

"Oh, one of *those* type of errands. Why don't you take the Jeep Wrangler?" George replied.

"Thank you, that will do nicely. And if anyone asks..."

"Let me guess. This never happened. Am I right?" he interjected.

"Thanks, George. I owe you one," Hunter responded.

"Just add it to the list," replied the attendant as he threw Hunter the keys.

Hunter climbed in the Jeep and was off. He hated to leave Spencer, his most trusted friend, out of the loop, but with him sometimes it was easier to beg for forgiveness than to ask permission.

It was a very nice April day. The sun was out and the temperature was heading up to 65 degrees. The traffic was lighter than expected and the drive only took Hunter about forty minutes. With time to kill, he figured he would give Amy a call and see how she was doing.

"You have reached the cell phone of Amy Evans with the FBI. Please leave a message," was the response from her voicemail.

"Amy, this is Eric Hunter. I hope you made it home all right and are feeling better. I am back in town. Give me a call and maybe we can get together for dinner," Hunter said.

As he was putting his phone away, he saw a man approaching his Jeep.

"Mr. Hunter?" he asked.

"Yes, sir. And are you Mr. Silver?"

"Yes but you can just call me Harold."

"Very well, please just call me Hunter."

"Let's walk down the exercise path," Silver said, leading the way.

Silver was not wearing the typical CIA suit. He was dressed in an exercise outfit and sneakers. This was an exercise path and he obviously did not want to stick out. Lucky for Hunter he almost never wore a suit. He was wearing jeans, a light jacket, and sneakers.

"Mr. Hunter, how much do you really know about the Oasis company?" Silver asked.

"Not a lot. Only that it is run by a man named David Bruner, a man I happened to meet yesterday," Hunter responded.

"Yes, I heard about that. Nice move if you want to be one of his targets," Silver said in a sarcastic tone.

"This guy has his hands in almost everything, from legitimate business to the deepest depths of the black market. He is as crooked as they come and will not hesitate to use any methods at his disposal to get what he wants. As you may not know, we at the CIA believe that he has already made an attempt on the President's life. We also believe he is going to make another attempt sometime within the next two weeks."

"Do you know why he wants to kill the president?" Hunter asked.

"We don't know much more than what you stumbled onto. We know he had been buying a lot of the world's stem cell samples and was furious when the President pushed for the research to be disbanded."

"Why can't he just get his samples on the black market or from other countries?" Hunter asked.

"Because part of the bill that the President had pushed through Congress made it illegal for any company that had the majority of business in the United States to buy it. This made it illegal for other countries to sell it to him and beyond what they say in the news; no country really wants to go against the United States. Besides, it wouldn't even matter because our country is currently the only one that would have enough samples for him to do his research," Silver responded.

"So, as long as our current President is in office he cannot continue what he started, and that's probably costing him millions of dollars. If he is the kind of man you say, killing the President of the United States to get what he wants is not something he would lose sleep over," Hunter said.

"Yes, and this is where you come in. Off the record, I am authorized to give you as much help as I can. You have been briefed on the situation and know that the President cannot go public with this until you have some solid proof. I can, however, aid you along the way and offer whatever information we have."

"So I have to pursue this without the official support of the government," said Hunter.

"That's it in a nut shell," he replied.

"Before you leave, you may want this." He handed over a large sealed envelope.

"What is it?" asked Hunter.

"By the time you get back to your office and open it you will be grateful that you have it," he answered.

"Here is my card and my secure line. Please feel free to contact me." He handed Hunter the card and walked away.

Hunter stood there a minute, taking in all of what he had heard. He still could not figure out why no one in Washington was willing to go after Bruner.

He walked back to his car, hopped in, and took off for the office, his mind racing in a hundred directions as he drove. Just as he entered his office, the telephone began to ring. He hurried to his desk, tossed the envelope, and grabbed the phone.

"Hunter here."

"Mr. Hunter, you don't know me. But I know you," a voice said.

"Who is this and what do you want?" Hunter asked.

"I am going to give you specific instructions and if you do not want any harm to come to your friend Amy Evans than I suggest you and Mr. Spencer do exactly what I say. You will buy two tickets on American Airlines flight 1745 with service to Los Angeles, California. Once you arrive in Los Angeles, a few of my associates will be there to greet you and take you to the meeting point. You will bring with you any reports or pertinent information that you have collected regarding the mishap in Vieques. If you contact anyone about this or miss your flight, we will terminate her life. This is the only warning we are going to give you. If you continue the investigation after our meeting, we will no longer be civil."

"Wait! How do I know she is still alive and you won't double cross me?" he asked as he finished writing down the information.

"You don't. But if you do not show, you can be sure that the worst will happen to her." With that comment, the man on the other end hung up the phone.

*   *   *

"Do you think they will come?" one of his henchmen asked Kyle London after he hung up the phone.

"They will come," he replied. "But they will try something. I don't see this man giving up without a fight, so we will have to be extra careful in our planning."

"What should we do with the girl?" he asked London.

"We should keep her safe and comfortable for now. We need to keep her alive and kill them all at the same time if we want it to look like an accident," London replied.

"No problem, boss. I'll take good care of her."

"No funny business. Just feed her and keep her calm until tonight," London said. "Now go and keep our prisoner company."

The man did as he was told and left the room. As soon as he shut the door, London picked up a phone in the small office and dialed Bruner's number.

"The package is locked down for the evening and the two pigeons will be on a plane headed my way soon," London said into the phone.

"Do you have everything ready for their arrival?" Bruner asked.

"Yes, sir. It will look like your everyday car accident. Even if they tell anyone what is going on, there will not be enough proof for anyone in Washington to want to go after you. I think this warning will halt any further investigations toward the Oasis Corporation."

"I hope for the government's sake you are right. How are things with the other project?" asked Bruner.

"Those are also moving along as planned, sir. In another couple of weeks we will not have that problem either."

"Great. Let me know how tonight goes after it is finished," Bruner said and hung up the phone.

"The world will be forever changed by my actions within the next few weeks," London thought as he cracked a little smile. For him, it was the pleasant calm before the storm he intended to unleash onto the world.

*   *   *

Hunter hung up the phone and sat back in his chair. How he was going to get Amy out of harm's way and live through the ordeal was anyone's guess.

He looked down at his desk and saw the envelope that Silver had given him. He carefully slid his letter opener through the top, making sure he did not damage anything inside.

In the envelope he discovered what appeared to be a folded blueprint of something. A Post-it note attached to the outside read, "Sorry this is all the help I can give you." There was no name on it, for obvious reasons, but Hunter was grateful for any help.

He picked up his phone and dialed Spencer's office. After a couple of attempts, Brad answered the phone.

"Office of Domestic Readiness. Operation Specialist Spencer speaking."

"Brad could you come to my office?" Hunter requested.

"Sure, what's up?" he asked.

"I'd rather tell you in person."

"I'll be right there!" Brad new if Hunter said he would rather say it in person that meant it was something serious.

Spencer made his way down the hall to Hunter's office. He entered without knocking to find his friend looking over schematics of some building.

"What's up?" he said as he entered.

"Amy has been kidnapped and if we don't go rescue her, she will be killed," Hunter replied in a serious tone that Brad rarely heard.

"What's the plan?" Spencer asked, knowing that Hunter was already hard at work formulating a rescue mission.

"Their instructions were that if we tell anyone they will kill her, if we miss our flight they will kill her, and if we do not come alone they will kill her," he replied.

"So what advantages do we have?" asked Spencer.

"Well, the flight they want us on does not leave until 6 p.m. our time and arrives in Los Angeles airport at 9 p.m. their time. I have already booked the tickets for the flight," Hunter said.

"But we won't be on that flight, will we?" Brad asked.

"Not if I can help it. I just haven't figured out how we are going to make them think we made the flight and leave earlier," Hunter replied.

Hunter sat in complete concentration for a few more moments, contemplating their next move. Then a mischievous smile lit up his face.

"I know that look," said Spencer. "What do you have up your sleeve?"

"Didn't I see a message that said Tom and Jim were due back today?" asked Hunter.

Tom Stone and Jim Radcliff made up another of the three teams of Operation Specialists that work for the ODR. They had just returned from a mission in the Middle East. Hunter hated to bring them in on this mission because they had earned a well-deserved rest, but he knew he couldn't pull it off without them.

"Yes, I just passed Stone's office and he was working away at his computer," said Spencer.

"Great!" Hunter said as he picked up the phone.

"Office of Domestic Readiness Operation Specialist Stone Speaking."

"Stone, Hunter here. Can you and Radcliff meet me in Clyde's office in about ten minutes? It is really important."

"Hunter, why do I know this is going to infringe on my time off?" Stone replied.

"Sorry, my friend. You know I wouldn't ask if there was any other way," said Hunter.

"I know," he replied with a sigh. "We will be there."

"Thanks a lot, buddy. I owe you one." Hunter hung up the phone, and then punched in another extension.

"Office of Domestic Readiness Adam Reinquest speaking."

"Sir, could you meet Spencer and me in Clyde Forman's office in ten minutes? It is of the utmost importance," he asked.

"Can you tell me why?" Reinquest responded.

"Not now, but I really need you on this one, Chief."

"OK, I will meet you there in ten," Reinquest replied as he shook his head.

"The boss is in. Now we need Marty," Hunter commented as he dialed Marty's office.

"Marty's office, Marty speaking."

"Marty, Hunter here. Could you meet me in Clyde's office in ten minutes?"

"Do I want to ask what for?"

"If you come to the meeting, you will find out. I want to brief everyone at once," Hunter responded.

"I'm in, see you there," Marty replied.

"All right, Spencer, everything is in order. Let's get down there and warn Clyde his office is about to turn into our war room."

Chapter 19

Clyde Forman's office started to fill shortly after Hunter and Spencer arrived. Hunter was in the back corner discussing his plan with Reinquest. He was just getting the OK as the last of the crew arrived. He motioned for Brad to join him at the front of the office.

"First, thank you for meeting us here on short notice," Hunter said.

"The reason I asked everyone to Clyde's office was, due to the fact he is a fanatic, I know this is the one place that is definitely not bugged. To fill everyone in, Amy Evans was kidnapped yesterday. For those of you not familiar with our case, she was an FBI operative working with us in Puerto Rico. Even though they have not revealed their identity it is certain the Oasis Company is behind all of it." Hunter paused for reflection.

"So what's the master plan?" Stone asked impatiently.

"I was just getting to that. I'm going to ask a lot of each and every one of you. To insure that the kidnappers do not kill her, no one outside this room can be in on the plan," Hunter said, looking as serious as anyone had ever seen him. They could see that this was personal for him.

"Tom and Jim you are our decoys. I need you two to get down to our props area and make yourselves look as much like Brad and me as you can. They will probably not approach you directly. You just need to fool them from a distance and make them believe that we made our flight. Your cover will be blown once you land, but that will hopefully buy us enough time," he continued.

"Sure," Tom replied.

"Clyde, I need you to make up fake identifications for them. I also need you to somehow disable the phone system on the plane so if they have goons riding along they can't contact headquarters until the plane lands."

"I think I can handle that," replied Clyde.

"Marty, I need you to book a private jet to leave within the hour under a couple of fake names. Do you have any connections outside of Los Angeles, preferably ex-military, where you can discretely get us a helicopter and a pilot crazy enough to fly us in and out of the compound?"

"I think I may be able to arrange that," Marty replied.

"Are there any questions?" Hunter asked.

"Yes. How in the hell are the two of you going to pull this off without getting yourselves killed?" Radcliff asked.

"Let me and Brad worry about that. Now any other questions?" asked Hunter.

"OK, if there are no other questions, you have your orders men, make them count!" Reinquest shouted from the back of the room.

Everyone headed to their perspective areas to prepare for the upcoming events. Hunter, Brad, and Reinquest stayed behind to finish discussing the role Spencer and Hunter were going to play.

"Do you realize how difficult and dangerous this mission will be," Reinquest asked. "You both may be killed, and you could get Amy killed in the process."

"Sir, I am aware of the risks. But if we do nothing, they will kill her. If we do what they want, they will kill her and us. Our only chance is to catch them by surprise and go in there first," Hunter said.

"Brad, are you OK with all of this?" asked Reinquest.

"Like he said, Chief, we don't have a lot of options. I'm not going to wait around and do nothing while they kill her."

"What do you guys need from me?" Reinquest asked.

He always got a bad feeling in his stomach when he asked them that question. The answer usually resulted in him having to do a lot of explaining to Washington. But in this case he could see no other way.

"I thought you would never ask," Hunter said with a big grin on his face. "First we will need access to our armory. We are going to need some major firepower on this one Chief. Second, you are going to have to authorize that helicopter, no matter what the cost, because my guess is we are going to have to make a quick and dramatic getaway. Last, we are going to need you to approve us temporary high level identification so we can bypass the security at the airport's FBO," Hunter finished.

"What about the warehouse?" Reinquest questioned.

"Sir if you authorize what we asked for, you can leave the rest up to us." Spencer chimed in.

"That is what I am afraid of. All right, you guys have what you want. Report to the armory and get your gear. The rest will be taken care of by the time you get back," Reinquest said.

He then turned to Clyde and said, "Can you handle the security and the badges for them?"

"I have already started working on it sir," responded Clyde.

"Very well men, good luck!" Reinquest stated.

Hunter and Brad left for the armory and Reinquest headed back to his office. Reinquest shook his head as he walked down the hall. He was worried he may never see his men again. He has sent them on many difficult missions in the past, but he just had a bad gut feeling about this one.

"Hey Jacob, we're here to pick out some weapons. Reinquest should have called down with the order," Spencer said to the man behind the cage.

"I don't know what mission he has you going on, but I have never had him say, 'give them whatever they want' before. You guys must have caught him on a good day," Jacob remarked.

"We need a couple of M-16's and four sidearm pistols. We need at least six remote activated mines and two grenade launchers. Let's grab as many rounds as we can hold. We also need to bring about ten hand grenades," Spencer said.

"Hold on you two! Are you going to war? Why do you need that much fire power?" Jacob asked in amazement.

"Sorry, Jacob. We can't let you in on this mission. We also need you to not speak of this to anyone. And I mean anyone. That is all we can say to you for now," Spencer responded.

"OK, grab that bag over there, let's fill it, and leave to get ready for our flight," Hunter said.

"Thanks for the toys!" Spencer said as they left the area.

"Any time," Jacob replied.

They rushed back to their offices to pack some more equipment and supplies for the mission.

"I will see you here in twenty," Brad remarked as he left.

"Sure thing," said Hunter.

After about twenty minutes the two emerged and rejoined in the hallway. Marty was standing there to meet them, with their itinerary in hand.

"Gentlemen, I have a private jet booked and ready to leave as soon as you get to the airport. They have the engines warming up as we speak. I will drive you to the airport in my station wagon. They are most certainly watching our office, so we need to get you to your destination without being detected. You can hide under a blanket in the back," he stated.

"I wanted to get closer to you Brad, and now here's my chance." Hunter said with a smile.

"You know I don't do anything on the first trunk date," he replied, continuing with the joke.

"We need to get going to give you two as much time as possible," Marty said, ignoring their humor.

They adjourned to the parking garage located in the basement of the building. It was fully enclosed and a perfect place to board the vehicle so they wouldn't be spotted. Hunter and Spencer hopped into the back area and Marty covered them with a blanket.

As Marty drove out of the garage, he gave a friendly wave to the guard. He took a non-direct route to the airport, which took a little extra time, but he wanted to make sure no one was following. After he was confident he was in the clear, he headed to Dulles Airport.

After forty-five minutes of driving, he arrived at the Fixed Base Operations (FBO) gate and showed his government ID badge. Marty made sure that the private jet he had reserved was still in the hangar so Spencer and Hunter could board undetected. He pulled the car into the hangar, and Hunter and Spencer jumped out the back.

"I thought that ride was never going to end!" Spencer proclaimed as he got out.

"Enough belly aching, Brad. We need to get our equipment loaded and get this bird off the ground," replied Hunter.

"Thanks again, Marty, for your assistance," Hunter said.

"You can thank me by not getting killed," responded Marty. "Now go, and good luck to the both of you."

They waved good-bye to Marty as they boarded the plane. Once they were seated they did not talk. Since both Brad and Eric were experienced pilots, they loved the feeling of the plane taking off, and neither liked to spoil the experience with mindless chitchat.

The plane approached the yellow hold line on the taxiway and, as ordered by ground control, the pilots held tight waiting for a 747 to land. They were the first in line for takeoff and would be cleared to do so as soon as the 747's turbulence dissipated.

Brad and Hunter requested that the captain broadcast the radio calls over the aircraft's speakers. The pilots throttled ahead and taxied the plane into position. Without delay they pushed the throttles forward and the sound of the engines filled the cabin. The power of the engines propelled the airplane forward, pushing everyone back into their seats. The plane drove ahead faster and faster while the whole thing shook as it rumbled down the runway. One hundred, one hundred ten the co-pilot announced. At one hundred twenty knots, the pilots rotated the controls and pulled the nose upward. They were quickly off, climbing higher and higher into the atmosphere.

After about fifteen minutes of climbing, the pilot announced that they were at their cruising altitude of 25,000 feet. Hunter and Spencer snapped out of their daydreams. It was time to get back to the mission at hand and they had a lot of planning to do before they landed in five hours.

"What's our best means of entry?" asked Brad as Hunter spread out the diagram of the warehouse.

"I think our best bet is to enter on this obscure side next to the trees. They are most likely holding her on the other side, which will allow us to get in undetected. It is a pretty big place and I doubt they will be guarding every room. I am willing to gamble that they are going to concentrate their men in this area and just do rounds on the rest," he said pointing to the area away from their entry point.

"What happens if we catch them on one of their rounds?" Spencer asked, already knowing the answer.

"Well, that's why we brought the silencers," Hunter continued. "Brad, this is a no holds barred. We cannot hesitate or take any chances on this one. Amy's life hangs in the balance and they don't give a crap about our existence. If you see one, take him out!"

Spencer had never seen Hunter hold a mission so close to the heart. He did not want to do anything to mess it up.

Five hours later, the captain interrupted their planning when he announced that they were preparing for landing. It was perfect timing because they were just wrapping up the final details. Neither could believe that the planning had taken the entire trip, but they were glad to have finished before the end of the flight.

There was only one more piece of the puzzle that had to be taken care of, and Marty assured them it would be ready and waiting when they landed.

Chapter 20

Leaving from the basement of the ODR building, Tom Stone and Jim Radcliff headed straight for the parking garage. They did not want to be late because the fate of two of their fellow operatives -- not to mention friends -- lay in their hands. If they pulled off this smokescreen, Hunter and Spencer had a fighting chance. If they were detected, their chance of survival was almost non-existent.

They entered the garage to find a car and driver waiting. They climbed into the backseat, gave the driver a nod, and they were off.

As soon as they left the garage, the driver noticed he had someone following him. He discretely signaled the two men that they had an audience and from now on they were going to be watched.

The make-up artist who had created Tom and Jim's disguises had done a good a job making them look like Hunter and Spencer. From a distance, the disguises would hold up. The main thing the two decoys had to do was make it on the plane before any of the pursuers could get a close look at them, which might be a lot easier said then done.

They had planned the trip to arrive at the last moment so they could head directly for the plane, forgoing any wait time in the terminal area. They were hoping to lure anyone from Oasis on the plane and have it take off before the gig was up.

The drive took forty-five minutes and the car that followed kept a distance and appeared only to be there to make sure they went straight to the airport. They were pretty confident that they had not yet been identified.

They approached the terminal and the driver sped up and got in front of a bus to slow down the progress of the car behind. This would give the guys a few seconds get out of the car and run in.

They had thirty minutes to get to their plane before take-off. If they planned it correctly, they would be arriving at their gate around the time of last call.

Tom and Jim headed straight for security and announced to a nearby security guard that their plane was about to leave and they were in a hurry. The guard acknowledged their haste, opened one of the security ropes, and waved them to the front of the line. They had already checked in online and had only a small carry-on bag each, but they were still cutting it close.

*   *   *

The two men in the car had been instructed by Kyle London to follow them from the ODR all the way to the security check point at the airport and identify that the two men were indeed Michael Hunter and Brad Spencer from pictures he had supplied them.

"Sir, the suspects are on the move and we are in pursuit," the men in the car relayed via cell phone when Mr. London answered.

"Good -- keep on them. Do not get too close, but when possible see if you can identify the passengers," he ordered.

"I will call you back when we have a confirmation on the suspects," the man said before hanging up.

"Don't follow too close," the passenger said to the driver. "We can get a positive ID when they get out at the airport."

They continued their pursuit, keeping their distance until they arrived at the terminal.

"Don't let that bus get in front of you!" the passenger yelled at the driver as they approached the terminal. "Great! Now we may not get a good look at them."

"What do you want me to do? Hit the bus?"

"I should be able to see them closer as they head toward security. I will jump out as soon as we get there, so hurry," the passenger barked.

They pulled up just as Tom and Jim where entering the terminal. All they could see were the backs of their heads.

As soon as the pursuers' car stopped, as anticipated, the passenger got out and headed toward security, trying to catch up to his prey.

He finally caught up with them as they were being waved to the front of the line. He grabbed his phone and dialed the boss.

"Sir, I could not get a definite visual on them before they entered the gate."

"I understand," London responded. "There is nothing more you can do. I will notify the next group that Hunter and Spencer are on their way. You are relived for now, but stand by in case you are needed."

London hung up and quickly dialed another number. "They did not get a positive identification on our passengers but they are headed your way," he said into the phone. "When you have a positive ID call me."

"As you wish, sir," the man responded.

*   *   *

"So far so good!" Tom exulted.

"Let's not count our chickens before they have hatched," said Jim. "I am sure they have a couple of guys stationed on the plane that we have to fool."

The two got to the gate as they were getting ready to shut the door.

"We almost gave up on the two of you," a perky lady said as she checked their boarding passes.

They entered the plane, heading directly to their seats trying to obscure their faces as much as possible.

*   *   *

"So far, we have not gotten a direct look at the two of them," he said as soon as London answered the phone.

"Well get up and get a good look at them! I want them identified before you leave the ground!" London shouted into the phone.

"Sir, I am going to have to ask you to please remain seated and turn off your cell phone," the flight attendant ordered.

"I am going to have to call you with a confirmation from the plane phone as soon as we get airborne," he said to London.

"You have to be shitting me. As soon as you can, get a good look and call me back," London replied and then hung up the phone.

They sat in silence as the plane pushed back from the gate and taxied to the runway. Tom and Jim knew they were being watched, so they sat facing forward in silence hoping not to be identified.

The plane took off and started to climb.

After about fifteen minutes, the flight attendant announced that approved electronic equipment could be used, including the plane's cell phone service. Neither thought they had been directly spotted, so whomever Oasis sent was going to have to wait until they could move around the cabin to get a direct visual.

Jim picked up the phone, ran his credit card, and attempted to dial headquarters, the whole time hoping the call would not go through.

"We are unable to process your call at this time," rang out through the receiver. That was one of the sweetest messages he had ever heard, since it meant Clyde had pulled off his mission and disabled the service.

"The call did not go through, but I am going to try the service again, just in case," he explained to Tom. He made one more attempt with the same result. Satisfied the service was not in operation, he hung up the phone and sat back in his seat.

Fifteen more minutes passed and the plane leveled out. The captain announced they were at cruising altitude and that passengers could walk throughout the cabin. They both knew that they were going to be identified soon.

"If we did our job, Hunter and Spencer have until we land to complete their mission," Tom said.

Shortly after making that comment, a man passed and looked back at them. He stared longer than normal and both could tell that he must be one of the men Oasis sent to verify Hunter and Spencer's presence on the plane.

By the look on this man's face, he was shocked to see them sitting there, which gave them a good sign that their friends in California did not know the truth as of yet. The man did not even try to conceal what he was doing and rushed directly back to his seat to make the call.

"I want to see if he has anyone with him," Jim said as he unbuckled his seat belt and rose from his seat. He turned and saw the man acknowledging another before heading for the plane's phone service. By the frustrated look on the man's face, he could tell he could not get service. The man tried two more times before admitting defeat.

"They could not get through, and I have a visual ID on the two of them. Once we land we will have them detained by the local police so we can further question them," Jim said after taking his seat.

"I think we have been double crossed. The two men are not our guys but decoys dressed up to look like our guys," the Oasis man said as he hung up the phone. "I saw one of them stand up and get a visual on the two of us. They will probably wait and have us picked up when we land. Our only hope is to blend in and make a run for it as soon as we can."

"You could not get through to London?" the other man asked.

"No, they must have disabled the service." he replied.

"I almost think we would be better off with the authorities than explaining our failure to London. He is not one to suffer failure from his men."

Chapter 21

The plane lined up for final approach on what appeared to be an old abandoned landing strip with two tattered buildings next to it. The co-pilot turned to Brad with a worried look on his face.

"Sir, it appears that the condition of the runway will do damage to our landing gear," he said.

"Don't worry," said Brad. "I talked to a pilot that landed here two weeks ago and he said it looks a lot worse than it is. Besides, the government will reimburse you for any damage."

"Are you sure it's safe?" Hunter whispered to him.

"Your guess is as good as mine. I don't know any pilots that landed here," Brad said, shrugging his shoulders.

Reassured, the pilots touched down with a surprisingly smooth landing and then taxied to one of the old buildings next to the runway.

"Are you sure this is the place?" Hunter asked the pilot as he looked out the cockpit windows.

"This is where Mr. Landover instructed us to land, sir," the pilot said. "He said you should walk into the hangar and the man you are looking for will be waiting for you."

When the co-pilot opened the cockpit door, Hunter and Spencer grabbed their gear and departed, giving a final wave to the pilots.

"This airport looks like it was deserted 50 years ago," Brad said as they walked toward what was left of the building's front door. To their amazement, the inside was not as raggedy as it appeared from the outside. Inside the hanger were a combined office-apartment and a very nicely equipped Black Hawk helicopter with machine guns and rocket launching capabilities.

They entered the office to find a man behind his desk with his feet propped up, taking a nap. He slowly raised his head and looked at the two of them for a moment before speaking.

"Are you the two from the ODR?" he inquired.

"Yes, my name is Eric Hunter and this is my partner Brad Spencer."

"You can call me Duke."

Both knew this was at best his pilot call sign, but neither wanted to pry. They figured he was an old CIA buddy of Marty's who was helping them as a favor.

"From what Marty tells me, you guys are in a bit of a pickle and need my help," Duke said. "I understand you are in need of a vehicle and a pick up after you are done with your exploits."

"Yes, we will probably be in quite a hurry," Hunter said.

"Ah, a smash and grab operation -- my favorite." Duke replied. "Gentlemen, you have come to just the place. Now, how much do I need and/or want to know?"

"The less you know the better, so if it all hits the fan you can claim ignorance," replied Brad.

"Works for me," said Duke. "If Marty trusts you, then I will as well."

They spent the next few minutes filling Duke in on his part of the mission. They left out the fact that they were going to illegally enter the warehouse and had very little support in Washington.

Duke agreed to the terms and led them out of the office toward a Jeep that was parked next to the helicopter.

"You can use this Jeep to get you within a mile of the warehouse. To stay undetected, you will have to drop it off just outside the tree line and hump it with all your gear through the mile of foliage. If you leave within the next half hour, you should arrive at the end of the trail around sunset and it should be dark just about the time you two reach the warehouse."

"Will this old thing run?" Spencer asked as he stared at the archaic vehicle.

"I have her looking like that for a reason. If you look under the hood, you will see she is in great condition and won't let you down." Duke said.

Hunter and Spencer spent the next twenty minutes getting on their gear and getting everything ready for the mission.

"Before you leave take these radios with you," Duke said, handing one to each of them. "They are loaded with a coded signal so we can talk without anyone listing to our conversation. I will be in the air and off to a distance the whole time you guys are in there, so if you have to make any changes, these will let us do so without being detected."

"Thanks for all your help Duke," Hunter said.

"No problem, I am glad to do it. But you just tell Marty this makes us even," he said with a smile. "Now get going so you can make the forest by sunset. Believe me, you don't want to navigate that trail at night."

They both gave him two thumbs up and then pulled out of the hangar. Spencer drove as Hunter navigated.

"What do you think our odds are on this one, old buddy?" Hunter asked partially returning to his normal jovial self.

"I don't know but I don't think Vegas would take any bets on this mission," Spencer replied.

"That's a heck of an idea Brad. If we make it through this, let's go to Vegas and do some gambling," Hunter said.

"I'm in, but let's complete the mission before we worry about where we are going to party after it's over," Spencer replied.

They bantered back and forth during the ride to take their minds off what was about to happen. They parked the Jeep in an area of bushes and trees so it could not be easily seen from above. Just in case they had men patrolling the perimeter, they did not want to take any chances.

They got out and headed to their target destination. After a 10-minute brisk walk through the trees, they reached the far entrance of the warehouse. They waited about 10 minutes under cover for the night to come, so as not to be spotted. Hunter pulled out his night vision binoculars and scanned the area.

"It looks like a simple key pad on the door. I don't think it will be any problem for you to handle," Hunter said as he continued looking around the compound.

"I just hope our element of surprise gives us the edge because we have no idea how many men are going to be in there," he continued.

"I'm sure we'll find out soon enough," replied Spencer.

"We still have about two hours to get in and out before they realize we are not on our flight, which should give us plenty of time," Hunter said.

"We should put on our silencers so we can stay incognito for as long as possible," he added as he screwed his on to the end of his gun barrel.

Spencer did the same and then grabbed two black masks out of his backpack, put one on and handed the other to Hunter. They did a few last minute checks to make sure all their gear was in place before continuing.

Brad led the way, crawling on his belly. He proceeded about ten yards, placed a mine, and then put some foliage around it for camouflage. He did this two more times, spacing them out about five yards from each other. If they needed to make a getaway through this area, this placement should slow down anyone trying to follow them.

Hunter and Spencer did a last weapons check to make sure everything was a go. Hunter looked up and gave Spencer the nod; it will be all hand signals from here.

Hunter took the lead and slowly crawled out of the tree cover. They had been watching the timing of the security camera and had already scouted out places to hide when it made its sweep through their position. They went slowly so as not to be detected. It took twenty minutes to make it to the back entrance.

Everything seemed to be going as planned as Hunter approached the door with Brad directly behind. But as he started to get up, he heard the doorknob twist.

The back door slowly creaked open. Hunter motioned quickly for Spencer to take cover behind a bush located just out side the door. Even in that hiding place, the guard would see them if he stepped beyond the doorway.

Spencer readied his automatic rifle, but Hunter gave him the hand signal to wait until the guard got closer. Brad's finger slowly pulled back on the trigger, waiting for the guard to take one more step. The guard stopped swung his flashlight around haphazardly and turned around, pulling the door shut behind him. He made this round every hour and had no ambition of working harder than he had to. He had no idea that the two men he was guarding against were lying just outside the door.

Hunter and Spencer both took a breath of relief. Hunter signaled for Spencer to head to the door and held his position to give him cover if needed.

Spencer did as he was told and broke open the control panel, placing a decoder device on the main wires. This device put random codes through the system until the correct one could be obtained.

It took about thirty seconds for the machine to break the code and open the door. Brad put the machine in his pocket and motioned for Hunter to join him. The two entered the warehouse, closing the door quietly behind.

Spencer took a small map out of his pocket, a guide through the labyrinth of hallways in the warehouse, which he had prepared on the plane ride. He took the forward position and motioned for Hunter to follow.

The plans he had drawn were only as good as the originals, he knew. If new cameras had been installed or walls erected or knocked down, that could prove to be fatal to the mission.

They proceeded down a couple of hallways with no resistance. The first half of the underground part of this warehouse was deserted, with only a few cameras to avoid.

They expected that the guards were going to be pretty relaxed because they thought Hunter and Spencer were still on a flight to meet them. The guards also believed that no one outside of their organization knew about the warehouse. They planned on using this to their advantage as much as they could.

Hunter and Spencer walked slowly toward an area where Amy was expected to be located. Spencer peeked his head around the corner slowly and spotted someone about fifty feet away and tied to a chair. She was facing the opposite direction so all he could make out was the back of her head, but he assumed it was Amy.

There were six guards in the general vicinity, but all were watching television and none were looking in her direction. He signaled Hunter to take a look. "What do you think?" Spencer asked in a whisper.

"I think I am going to sneak up there, untie her, and then casually stroll back here. I am going to need you to take position over there to cover me in case one of those guards catches wind of what I am doing," Hunter whispered back, pointing to an area close to Miss Evans where Spencer would have sufficient coverage.

Brad gave him a nod of agreement and then proceeded to the position and took cover. After he was set, Hunter slowly crawled toward Amy.

The tension built as Hunter approached. Brad could feel the sweat drip down his neck as he anxiously waited for Hunter to get into position. Hunter crept behind Amy and gently touched her arm to get her attention.

Her eyes lit up and he quickly put his finger to his mouth, signaling her not to make a sound. He pulled out his knife and cut the ropes that bound her, trying his hardest not to make a sound.

The first cut broke through and the rope fell to the ground with a small thud. Hunter stopped for a second, hoping the guards did not hear the sound over the television. He was in luck. None of them stirred.

A couple more cuts and the ropes were off. Hunter motioned for Amy to slowly get up and join him on the floor.

She did as instructed and the two crawled on their bellies toward Brad's position. They traveled across the floor at a snail's pace as to not alarm the guards. They were almost to Brad's position when one of the guard's cell phones started to ring. The two of them froze and turned to look, both too terrified to move.

Chapter 22

"All right, men, the time is getting near. I want you four to come with me. The rest of you stay here and guard our captive," Kyle London continued. "I have not heard from our guys on the airplane, so be ready for anything. It may be the cell phone system is down on the plane, or they may be planning a rescue attempt."

"Sir, they don't know where we are. We have nothing to worry about," one of the men commented.

As a result of that comment, London's casual demeanor changed drastically. He reached for his handgun, grabbed it out of its holster, and struck the man across his head. The man quickly hit the floor and lay there in pain, holding his bleeding wound.

"Let me make this clear to everyone. We need to be on high alert. I don't want to underestimate these men. Everyone will keep a vigilant watch. I want a pair of eyes constantly on this woman. Failure is not an option."

The men were silent. After the display they had just witnessed, no one was going to speak out.

"All right, we are out of here. Someone attend to him," London said as he left the room.

London and four of his men got into a black SUV and pulled out for the airport. He knew something was wrong because his men should have checked in by now. He could not dispose of the girl until he was certain of the situation. He was not used to failure and would not accept it. He could feel his frustration grow as they made their way to the airport.

"I will know for sure in about forty minutes," he thought to himself.

They arrived at the airport shortly after the flight was scheduled to land, and he and three of his men got out and headed for the terminal.

"Stay out here as long as you can. If they make you leave, go around and park in the short-term parking lot. I will call you as we are walking out," London instructed.

The driver gave an approving nod as Kyle London turned and headed into the airport. He joined his men in the lower-level baggage area, which was where he had instructed Hunter and Spencer to meet them. They took positions around the area and tried to blend in. They did not want to give up their identities but wanted to be ready to greet their guests as soon as they walked by.

After about fifteen minutes, London's patience was wearing thin.

"Has anyone had a visual on our package?" he said into the radio communication system they all wore.

All calls came back negative. He then attempted to call his men on their cell phones, but received no answer.

"Something is not right here. I need the two closest to proceed to the baggage conveyer and look for them," London barked over the radio.

London signaled his other associate to follow, and the two of them proceeded up to the departure level. London held back while the other man went to the counter to check on the flight.

"Excuse me ma'am," he said as he approached the counter. "Could you tell me if flight 1745 has landed?"

She typed the flight number into the computer. "Here it is, sir. They have landed and disembarked."

"Thank you." He walked over to where London was standing.

"Sir, she said the plane landed and everyone is at the baggage claim collecting their bags."

"Do any of you have a visual on our guys or the two we are here to collect?" London asked over the radio.

"Sir, still no visual," they all replied.

"Keep looking!" London stated.

He stopped for a moment and took a look around. "Where could they be?" he whispered under his breath.

Out of the corner of his eye, he witnessed a group of men heading toward a back room. He quickly saw that two of the men were in hand cuffs and that those men were in fact the two he had sent on the plane.

London quickly reached for the radio. "All men reassemble out front. We are getting out of here."

He then grabbed his cell phone and called the guards back at the warehouse.

"Do you have a visual on our prisoner?" London demanded.

"Yes, sir. She is right ... " He stopped in mid sentence as soon as he saw the chair was empty. He turned to his left and spotted his prisoner escaping with a man he recognized from a photograph he had been given.

The guard quickly pulled his weapon. He aimed and squeezed the trigger. Hunter jumped in front of Amy so she would not take the hit.

A shot went off! Hunter cringed and grabbed Amy tight.

Since he felt no pain, he glanced up.

The guard grabbed his chest and dropped to the floor. In all the excitement, Hunter had briefly forgotten that Brad had him covered.

Amy looked up to see Spencer emerge from the shadows. She was still surprised to be alive.

"Let's get out of here. Unless you want to wait around for the rest of them!" Brad shouted, giving Amy a hand up.

The shot roused the rest of the guards, who charged in to investigate. Brad laid down some suppressing fire to send all of them to their bellies as Hunter and Amy took cover behind him.

"Run, you two! I'm right behind you!" Spencer shouted between bursts.

Hunter and Amy started to get up but had to quickly hit the deck to avoid the onslaught of gunfire from the guards. The guards shot out three large windows that separated the two areas, sending glass flying all around them.

Brad returned fire as they took shelter behind the room's furniture. He shot one of the guards in the shoulder. The guards returned fire and now all three of them kissed the concrete to avoid the barrage of bullets.

"I am getting about sick of this, aren't you, buddy?" Hunter asked Spencer.

"I sure am. What do you have in mind?" asked Spencer.

"I'm going to throw one of these flash grenades, then we'll take them down as they come out from hiding," Hunter said.

Hunter grabbed one of the grenades from his bag, pulled the pin, and readied himself to make the throw.

The guards had ceased firing and the room was silent. Hunter was not about to wait around to figure out why. But as he stood up to throw the grenade, the reason for the cease-fire became evident. He stood face to face with a guard that was getting ready to fire.

With the kind of reflexes that only come from years of training, Hunter quickly grabbed and pushed the guard's gun into the air. The gun fired into the ceiling.

At the same time, Hunter threw a hard right to the man's Adam's apple, caving it in and knocking the man to his knees.

Since Hunter had grabbed the gun with the same hand that held the grenade, it dropped to the ground and rolled a few feet away from where he was standing. He and the guard, who out of fear had to quickly recover, each jumped in opposite directions.

With a large flash and loud explosion the grenade went off, temporarily blinding and deafening all in the area. From his place on the ground, Hunter looked over toward Spencer and Amy.

"Let's get the hell out of here while we still can!" he shouted.

"What? I can't hear you!" Spencer responded, still deaf from the blast.

Hunter did not respond but simply motioned for Spencer to cover him as he helped Amy to her feet. The blast had confused the guards long enough for the three of them to get up and make a run for the back door. Hunter led with Amy by his side as Spencer covered the rear.

"Duke, do you read me?" Hunter barked into his hand held radio as they ran.

"I can't get a signal down here. I just hope he is already airborne," he said aloud.

They made it to the back door and Hunter forcefully pushed it open.

"Amy, we have to make about a mile jog through these trees to a Jeep we left parked on the other side. Do you think you can make it?" Hunter asked.

"Are you kidding me? I have so much adrenaline I could run a marathon," she responded.

The going was not easy. They had navigated this forest quite easily during the day, but under the darkness of night it proved quite difficult.

They were only running for a couple of minutes before they saw that four of the guards were giving chase. Hunter picked up the radio again and made another attempt.

"Duke! Are you there?" he asked. No response.

He tried two more times and was ready to give up. He decided to give it one more try.

"Duke, this is Hunter. Are you out there?"

"Hunter, I thought the worst for the two of you. How can I assist you?" Duke replied.

"We're making our way through the forest to where we left the Jeep. We will be leaving very rapidly along the same dirt path we came in on and could use some air support and possibly a pick up. Do you think that could be arranged?" Hunter asked.

"I think I can help you out. Just stay on the path and I will find you," Duke replied.

"Thanks, Duke. We owe you a big one."

"Just get out of there alive. That will be enough for me. Duke out."

They continued to travel through the woods toward the Jeep.

After about fifteen minutes, the three of them, exhausted and aching, reached their destination. Spencer jumped in the driver's seat while Hunter got in the back and readied himself in case the guards made it through before they could get away. Amy took the passenger seat and fastened her safety belt in preparation for what she believed would be a rough ride.

Spencer put the key in the ignition and turned. Luck was not on their side because the Jeep refused to start.

"I am going to kill him. He said this Jeep was in good running condition," Spencer commented as he tried it again.

"You flooded the thing. Just floor the gas and try it again," Hunter said, trying to stay calm.

"Don't you think I already tried that?" Spencer replied.

"Well try it again and quit acting like a Nancy!" replied Hunter.

"Do you want to come up here and drive?" Brad replied.

"Yes I do," Hunter bantered back.

"Guys, guys, we have people following us," Amy interrupted.

Spencer tried it one more time and the Jeep spit and sputtered, then came to life with a loud backfire. Spencer quickly put it into gear and peeled away, leaving a cloud of dust.

They couldn't have cut it any closer. As they pulled away, the guards broke through the foliage and commenced firing on the unprotected Jeep.

"Go, go!" Hunter screamed as the bullets rained down.

"I'm going. Amy, keep your head down. Hunter, give them some of it in return," Brad, screamed back

Hunter returned fire and sent the guards to the ground. But soon they began to fire from the ground. One bullet nearly grazed the side of Brad's face.

"That one almost got me!" Brad said frantically.

"I think we're out of range now," Hunter replied.

"I'm sure they won't give up without a fight," Brad said.

As soon as the words left his mouth, two Jeeps appeared from the darkness.

"It looks like the reinforcements must have gotten back from the airport," Hunter said. "Duck!" he screamed and covered Amy as bullets flew overhead.

"I don't think we can take much more of this," Spencer replied.

They continued to take on fire with Hunter returning the punishment the best he could.

"I have had about enough of this!" Hunter said. He reached in his bag, pulled out a grenade and loaded it into the launcher on the bottom of his weapon.

"Take this, you bastards," he said, launching the first grenade. It was a little off target and only disrupted the flow of bullets for a moment. He took cover and loaded again.

At this point, the Jeep looked like Swiss cheese, riddled with bullet holes and missing the front windshield.

From back at the warehouse, Kyle London was coordinating the strike.

"Don't let them get away or it is your ass!" he shouted to the head of the guards via the radio. "Bring out the heavy artillery and take them before they get to the main road."

The guard did as he was told and opened a crate containing an anti-tank missile launcher with target-locking capabilities that could mark and follow a target for miles. There would be nothing left of Eric, Brad and Amy if this rocket made its target.

"Oh my God! They are pulling out the heavy artillery!" shouted Hunter.

"How many grenades do you have left?" asked Spencer.

"Just one, partner. I have to make it count," Hunter said as he loaded the last one into the chamber.

Another barrage of bullets struck the front of their Jeep. It began to smoke.

"This thing is not going to hold together much longer," Spencer said. "We're losing oil pressure."

"She just needs to last a little longer," Hunter said.

He took aim and fired his last grenade. Just then, the two Jeeps switched positions, so the second was covering the first.

The first Jeep took the hit directly on the front. It spun out of control and flipped, exploding into a fireball as it smashed into a tree.

"I got one of them, but not the one with the rocket," Hunter said, a bit discouraged. "We're out of rockets and I only have twenty more rounds of ammunition."

"What are we going to do? Our jeep is slowing!" Amy asked in a frantic tone.

"Brad, pull the Jeep over by that embankment so we can take cover," Hunter ordered in his normal, calm voice.

Brad did as he was told and they reached the embankment just as the Jeep lost the last of its oil pressure. The engine seized and the Jeep crawled to a halt.

"Everyone take cover," Hunter yelled, jumping out of the Jeep and then turning to give Amy a hand. They ran to an embankment around 20 yards from the vehicle and jumped for cover as a rocket launched from the second Jeep, exploded and blew their transportation into a million pieces.

"We destroyed their Jeep sir, but I think they got out before we did so," the head guard reported to London.

"Continue until you have a visual confirmation of their deaths. We don't want any loose ends," London replied.

The men did as they were told and approached the area. They slowed their Jeep and one of the guards grabbed a spotlight while two more covered him with their machine guns.

"What is the game plan?" Spencer asked.

"How many bullets do you have left?" Hunter asked.

"I am out," replied Spencer.

"I have a full magazine," said Hunter. "Here, take half of mine. Now, that leaves us with only ten shots each, so we need to make them count. Set your M-16 on single shot and try not to fire until you think you have a good one. I am going to the left and I want you to get around to the right and cover me."

"What am I supposed to do?" asked Amy.

"You need to stay here and pray!" Spencer said with a laugh.

"On the count of three, we go," said Hunter.

"One, two, three go, or when you say three?" asked Spencer.

"Do we have to go through this every time Brad? It is one, two, and go on three," Hunter explained.

"Ready three!" Hunter screamed and began running in the darkness and taking position about twenty yards to the rear of the Jeep."

"I hate when he does that," Brad said as he jumped up and ran over to his position.

At this point, London's men had stopped their vehicle and were out inspecting the area around the burned-out wreckage that once was their Jeep. Finding no bodies, they decided to take a look around and see where the occupants had gone.

"They have to be near. I want us to split up in two groups. You two cover that area over there, and we will head this way," the head of the guards ordered. "They might still be armed, so be careful."

One group headed toward Spencer's hiding place, while the other two headed toward Hunter. Since they were carrying portable spotlights and the area was flat, Hunter knew it was just a matter of time before he was discovered.

He waited until the two men were close enough for a good shot, then raised his weapon and took aim. He slowly pulled back on the trigger, sizing up the two men and readying for the kill.

He took a long breath, breathed out half way, and then held it before pulling the trigger its remaining distance.

"Click!" the hammer went as it struck the bullet.

"Oh shit! A misfire," Hunter said under his breath.

His pursuers were closing in, so he rose to his feet and charged the two guards, hoping the element of surprise would work in his favor. He managed to hit one in the shoulder, making him drop his weapon.

He was not so lucky with the other guard, who unloaded his magazine, sending three bullets into Hunter's chest and knocking him down.

"No!" Brad cried as he charged the man who just shot his friend. He managed to get off two clean shots, killing him instantly. By this time, the wounded guard Hunter knocked down had regained his composure and turned toward Spencer. Spencer emptied the remaining shots into his chest. The man fell back dead.

The other two guards heard the commotion and turned running back toward Spencer and Hunter. Spencer, still in a fit of rage, grabbed the dead guards' weapons and, without taking cover, fired both of them in the direction of the approaching guards. He kept firing until he exhausted both magazines. The bullets ripped through the charging guards dropping them both.

After the job was finished, he turned all his attention to his wounded friend. Hunter was unconscious but still alive.

"Hey, are you there?" came a voice over the radio.

Brad grabbed the radio from Hunter's belt and replied. "We are desperately in need of some assistance."

"Is that you next to the burning Jeep?" Duke asked.

"Yes, you are clear to land. We have eliminated the danger," Spencer said.

Amy was close enough to hear the helicopter and since the gunfire had stopped, she figured she could come out of hiding. She turned pale white as she saw Brad hovering over what appeared to be Hunter's dead body.

"Is he dead?" she asked.

"No, just extremely wounded and unconscious."

As soon as the helicopter touched ground, the two lifted Hunter and gently placed him inside. "We need to get him to a doctor," Brad said to the pilot.

"He looks pretty bad. There's a medic kit behind my seat," Duke said.

Brad grabbed the kit and took out a shot of adrenaline. He pulled back the sleeve on Hunter's right arm and readied the needle.

Just then, Hunter woke up. "You always had a flair for the dramatic, Brad," he said.

"I don't need a doctor, but what I do need is a nice stiff drink and cigar," he continued with a smile.

"You son of bitch! You are all right," Brad said, trying to hide his excitement.

"I am so happy you are OK," Amy said, lunging at him and

laying kisses on his face, not even trying to suppress her signs of happiness.

"I told you these vests would come in handy on this mission," Hunter said, breaking Amy's embrace so he could sit up. Then he held her near again.

"I thought you were dead!" Brad exclaimed.

"No, my friend, you can't get rid of me that easily," Hunter said as he sat back to enjoy the ride.

Chapter 23

"I hope you're calling to tell me that the mission was a complete success," said Bruner as he answered his secure line.

"Well, sir, not exactly," London replied.

"What went wrong?" asked Bruner.

"Pretty much all of it, but I am formulating a new plan and this time it is personal. Don't worry -- I will still make it look like an accident."

"No, you had your chance to go after them. Any more attempts at this time will attract too much attention," Bruner replied.

"We're less than a week from our main project and we can't afford any more mistakes," he continued.

"But sir, I know I can have them dead within the next forty-eight hours and make it look accidental," he said.

"I know you can, but you're going to have to set your pride aside for now and focus on the mission at hand. If I have read these men correctly, we won't have to go after them. They will come right to us," Bruner said.

"I think I know what you mean, sir. Will I be meeting you in Puerto Rico?" he said already knowing the answer.

"My plane is being prepared as we speak. I want to see you down there as soon as you can."

"Consider it done," London said and then hung up.

Bruner made another call.

"Serpentine, Captain Gevalia speaking."

"Captain Gevalia, this is Mr. Bruner." He replied.

"Mr. Bruner, how are you today?" His stomach dropped, as it did every time he received a call from Bruner.

"I need you to take the Serpentine to the west side of Puerto Rico, anchor it in the Mayaguez Harbor and wait there for orders," barked Bruner.

"Yes sir. Would you like me to pass through all the appropriate custom stops, or will this be a stealth mission?" he asked.

"I want you to be as traceable as possible. Don't miss any required stop on your way out of the British Virgin Islands en route to Mayaguez."

*   *   *

"Did you manage to get any sleep on the flight back?" Marty asked as he helped Amy with her bags.

"Yes, thank you," she replied with a big yawn.

"Marty, you are making a habit of these visits," Hunter said.

"Anything to help out. And to get me out of the office," he replied.

They all caught some much needed rest on the ride back to Washington DC. Amy and Brad were sound asleep before the plane left the ground. Hunter, not wanting to miss takeoff, waited until shortly after the wheels were up, and dozed off while the plane was still climbing.

"Where would everyone like to be dropped off?" asked Marty.

"At headquarters, so we can pick up our vehicles," replied Hunter.

"Amy, if you don't object, I would like to escort you to your town home, where you can pick up some clothes and then drive to my place where you can get ready. You can take a nap, have lunch, or whatever you want. I don't feel comfortable leaving you alone with those guys still on the loose."

"I appreciate that," she replied.

"Would you like me to join the two of you for extra safety?" Brad asked in a joking tone.

"No Brad, I have another mission in mind for you," Hunter said.

"You want me to find out were Bruner is and start formulating a plan to go after him, don't you?"

"Right you are, my friend. I want to be where Bruner is, no later than tomorrow afternoon," Hunter replied.

"Do you think Reinquest is going to go for it?" asked Brad.

"That's what I want you to find out," Hunter said as they entered the garage.

"Looks like I have a fun-filled day ahead," Brad grimaced. "Amy, are you sure you wouldn't rather have me watch over you?"

"No thank you, Brad, I think Hunter has it covered," she replied giving Hunters arm a small squeeze.

He and Marty gave Amy a hug goodbye and then headed toward their offices. Hunter led Amy to where his car was parked.

"This is your car?" she asked as they approached.

"Yes, I restored it myself."

"I am impressed." She replied.

"Well will you do me the honor?" Hunter asked as he opened the door and helped her in.

They departed the garage in style in his silver convertible 1952 Porsche 356.

"This is a really nice car," Amy commented again as they pulled away.

"Thank you. I am sort of a Porsche collector. This one I found at an estate auction in Ohio."

"So where are we heading?" He asked.

"I don't live far from here. Just ten minutes away," she replied.

Amy guided him turn by turn to her town home. She ran in, grabbed some clothes and personal items, and then Hunter drove off again, heading out of town.

"I thought you said you lived close to Baltimore," Amy commented when she noticed that they were heading east on I-50 toward the Bay Bridge.

"I do but that would be the first place they would check if they where looking for us."

"So where are you taking me? Am I to be your captive?" she asked in a flirty tone.

"It's a surprise. Brad is the only other person who knows about this place. Even the ODR does not know it exists," Hunter said. "It's the only place I feel confident you'll be safe for a couple of days until we get back."

"You're not staying?"

"Unfortunately, I can't. Brad and I have to travel to wherever Bruner is tomorrow and try to stop him before he makes another attempt on the President's life. Trust me, you'll be safe until I get back. No one will think to look for you where we are going."

On the way, they stopped for groceries. Hunter purchased enough to last Amy a week just in case something went wrong and he couldn't make it back as soon as planned.

After the grocery store, they traveled through a few back roads toward Annapolis and finally came to an out-of-the-way marina located just outside of the city limits.

They continued through the slew of boats until they arrived at the water's edge. Hunter parked the car and got out, grabbing the bags of groceries he had purchased. He led Amy down a pier until they came to a slip, which held an old sailboat that looked to be in the middle of a restoration.

"Here we are, home sweet home," Hunter said as he headed toward the gangway.

"Is this what you had in mind?" Amy asked as she looked at the ship in front of her.

"What's the matter? No sense of adventure?"

"No," she replied, "I can handle it. I just wasn't imagining an old sailboat when you spoke of a hiding place.

"Give me your hand and come aboard," Hunter said as he set down the groceries.

"I think you will be pleasantly surprised with my lady once you get a look around. Her outer hull just needs to be pulled out of the water, sanded down and painted, and she will be as grand as the day she was launched."

"Wow," Amy exclaimed as she stepped on deck. "You were right. The top part has been redone beautifully. Who did this for you?"

"I do my own work, Hunter said. Brad comes out to help from time to time when I have a two man job, but mostly it's just me."

"How long have you been working on this?" Amy asked.

"I started eight years ago. Because I'm away so often, it took me six years to finish the inside and the last two to finish the top deck. I have been slapping paint on the hull each year just so she would not get any worse, but I intend to finish her this summer."

"Well I must say she has a beautiful deck."

"Oh, you know the terminology."

"I am a little rusty, but as I told you before my father used to take me sailing when I was younger," Amy said.

"Well, lets get these groceries inside before they spoil," he replied leading the way.

They adjourned below decks with the groceries and Amy's belongings. The cabin was more impressive than Amy would have thought. The 1945 fifty-foot sailboat had been redone from top to bottom in a nice oak finish. The inside still smelled as if it was redone just yesterday.

A few modern conveniences were added, including a wall mounted plasma television, a stereo system that ran throughout the boat, six speakers, and an entertainment system with a DVD/VCR combo, tape, and CD player. The galley was redone with all the modern conveniences, including a separate refrigerator and freezer that operated on both generator and shore power.

He had even installed an air conditioning/heating system that could be run under generator or shore power.

"You have really outdone yourself," Amy commented with an impressed look on her face.

"Thank you. It has been a labor of love."

"Why don't you get situated in the master stateroom and I will take a shower in one of the forward heads," Hunter suggested.

Amy started the shower to warm up the water before getting in, then took off her clothes and stepped into the soothing water. After the long adventure and her rough time in captivity, she longed to be clean and refreshed. She took a longer time in the shower than usual, enjoying every moment.

Hunter was doing the same in the forward shower. This had been a long adventure for him as well, and he was in no hurry to leave the comfort of a warm shower.

When she finally got out, Amy decided not to put on a full set of clothes, but instead rummaged through the drawers in the aft cabin looking for something comfortable to wear. She found one of Hunter's old sweatshirts with Ohio State written across the chest.

She pulled the sweatshirt over her head and it covered most of her body. Satisfied with her comfort level, she went back to the ship's head to finish drying her hair.

Meanwhile, Hunter was finishing up in the forward part of the boat. He stepped out to towel off, taking a moment to notice three large bruises on his chest where the bullets had struck his vest.

"Another close call," he thought to himself.

He wrapped his towel around his waist, then gathered his dirty clothes and headed to the master stateroom for a clean set. He knocked on the door and waited. After a few moments had passed, he figured Amy was out of earshot, probably still in the shower or drying her hair, so he entered.

He opened the drawer where he kept his favorite sweatshirt and noticed its absence. He figured Amy had borrowed it, and started daydreaming about how she would look in the sweatshirt and nothing else. He would have gone on dreaming about it for a while longer if not for the fact that Amy was standing in the doorway. He glanced up to find her wearing only his Ohio State sweatshirt.

"She looks even better than in my dream!" Hunter thought.

Amy motioned for him to come over. He walked over and gently caressed the side of her face slowly leaning in putting his lip to hers. They passionately kissed for a short while and then Hunter reached down and hoisted her in his arms. He carried her to the bed and laid her down, being as gentle as possible. They continued their passion for the next few hours, falling asleep in each other's embrace.

*   *   *

Hunter awoke the next morning early to find Amy still fast asleep. He didn't want to wake her, so he quietly got out of bed and headed to the forward stateroom to shower. After he got dressed, he went to check on Amy one last time before heading to the office.

She awoke still groggy and looked up at him with barely open eyes. He leaned over and gave her a kiss on the lips.

"I have to go to the office to meet up with Brad and should be back in a couple of days. It is only a ten-minute walk to downtown Annapolis. I don't think anyone will be looking for you in this area, so you should be safe. Call anyone you like but don't let anyone, including your family, know where you are staying. It could put them in harm's way."

"You promise to come back to me in a couple of days?" Amy asked.

"Of course, I still have to take you sailing," Hunter responded with a smile before he reluctantly turned and walked out the door.

Chapter 24

Eric Hunter arrived at the office early, expecting to be the only one there. He walked by Brad's office to find his door slightly cracked open. He peeked in and saw his partner sleeping on the couch. The light from the hall woke Brad as it shined on his face, and a drowsy Spencer opened his eyes and looked up.

"What's going on?" Brad asked as he sat up.

"I was going to ask you the same thing. Why didn't you go home last night?" Hunter asked.

"Why didn't you have your cell phone on?" he returned with a question. "I tried to call you ten times."

"What's up?" Hunter asked, noticing the distraught look on Brad's face.

"I booked us on the 7:05 a.m. flight to Puerto Rico out of Baltimore Washington International Airport," Brad said as he rubbed the sleep from his eyes. "By the way, where were the two of you last night? The boat?"

"Of course. Why didn't you come by to tell me if you were so worried?"

"Did you really want me to bother you when you were alone with Amy? Besides, I figured you would be in here early."

"Good point. I'm glad you left me alone," said Hunter.

"So you had a good night?" Brad asked.

"You know my usual answer."

"I will take that as a yes and leave it at that," Brad replied.

Brad never really had to ask Hunter how his night went. After 14 years of friendship, he could tell just by the look on his face. Besides, he knew Hunter was not big on discussing what went on behind closed doors. Even though he knew a lot of women, he never talked about them in a negative way or said anything derogatory about any of them. It was a trait that Brad respected.

"What do you need me to do before we leave?" asked Hunter.

"Do you have two or three days worth of clothes packed in that bag you are carrying?" Spencer answered with a question.

"Yes sir," responded Hunter.

"Well in that case we're all set. I have everything else packed and ready to go in my Jeep. We should leave within the next twenty minutes so we have enough time for check-in."

"I just want to log in and check my e-mails before we leave," said Hunter.

"That's fine. I need to take a quick shower," Brad replied. Meet me at my Jeep in twenty."

Hunter walked down the hall to his office. He clicked the power button on his computer and was soon sorting through his inbox. It seemed to be the regular old crap, department notices and the occasional joke e-mail. Then he saw a message from his new friend at the CIA, Harold Silver.

"I thought this might come in handy. Sorry I can't do more," was the message with an included attachment.

Hunter clicked on the attachment and waited for it to download. To Hunter's amazement, Silver had sent him the schematics to Bruner's factory in Puerto Rico, along with the floor plan and address to the home Bruner owned and stayed in while visiting the plant.

"He arrived in Puerto Rico yesterday and was last spotted heading west toward his factory," was written at the top of the first page of the attachment.

Hunter printed all twenty pages Silver had sent him, gathered them up, and studied them for a moment. He always liked a good adventure and this trip was shaping up to be one he would not forget.

He glanced at the clock and realized it had already been twenty minutes. He shut down his computer and headed out the door.

As expected, Spencer had the car pulled up to the door and ready to go. Hunter threw his bag in the back and got in the passenger seat.

"Did you bring our dive gear and a couple of weapons we can dive with?" asked Hunter.

"Yes on the dive gear but no on the weapons. What did you have in mind?" Brad asked.

"I think you should drive so we don't miss our flight. I will make a call to our new friends down there on the way to airport and request a few additional items," Hunter said.

As Brad put the car in drive, Hunter dialed his cell phone. "Captain Harkin, this is Eric Hunter," he said as Harkin picked up the phone.

"Hunter! How the hell are you?"

"I am doing well, sir, we are heading your way again and need a little help."

"The last time you said that we had a hell of a time. What can I do for you?" Harkin said.

Hunter responded with a list of items he would need once they arrived in Puerto Rico.

"That sounds like a heck of a tall order, but I'll see what I can do," Harkin said after Hunter had finished.

"Thanks, sir. We'll see you in a few hours," Hunter said before hanging up the phone.

"So is he on board or not?" asked Brad.

"I think our new friend will come through," replied Hunter.

The remaining ride to BWI Airport gave them enough time to talk about the e-mail and some ideas Hunter had about getting into the factory.

After leaving the Jeep in long-term parking, they boarded the bus for the terminal and were on their way.

Chapter 25

Amy awoke to the sound of waves lightly slapping against the hull of the boat. It was a very pleasing sound, and it had given her one of the best sleeps she had had in quite a while. She arose slowly, giving her body a big stretch. Looking at the clock on the wall, she was amazed to find that she had slept until ten o'clock, getting more than nine hours of sleep.

"I have not slept that long in years," she thought to herself.

Not wanting to waste any more of the day, she pulled herself out of bed and headed to the bathroom to freshen up. After about forty-five minutes, she emerged showered and was ready to take on the world. She planned on walking to the waterfront in downtown Annapolis to do some shopping. She could not remember the last time she'd had a couple of days off with nothing to do and she wanted to make the most of it.

The walk downtown was wonderful. It was a beautiful seventy-five degree day and everything smelled so fresh. It took her approximately twenty minutes to make the journey, since she was in no hurry to get anywhere. It was just past eleven and she decided the first thing she wanted to do was get something to eat. She walked around the downtown square before venturing into one of the local restaurants.

The hostess greeted her with a smile and was kind enough to sit her by the window so she could look out at the boats on the water.

Amy was enchanted by Annapolis, which had a laid-back feel so different from the bustle of downtown DC. She felt safe again and could finally let her guard down for some much needed R & R.

As she watched the passing boats, she dreamed of sailing with Hunter on the bay, wind blowing in her hair. She continued her daydream until the waitress, who had been patiently trying to get her attention to take her order, startled her. Amy quickly ordered. As she was handing the waitress her menu, she noticed a man with very sharp features and a disposition that she had only seen held by soldiers or men who had been through a lot of hard times. Her heart rate began to quicken and she started thinking the worst.

"How did they find me?" she asked herself. "Hunter was so careful."

Just then, a young man in a white uniform approached the table of the older man. In her excitement, she had forgotten that the Naval Academy was located not more than a block away. This man was probably visiting his son for lunch.

"How silly of me," she thought, and went back to her daydreams.

She took her time finishing the crab cake sandwich she had ordered, trying to savor every moment. After finishing the last bite, she put down her napkin and reached for the check that the waitress had already placed on her table. It kind of annoyed her that she did not wait until she was finished but quickly brushed it off and reached for her wallet.

Amy tossed twenty dollars on the table and did not wait for change. Her next stop was the water's edge, where she found a bench and sat down, tipping her face up to the sun.

"I could stay here all day," she thought as she again drifted off into a daydream.

Before long, a man approached and sat next to her on the bench.

"Nice day today," he said as he sat down.

"Yes, wonderful weather," she replied.

"A great day for a boat ride," he continued.

"I was just thinking that myself," Amy replied.

"Well, Mrs. Evans, would you like to go on a boat ride with me?" the man asked, his eyes still focused on the water.

Amy felt all her strength leave her body. The anxiety from the restaurant returned with ten times the force. She started to stand up, but the man grabbed her arm and pulled her back down.

"No, Mrs. Evans, you mustn't go. I insist that you go on a ride with me."

With her free left hand, Amy clawed at the man's eyes.

He was not prepared for such a combative women and he released his grip to defend himself. Amy ran toward the center of town, with the man hot on her trail.

The commotion attracted more attention then the man had intended, but still he pursued. Amy kept running, scanning the area for any signs of help but to no avail. She continued around the circle where most of the downtown restaurants were located. As she passed the center market and turned left, she noticed another man standing in her way, ready to grab her as she went by.

"I have had enough of this," she thought. She steadied herself, knowing she could not outmaneuver this highly trained man, and went for the only weapon left in her arsenal. As he came in to grab her, she kneed him in the groan with all her might.

He fell to the ground in agony, and she continued on her way. As she rounded the next corner, she saw a police car stopped at the crosswalk. She ran to it, waving her arms to get the attention of the officer inside.

"Oh thank God officer. My name is Amy Evans and I am a forensic expert for the FBI and there is a man trying to kidnap me," she said, showing him her credentials.

"Get into the car, Ms. Evans. I will handle this," the officer said.

He immediately reached for his gun, pulled it from its holster, and aimed at the man heading their way.

"Freeze! Police!" he shouted.

Bang! Bang! Two shots rang out. The officer grabbed his chest and fell to the ground.

Just then, a boat pulled up with two men inside.

Amy screamed as the man she had kneed in the groin and her pursuer reached the police car. She quickly locked the doors.

Two more shots rang out and the passenger window shattered into a million pieces. The man Amy had attacked reached in and grabbed for her while the other man smashed in the driver's side window with his elbow.

"You can go the hard way or the easy way," he insisted.

Of course the easy way was not an option for her and she started kicking and screaming. The man pulled his rather large arm back and cold cocked her in the head.

He grabbed her by the wrist and before she could react, pulled her to the water's edge and flung her into the boat. She hit her head and became dizzy from the blow. She stumbled to get up and was pushed back down to the deck.

The last words she heard were "hit it" and the engine roared to life as a rag was placed over her mouth and nose. Her next breath was filled with a smell she came to know all to well. As the chloroform entered her lungs, she gently passed into a sea of blackness, not knowing what would happen next or what these men had in store for her.

Chapter 26

Hunter and Spencer got off the plane to the musky smell of the San Juan airport. The weather was so humid in the Caribbean that not even the air conditioning systems could pull enough moisture out of the air. The result was a unique smell that anyone who had spent time in the Caribbean could identify.

After proceeding to baggage claim and picking up their bags, they exited to find Lieutenant Hernandez awaiting their arrival.

"What the heck are you doing here?" Brad asked as he gave him a big handshake.

"A little birdie told me you needed help and so here I am."

"Would that little birdie be Captain Harkin?" asked Hunter.

"It was indeed. How are you?" he asked, extending his hand.

"I am great. How are things in paradise?" asked Hunter.

"Things have been quiet around here since you two left, but I am sure they are about to get lively again," Hernandez replied.

"We have been known to bring the party with us," remarked Spencer.

Hernandez returned a smile and then motioned them toward a car that was parked a very short distance from the exit.

"How did you get a spot so close?" asked Brad.

"Police pass," answered Hernandez. "The captain managed to score a couple and we use them when we need to pick up anyone of importance that arrives here."

"So we rank up there with the big wigs it seems," Spencer joked.

"Nice wheels you have here," Brad said.

"Thank you. This is the new Seven Series BMW. I had it shipped from the States. It is not a common car down here, which makes me kind of stick out, just the way I like it," Hernandez replied.

"I take it this is not a government vehicle," observed Brad as they pulled away.

"So did you get the items we needed?" Hunter interjected. He liked the small talk, but knew time was tight and they needed to get moving.

"Most of it. The rest should arrive once you get back from your surveillance trip," Hernandez replied.

"Oh great, another trek though the Puerto Rican jungle." Brad said.

"Brad, I suspect from the look on your face Hunter has not told you how you will be traveling this evening," said Hernandez.

"We have arranged a nice twin engine plane for the two of you to do a flyover. Your flight departs an hour before sunset, which should place you at your destination shortly after nightfall. I also have two sets of dive gear fully equipped with the rebreathers that our Navy Seals use, so you can go undetected for the second part of your mission."

"We have rebreathers on this mission?" Brad said with excitement.

"How much did you tell him?" asked the Lieutenant.

"Enough not to ruin the surprise." Hunter replied. "Brad, I will brief you on the entire mission once we get to our hotel room."

Hernandez continued: "As promised, the plane will be waiting at the airport fully loaded. Everything is taken care of with the Coast Guard as well. I have to pick up a few items in town, but I'll meet up with you at the plane."

"Will you be going with us?" asked Spencer.

"No, but I'll make sure you get off without a hitch. Don't hesitate to call if you need anything else before tonight," Hernandez answered as he pulled up to the hotel.

Captain Harkin himself had arranged the five star accommodations, located near the airport on Isla Verde Avenue.

"Here are your room keys," Hernandez said. You're already checked into Room 517. I will be here at 4 to take you to the airport.

Hunter looked at his watch to discover it was already one o'clock. "We have three hours until he comes back, so let's talk about our game plan," Hunter said.

They decided to talk over lunch at the hotel's beach restaurant. Hunter discussed in great detail every facet of his plan while Brad focused on every word. After about an hour Hunter finished and they both sat back, bellies full from a delicious meal.

"What do you think our odds are that things go as planned?" asked Brad.

"About the same as always, I guess," replied Hunter.

"We have about an hour and a half until the mission goes down. I'd like to get in a shower and maybe lay down and rest for a little bit before we start," Brad said before he headed to the room.

Hunter stayed long enough to pay the check and then headed to the beach for a stroll. Neither one had said it, but they knew this was going to be a very difficult mission, one of their most dangerous yet.

Hunter was looking forward to it, but he liked to take moments like this to reflect on his life, just in case he didn't make it back.

As he walked down the beach, he realized how blessed he had been to live a life that not many could even fathom. He had never known the daily grind of an office worker and had never been bored by his work.

After a half hour, he decided to head to his room and get cleaned up before the mission.

He walked from the beach through the main pool area toward the hotel's beach entrance. He thought to himself how amazing these resort hotels had become. The main pool area had two large swimming pools connected by a small swim through-area. A waterfall fell into each of the pools, and a large hot tub at one end looked like it could seat as many as thirty people.

"I will have to use that after the mission," he thought as he passed.

He arrived in the room to find Brad already showered and taking a nap. Hunter took a shower and was shaving when his cell phone rang. He recognized the number as belonging to his boss, Adam Reinquest.

"What's up, chief?" he asked as he answered.

"Just calling to see how everything is coming along," Reinquest said.

"So far so good."

"How is Amy faring in her hideout? By the way, where are you keeping her?" asked Reinquest.

"My sailboat in Annapolis," Hunter replied. "In fact, would you mind checking in on her on your way home?"

"Sure. Just let me know where you keep your boat."

Hunter passed along his slip information as requested, plus gave Reinquest her cell phone number in case she was not at the boat when he arrived.

"Anything else?" asked Reinquest.

"I think we have it under control, but we'll keep you posted on our progress," replied Hunter.

"Well, if it's the way you usually keep me updated, I won't hold my breath awaiting your call. Good luck on your mission and I know it goes without saying, but be careful."

"Thank you, sir. We will make you proud," Hunter said and then hung up his cell phone.

He finished shaving, got dressed and headed out of the bathroom about the same time Brad was waking up.

"How much time do we have?" Brad asked.

"About a half an hour before we get picked up," Hunter replied.

"Great, just enough time," remarked Brad. He got out of bed, stretched, and started to gather his gear while Hunter studied the aerial map of Bruner's layout.

At the appointed time, they headed to the main lobby, each carrying a black utility bag.

As promised, Lieutenant Hernandez was waiting for them in

his BMW, parked just outside the front doors. He was sitting in the front seat with his head back, enjoying music playing over the radio.

Brad knocked on the window to get his attention, which startled the half-asleep lieutenant. Instantly he unlocked the doors and got out to greet them.

"Sorry if I startled you," said Brad.

They all got in the car and off they went. It was a short ride to the San Juan Airport. They arrived at a private aviation gate and were greeted by the gate guard.

Lieutenant Hernandez spoke to the gate guard in Spanish so fast that Hunter, even though he spoke a little, could not make out their conversation.

Hernandez had grown up in Puerto Rico but had left to go to the Naval Academy in Annapolis, where he perfected his English and spoke with hardly any accent. He had lived in the States for many years after graduation and had taken a position at Naval Station Roosevelt Roads two years ago when his father had become ill.

Since he was from Puerto Rico, he was a great asset to the Navy because he knew how to cut through red tape and get things done on the island.

"I may just have to spend more time here to get to know the culture," Hunter said.

"Get to know the culture or the underwater environment?" asked Hernandez.

"I think a little of both."

They pulled up next to a twin engine Cessna 310. From the looks of it, Hunter placed it as a mid 80's vintage, a common production year for 310's.

"With your flight experience, the captain figured you were certified on this type of bird," said Hernandez. "Was he correct?"

"Hunter has hundreds, maybe thousands, of hours on this type of craft," Brad replied. "Heck, I think he is close to instructor level."

Hernandez accepted the answer and left them to take care of some final rental details.

"You know I have only flown a Cessna 310 once about five years ago," Hunter said to Brad under his breath.

He had been expecting a single engine craft. He was certified in a few twin-engine planes, but was a little rusty. He and Brad had been flying acrobatic single engine planes for the past five years and only flew twin engine planes once in a while.

"Do you think you can fly it?" asked Brad.

"I can give it a try!" said Hunter.

"That is all I ask," replied Brad.

"Everything all right?" asked Hernandez when they approached.

"No problems whatsoever," replied Brad Spencer.

Hernandez gave an approving nod and then turned his attention to the airplane to go over the inventory on board.

"OK gentlemen, I have all the items you requested. I managed to pull some strings and get the remaining gear. In this bag, you have your rebreathers. These bags contain your wet suits and spear guns. I took the liberty of taping your names on the outside."

"In this bag are your weapons. I have included two machine guns, four side arms, eight remote detonated mines, ten grenades, and four knives. I think the only thing you did not ask for were rocket launchers," he continued.

"By the way we may need ... " Brad started and was cut off.

"Don't even think about it!" Hernandez interjected. "There is no way the Captain is going to give me permission for those.

Brad shrugged his shoulders, pretending to be upset.

"In the back is an inflatable raft with an electric motor that will take you up to speeds of twenty knots for five miles. It is the same kind that the SEALS use. For weight and space reasons, I did not include a gas motor so when the battery runs out, you better be at your destination or it it's time to paddle."

"All your night vision gear and other items you requested are in the last set of bags. Did I miss anything?" asked Hernandez.

"I feel like James Bond must feel before a mission," said Spencer.

"I think you have more equipment then he usually gets," retorted Hernandez.

"It all looks to be in order," said Hunter.

"Great. Then I need you to sign for it. You know the Navy does not let you go to the bathroom without a release form."

Hunter signed the form, shook hands with the Lieutenant, and jumped into the captain's seat.

"Sorry. He gets excited around aircraft," Brad said as he shook Hernandez's hand goodbye.

"Have a great flight and be careful," Hernandez said as he shut the airplanes door.

Chapter 27

"San Juan Ground this is November One Seven Seven Bravo Delta sitting at the west hanger on Apron Six awaiting taxi to Runway 28," Hunter said into the radio.

"November One Seven Seven Bravo Delta, taxi and hold Runway 28." Replied ground control.

"Taxi and hold," Hunter returned.

He reached for the throttle and applied pressure. The Cessna's engines came to life with a sound that was pure music to flight fanatics like Brad and Hunter. It signaled the start of another mission, which meant during the next few hours anything was possible and the improbable would probably occur.

Hunter taxied to the edge of Runway 28 just outside the hold line as Brad rattled off the preflight checklist. They were most of the way through the checklist when they arrived at the runway's edge.

"Ready for run up?" Hunter asked Brad through the intercom system.

"Ready. Brakes applied and holding run up to 2500 RPM," replied Spencer.

Hunter did as instructed and applied enough throttle on both engines to take them to the appropriate levels on the RPM gauges.

"All systems in the green checking left magneto. Noticeable drop in RPM testing right magneto. All systems in check pulling back throttles to 1000," Hunter said.

Hunter switched the frequency from San Juan Ground and dialed in the tower.

"San Juan Tower this is Cessna November One Seven Seven Bravo Delta at the end of Runway 28 awaiting takeoff," Hunter said.

"Cessna Seven Bravo Delta taxi in position and hold," came the response.

"Taxi and hold Seven Bravo Delta." Hunter replied.

He again applied pressure on the throttles and the engines roared in response, propelling them to the center of the runway. Hunter turned the plane to line up with the centerline and held position.

"Cessna One Seven Seven Bravo Delta cleared for an immediate takeoff on Runway two eight," came the instructions from the tower.

"Cleared for take off Seven Bravo Delta," Hunter replied.

He immediately grabbed the throttles tight and pushed them to full power. The thrust of her mighty engines kicked them forward and they began to march down the runway.

"Brad, to answer your earlier question, I am sure I can take this bird off. I just don't know if I can land her," Hunter said as they gained speed.

"That makes me feel great!" Brad replied.

Hunter did not reply, but pulled back on the yoke. The plane's front wheel lifted off the ground and they remained suspended with only one wheel in the air for a few moments.

The speed increased, creating the added lift and the rest of the wheels lifted off the ground. They started their climb at 1000 feet per minute and then lowered the nose to a more modest 750 feet per minute climb rate.

Brad went through the post take-off checklist as Hunter checked their course and acquired the appropriate permission to proceed to their intended destination. After getting the clearance, they made one final turn en route the west coast of Puerto Rico and toward their target.

The sun was just about to set and the sky over San Juan was a beautiful sight. They both took a quiet moment to enjoy the sunset before returning their focus on their mission. They planned to see many more like it, but wanted to enjoy this one just in case.

"Brad could you load our waypoint into the chart plotter and give me a heading to steer?" Hunter said, breaking the silence first.

Hunter, being a sailor first and a pilot second, like to throw in boating analogies whenever possible.

"Course to steer two five five degrees true," said Brad.

"Adjusting course to two hundred and fifty five degrees true," Hunter repeated.

"What is our ETA to the factory?" Hunter asked.

"The GPS has us at thirty three minutes."

"Good. We should be there right as the last light leaves the sky," Hunter said.

"Brad, I think we should start breaking out all the night gear, including the camera, so we're ready when we get there. I want to do this as quickly as possible and make only a few passes so we are not detected."

"I agree. Don't worry, old man, I will have everything ready by the time we get there."

"Old man? If I recall correctly, you are only three months younger than me," replied Hunter.

Brad did not respond. He was too busy rustling through bags and getting the required gear. It took him approximately thirty minutes to get the gear out and set up.

"OK, I am ready," Brad said as he lifted the camera with the night scope.

"Not a minute too soon. We'll be in visual range in four minutes. Time to turn out the lights," Hunter said as he flipped off several switches on the panel.

"I see it straight ahead," Brad said. "Bring your altitude down to five hundred feet and slow down to one hundred and twenty knots."

Hunter did as he was instructed.

"We are currently at five hundred feet at a speed of one hundred and twenty knots," Hunter announced.

They flew over Bruner's mansion first, in case they would get only one pass. Brad took picture after picture, and since the digital camera could hold over five hundred he did not have to hold back.

Hunter made a full circle, then continued on course to the main factory.

"The factory will probably have guards on watch. We need to climb a little higher so we don't tip them off," remarked Hunter. "How high can I climb and still keep your camera in range?"

"This zoom lens is good for about five hundred feet, so level off at 1000 feet and glide in with the engines at idle. At that low engine speed we will sound like we are much further away and that should keep us from attracting attention," said Brad.

*　*　*

"Are you sure it's the same plane? I don't want any mistakes," David Bruner asked his right hand man, Kyle London.

"I've already taken more of a risk than I like, letting you kidnap the FBI agent for a second time," he continued, not waiting for an answer.

"Sir, I am sure it is them. My men have confirmed it is a Cessna 310, the same airplane our sources say they took off in an hour ago," replied London.

"What do you have in mind?" asked Bruner.

"With your permission, sir, I would like to take care of this problem once and for all."

"By take care of, you mean blow them completely out of the sky," said Bruner. "That was my thought."

"Do what you have to do. I want this finished now and for good."

"That is all I needed to hear," London said and hung up the phone.

"Get the rocket launchers!" London screamed as he turned to face one of his top men. The man did as he was instructed and grabbed three others to help him with his task.

London grabbed the night vision binoculars and stared at the approaching plane.

"They are totally unaware of how close they are to death," he whispered to himself.

*   *   *

Hunter positioned the airplane on final approach for the factory and pulled back the throttles to the lowest power setting. He wanted to give Brad enough time to get as many pictures as possible.

"All right, Brad, we will only be able to do one pass at this so make it count," Hunter said. "By now, they have got to be on to us."

Hunter flew overhead as Brad snapped pictures as fast as the camera would allow.

After he completed one full circle, Hunter returned to their original course, which took them out to sea. He pushed the throttles forward to increase their speed and pulled back on the airplane's yoke to increase their altitude.

"That seemed to go off with out a hitch," Brad commented as they made their climb back to a safe altitude.

"Let's not get too confident until we have a little more distance between us and the factory," Hunter said.

"You were always a worrier," Brad said.

As Brad turned to put his camera away, he noticed two flashes of bright light leaving from the warehouse roof.

"I hate it when you're right," Brad said pointing to the warehouse.

"What is it?" Hunter asked, excited.

"I think they just launched two missiles from the roof!" Brad yelled.

"Hold on!" Hunter screamed as he pushed the controls down, putting the plane in a nosedive toward the ocean.

As soon as the rockets launched, they locked onto their target. They were designed to track the heat trail left by the plane's engines.

"We need to ditch this bird into the ocean," Hunter said.

"We need to do what?" Brad asked, holding on for dear life as Hunter increased his downward angle of decent.

"The missiles are zeroing in on our heat signature and the only way to shake them is to put this plane in the ocean," Hunter screamed.

He pressed the plane's limits even further, increasing the speed of the dive and passing the red zone on the speed gauge.

"Won't we rip the wings off at this speed?" Brad yelled into the intercom.

"She just needs to hold together for a few more seconds," Hunter screamed back.

"I don't think we are going to make it to the water first." Hunter said as he pushed the plane even further.

Before either could speak another word, the first of the two missiles flew by, passing just feet from them.

Brad looked at Hunter in raw disbelief.

Their celebration was short lived because the second missile locked on them and exploded, leaving a large fireball in the sky where their plane had been.

*   *   *

"We scored a direct hit!" London yelled, unable to contain his elation. He called his boss to relay the news. "Sir, I am happy to report they won't be a problem to us any more."

"Are you sure?" Bruner asked.

"Yes sir, they are done. I am watching the debris fall right now," London reported.

"Great work!" Bruner said, paying London a rare compliment.

"Thank you, sir," replied London.

"Now get rid of those rocket launchers. The last thing we need is for this to get traced back to us," Bruner ordered, returning to his usual rough self.

"No problem, sir. I will take care of it." Replied London.

Fortunately for Hunter and Spencer, it had not been a direct hit. The explosion had blown off a portion of the plane's roof and had torn the tail assembly to pieces. The remaining part of the roof was engulfed in flames.

Brad grabbed the plane's fire extinguisher, located behind his seat, and began to battle the fire. The extinguisher filled the cabin with powder, making it almost impossible to see and hard to breath.

"I can't believe we are still alive," Spencer screamed, coughing between words.

"We won't be for long unless we get out of this plane. The first missile is making a loop around and coming back for a second try!" Hunter yelled. "Grab the gear and jump," he commanded.

"You want me to do what?" Brad asked, shocked.

"I am going to slow the plane down and we are going to jump before the second missile locks on, so grab you parachute," Hunter shouted.

Without responding to Hunter's crazed idea, Brad grabbed a case from behind his seat and opened it, revealing a pair of flares guns.

"What do you intend to do with those?" asked Hunter.

"Shoot them like counter measures and hope the missile will lock on to them instead of us," he replied.

"It is our only chance. If we jump from this altitude, our parachutes will not have time to open and we will make a death splash in the water," shouted Brad.

"Level off at five hundred feet. When I give the word, kill the engines and dive as fast as the plane will allow," Brad ordered.

"Do you really think that plan will work?" asked Hunter.

"If it doesn't, you won't have long to complain about it."

"That's comforting," Hunter said under his breath.

"This has to be exact, so ready yourself. Here comes the missile," Brad continued.

Brad sat in silence for the next few moments, waiting for the right time to act. The missile circled around, locking on and lining up for the kill.

"Kill the engines and drop; Now!" Brad yelled out.

Hunter hastily pushed the controls forward and put the plane into a nose-dive while simultaneously shutting down the engines. At the same time, Brad fired off both flares.

The force was so intense on their bodies that the only thing keeping them from flying out of the plane was the well-designed seatbelts they wore.

Luck was on their side. The missile locked onto the flares and exploded as they continued their descent toward the water.

Hunter held his decent for a few more moments before leveling the plane at one hundred and fifty feet above the water. He immediately attempted to restart the engines. He only had a few moments, or they would crash into the sea.

To their immense relief, Hunter managed to fire up the Number One engine. He pushed the throttle to full power to maintain the plane's altitude while he attempted to start the second.

Unbeknownst to the two of them, shreds of metal and fire from the missile had rained down upon them, ripping through the right wing and completely destroying the Number Two engine.

"Are we still alive?" Brad asked.

"Yes, but don't celebrate just yet, my good friend. I can't get the Number Two engine online," replied Hunter. "Look outside the tell me what you see."

Brad looked out his window to inspect the engine. "You can try all you want. It's never going to start," he said. "Not only is the engine torn to pieces, so is most of the wing."

"More good news," Hunter said, struggling to keep the plane level. "I'm going to turn this plane around and head toward land. Maybe we can make it and ditch this bird in a field somewhere." He made the turn, but quickly realized the plane's structural integrity was holding on by a string.

"I don't think she is going to hold together long enough for us to make it back," Brad said.

"I think you're right. We may have a couple more minutes if we are lucky. Gather up all our gear and lash the bags to the inflatable raft," Hunter commanded.

"Put on your life jacket and hand me mine. I will slow down as much as possible, but when we crash my hope is the auto inflate will blow up the raft and all the equipment will float to the top through the hole in the roof."

"That is one of the craziest ideas you have ever come up with. I don't think it will work. But what the hell," Brad said as he removed his seatbelt and did as instructed.

He handed Hunter his life jacket before continuing on with lashing the gear to the raft.

Hunter slowed the plane, keeping it level about a hundred feet above the water as Brad continued his job in the back.

"How are we doing back there?" Hunter asked.

"Just a couple more seconds," Brad said as he tied the last bag to the raft. "All finished."

"Great, now get your butt back up here and strap in," Hunter ordered.

Brad climbed into the co-pilot seat and tightened the straps.

"I really hope your plan does not get us killed," he said.

"Me too. Now hold on. I'm going to slow us down and try to stall the wings a few feet above the water and drop us down as smooth as I can," Hunter said.

Hunter positioned the plane as he had intended, slowing it down about ten feet above the water. The plane slowly creped to stall speed as parts of the right wing ripped off at an ever-increasing pace.

As soon as the plane's speed could no longer maintain the amount of lift it needed to continue flight it dropped like a log head first into a five-foot wave.

It was not the smooth landing they wanted. The impact was so great it caused Hunter's head to hit the dash, slashing it open and rendering him unconscious. Brad took a hard hit as well, but managed to remain coherent as water flooded the cabin.

After grabbing the release on his seatbelt and shoving the belt aside, Brad turned to check on his friend. His eyes widened as he saw that Hunter was slumped over and bleeding badly, unable to save himself from the onslaught of rushing water.

"Hunter wake up!" Brad screamed just before the last of the air in the cabin vanished.

He might as well have been talking to himself because Hunter did not budge an inch. Brad swiftly reached for Hunter's belt and pushed the button to release the clasp. The force from the impact must have damaged the release mechanism because no matter how hard Brad tried; he could not get his friend free.

By this time the plane had almost completely filled with water and it was beginning its descent to the bottom.

Brad continued his efforts until he was out of air in his lungs. His only choice was to make an unwilling ascent to the surface for air, leaving Hunter falling further and further to the crushing depths of the abyss.

They were still close to the surface and with the added lift he got from his life jacket; it only took Brad a few moments to reach the surface.

As soon as his head broke the surface he took a deep breath, tore off his life jacket, and was about to make another rescue attempt when he spotted the black life raft fully inflated just a few feet away.

"I can't believe that worked," he said out loud.

Knowing he would not have time to put a tank and regulator together, he reached for a can of spare air, a dive knife and a flashlight from one of the bags.

The spare air would only provide enough oxygen for about twenty breaths, but it might be enough. Brad plunged below the surface to make one final attempt to save his friend.

He swam down as fast as his legs would allow, taking a breath only when he desperately needed it. He continued deeper and deeper until he came upon the plane.

Because of an air bubble trapped in the luggage compartment, the airplane was descending at a slower than normal pace, which gave Brad a few more moments to work.

He rushed into the cockpit to find Hunter still unconscious and bleeding. He quickly cut the seatbelt straps with the dive knife and dislodged his friend from the captain's seat.

He pulled Hunter out of the airplane and began his ascent,

swimming as fast as he could. As before, Hunter's life vest allowed them to travel toward the surface at a much faster rate, giving them valuable seconds that Brad knew he would need if he were to resuscitate his friend.

They broke through the surface and Brad immediately pushed Hunter into the inflatable raft. He hastily jumped in and checked Hunter's vital signs, hoping for a miracle.

Hunter was not breathing but Brad was relieved to find a pulse. It was weak, but it meant Hunter still had a chance. Without delay, Brad began to administer CPR to revive his fallen comrade.

He continued on his mission and was determined not to stop until either Hunter was revived or he passed out from exhaustion.

"Come on, damm it, don't give up on me!" Brad screamed as he administered his chest compressions.

"You have never given up on a fight, so don't start now!" he screamed even louder.

Brad began to administer mouth to mouth once again when he noticed Hunter's hand move. At first he thought he was delirious from exhaustion but realized it was not his imagination when he felt that same hand push him away.

Hunter rolled over and coughed out what appeared to be a gallon of water. He took a couple of deep breaths and tried to regain his composure.

Before Brad could say anything, Hunter sat up, resting his back on one of the inflated sides of the raft.

"This does not mean we are going to start dating. I don't care how much time we spend together," Hunter said, trying to muster a smile between bouts of coughing out more water.

"You son of a bitch! I thought you were a goner for the second time," replied Spencer.

"How many times do I have to tell you? It's not that easy to get rid of me," Hunter said as he leaned back to rest.

"I'm glad to see you still have your sense of humor," Brad replied as he laid his head back to recover from his exhaustion.

Chapter 28

It took about an hour for the nearby Coast Guard cutter to receive their locator beacon and arrive. By that time, Hunter had returned to his normal chipper self.

"You two need a lift?" Lieutenant Norman called out from the port bridge wing as the ship approached.

"If it would not be much of a bother," Brad called back.

"No bother. We were already in the neighborhood," the captain yelled.

In short order, Spencer and Hunter were safely aboard.

"Don't worry about your gear, sir. We will have it all brought onboard and secured," Chief James said to Hunter.

"Thanks, Chief. It's good to see you again," Hunter said.

"You too, sir. I'm glad to see you guys in one piece. The Captain is waiting for you on the bridge. Give me a minute to secure your items and I will lead you there," said the chief.

"I am sure you two will want to clean up after you talk to the Captain.

"Thanks, Chief. A shower sounds great right about now," said Spencer.

Chief James led them to the bridge wing, where the Captain was waiting.

"Captain, I didn't think we would see you again so soon. How did you get this assignment?" asked Hunter, holding out his hand.

"After I heard about your plane crash, I thought that was the last I was going to see of your two ugly mugs. I'm glad to see you escaped unharmed once again," he replied, shaking Hunters hand.

"And to answer your question, I volunteered for this assignment. From your reputation, I thought it was the best way to see some action," the Captain continued.

"Well, I hope we don't disappoint you, sir," said Hunter.

"I am sure you won't. Now let's go to the bridge and discuss your plan," the Captain replied.

"What makes you think we have a plan?" Hunter asked.

"You strike me as a person who always has a plan," said Norman. "Plus, you had over an hour to wait before we arrived, and I am sure you didn't talk about the weather."

A smile formed on Hunter's face as he thought about what he was going to say.

"Captain, before I get into my plan, can I use the ship's cell phone to make a couple of calls?"

"Sure, I have a feeling it is going to be a long night," he replied as he led Hunter to the cell phone station located in the electronics space just below the bridge.

He left Hunter and returned to talk to Spencer on the bridge.

"So what do you two have up your sleeves?" he asked.

"I am not exactly sure what Hunter is going to come up with. We talked about different scenarios but didn't settle on one in particular," replied Spencer.

Twenty minutes and two phone calls later, Hunter returned and joined Brad and the Captain by the chart table.

"It is all settled. They arrive tomorrow morning," Hunter said.

"Who is coming and what are we in for tomorrow morning?" asked the Captain.

"Two teams of Navy SEALS. We meet them at this location in seven hours," Hunter responded, handing Captain Norman a piece of paper with latitude and longitude positions.

"You said you wanted some action," Hunter continued with a serious look on his face.

"Yes I did," replied the Captain with a sigh. "Any chance you're going to tell me what I am getting my ship and crew into?"

"If you don't mind, I will give a full briefing tomorrow when the SEALs arrive. We have a long day ahead of us and I for one need to get cleaned up and get some sleep," said Hunter.

"Good enough. I will see you in seven hours," replied the Captain.

Chapter 29

Seven hours later, it was still dark. Captain Norman entered the bridge, holding his morning cup of coffee.

"I still don't see anything, sir," the Chief of the boat reported. "I can't imagine a SEAL team would be late."

"When were they supposed to arrive?" asked the Captain.

"They should be here in the next minute or two, but the radar is not picking up any air or water traffic for miles."

"That is strange," the Captain said under his breath.

As the words were leaving his mouth, he noticed a movement out of the corner of his eye in the dark. He snapped around to investigate.

"What is it, Captain?" the Chief asked.

Without saying a word, Norman scanned his eyes across the deck. At first he thought he was seeing things, but then he saw it again. It was a flash or blur -- there one second and gone the next.

"Sound general quarters, Chief!" the Captain said with excitement, almost dropping his coffee.

"Sir, please repeat the order," the Chief responded, not believing what he had heard.

"Sound the general quarters alarm now!" shouted the Captain.

As the Chief reached for the alarm, a figure dressed in a black uniform, with black face paint, and an M-16 rifle, emerged from the shadows of the bridge.

"Chief, that won't be necessary," said the man as he grabbed his hand.

The Chief nearly jumped out of his skin. Before he or anyone else could do anything, three more men abruptly entered. No one said a word but just froze in pure terror.

"Sorry if we startled you, Captain. My name is Lieutenant Jack Hardy and I am the leader of the SEAL team you requested."

"My God, man. You almost gave me a heart attack," replied the Captain.

"Again my apologies. I like to keep my men on their toes and what better way than to storm a Coast Guard ship? I am impressed, though. Most people don't even know we are there until it is too late," Hardy commented.

"I would hardly say that I acted in time to do anything."

"Yes but you did spot my men, and if you were a second earlier you would have sounded that alarm," Hardy continued.

"Thank you, but I still think I need a change of underwear. Where are my manners? My name is Lieutenant Harry Norman and as you know, I am the Captain aboard this vessel." The two men shook hands then got down to the task at hand.

"We would like to set up our equipment on the stern of your ship," Hardy said. "Could you have the necessary crew ready for a briefing in forty-five minutes?"

"That would be fine Mr. Hardy," replied the Captain.

"Captain, please call me Jack," Hardy replied.

"Thank you, Jack. Please call me Harry."

"Thank you Harry. But before we go any farther, where is this Hunter character?"

"I sent a man to wake him and his partner about a half hour ago, so I think he will be emerging shortly," replied the Captain. "Why do you ask?"

"I just want to meet the man who made a full bird Captain and head of the Naval Station jump at his command," he replied.

"I don't think it happened quite like that, but here he comes now," said Norman, pointing to the bridge entrance.

Hunter climbed the ladder to the bridge slowly, savoring his cup of coffee and still wiping sleep from his eyes.

"Mr. Hunter. Good morning, sir," Hardy said as Hunter reached the top bridge step.

"Captain permission to come on the bridge?" Hunter asked before responding.

"Permission granted, Mr. Hunter," responded the Captain.

Hunter entered the bridge and turned toward Hardy, not speaking right away, just sizing up the man who stood before him. He took long enough to achieve his mission but not so long as to offend.

"My guess is you are the leader of the SEAL team I requested," Hunter said.

"Yes sir, my name is Lieutenant Jack Hardy."

"Can I call you Jack?" Hunter asked, awaiting a nod of approval before continuing. "Please call me Hunter."

"Very well, Hunter." he replied.

"I appreciate you guys getting here on such short notice," Hunter said.

"About that, sir, how did you get the Captain of the base to act so quickly?" Hardy asked.

"Well, you call your boss, who in turn calls the President, who rings the Captain personally, things get done pretty quickly," Hunter responded.

"To get the President on such short notice, you must be someone very important," Hardly commented.

"We will get to that, but for now lets go over the plan," Hunter said, leading the men to the chart table. "Please let me know if you see ways to improve on it."

Brad walked up to the bridge just as Hunter was starting his briefing. Rubbing his eyes and barely awake, he proceeded toward the three men.

"So am I invited to this party or will I be sitting this one out?" he asked.

"Brad it is good of you to join us. I am just going over the first part of the plan that we discussed last night. Please hop on in here and make sure I don't forget anything," Hunter replied.

For the next forty-five minutes, they went over the plan, discussing it in intricate detail until everyone understood what was expected of him.

At the end of the discussion, they separated to get ready for the mission.

The Captain of the Cushing called his chief, the operations boss, and the head of the deck department to the bridge to discuss the plan. The Navy SEAL boss went to the stern to brief his men, and Hunter and Brad returned to their stateroom to get their equipment together.

They had agreed to meet on the stern of the ship, and after about twenty minutes they all mustered for one final briefing by Lieutenant Hardy.

"Men you have all been briefed individually, but I want to make sure we are all on the same page. My men, with the help of Mr. Spencer and Mr. Hunter, will be deployed fifteen miles outside the factory. We will travel by our boats until we get within 1,000 yards. We will leave the boats behind a pre-determined rock formation and out of sight. We then will precede under water the rest of the way to our penetration point. Captain Norman of the Coast Guard has agreed to maintain what will appear to be a standard patrol within twenty miles of the factory. He will be our support and exit plan if we need to get out of there in a hurry. Are there any questions?"

After a small pause and no questions he finished his speech.

"Gentlemen, this is not an exercise. This is a live operation, so we need to be on our toes."

Eighteen men, including Hunter and Spencer, separated into three boats. The Lieutenant led the first boat, with Brad and Hunter heading the other two.

The waves were calm, which was uncommon for the Mona Passage but would help them make their rendezvous point within the hour. All the men laid low in the boats so as to not be detected. The SEAL boats were designed to blend visually with the water, making them almost impossible to see from a distance. They approached from the south, which gave them adequate cover as they closed in on their destination.

The team reached the rocks 1,000 yards from the factory and tied the boats up, disguising them for a possible escape if needed. As soon as the boats were secure, the men donned their scuba gear and executed the final preparations for departure.

After they finished getting their equipment together, Spencer and Hunter performed a final check of their weapons and equipment before entering the water. They were a little nervous and wanted to make sure they dotted all their I's and crossed all their T's before continuing.

Led by Hardy, they entered the water. Hunter and Spencer could barely contain their excitement. This was the first operation they had done with the SEALs, and both hoped they could live up to the SEAL reputation. Neither wanted to be the weakest link and the cause of a failed mission.

"Men, give me the OK signal if you are ready," Hardy ordered.

One by one each man did so.

"From here on out, it will be hand signals until we reach the factory," Hardy announced.

Hardy pointed his thumb down, the diver signal to submerge, and slowly sank below the surface.

One by one they gently sank and fell in line, keeping pace behind their leader and swimming in perfect unison toward the factory. It took them around twenty minutes to get to the penetration point, an underwater gate that guarded the factories water drainage pipe. Hardy swam to the side as the group's two specialist in underwater construction approached. They were in charge of getting the gate open.

It took them only a couple of minutes to cut through the locked portion to release the gate. One by one they entered the pipe, which was only big enough to hold a single file line. Hardy swam until he found the drainage area marked on his map. This is where they would prepare for the next phase of the operation.

From the side pocket of his scuba vest, Hardy removed a small camera he had brought for this purpose, and slowly extended the miniature telescope lens, bending it so he could get the full 360-degree view of the room.

After a successful swing around the room, he was satisfied there was no one occupying the space. He slowly lifted the drain gate and softly pushed it to the side, trying to make as little noise as possible.

After taking a deep breath, he handed all his gear except his rifle to one of his men and pulled himself through the small opening.

According to the map, which Hunter had shared with them, this was a room used to house the liquid cooling systems for the plant. Hunter's intelligence had discovered that the maintenance employees only came in twice a day to inspect the equipment. It took a long time to get all the men and equipment into the room. Hunter and Brad were the last two to leave the pipe and both were relieved to be out.

By the time Hunter and Brad surfaced, most of the unit had changed and were waiting for the next evolution of the mission. The plan was to check certain key rooms in the factory that were not defined on the layout, subdue the guards, and then all three teams were to meet at the lab where Hunter and Brad had entered during their first visit.

"OK men, our intelligence estimates there are fifteen guards currently on duty. Since it is Sunday we should not encounter many -- if any -- factory workers. We do not want to kill anyone, just take them down and secure them. You have all been briefed, so from now on we will observe radio silence. Good luck and I will see you all back at the lab," Hardy announced.

"Hunter, are you and Brad ready for this?" he asked pulling them aside. "I have a lot of good men I am putting in your charge."

"We won't let you down," Hunter stated. Brad also gave a convincing nod, which helped to ease Hardy's mind.

"Let's do it. I will lead out first, then Hunter," Hardy said, gathering his equipment.

They left the room slowly, using only hand signals to communicate. Hardy and his men went left. Hardy had the hardest job because his men had to cover the factory floor, which left them exposed and easy to spot from above.

Hunter and Spencer went right and would split at the end of the hall. Even though they were technically in charge, neither wanted to call the shots because of their lack of experience. Instead, the next in charge would lead, and Hunter and Brad would follow, making the decisions if any deviation from the plan occurred.

At the end of the hall, Hunter and Brad took a moment to shake hands for luck before the two teams separated. Hunter's team turned left, heading north before circling around, while Spencer's team went right, heading directly for the lab.

Hunter's team slowly crept through the passage. Two men went forward as the rest covered them. After the hall was clear, two more moved into position as the front two covered them, leaving the remaining two to cover the rear. They did this again and again, moving the last two men up as they marched down the hall.

Hunter's team found their first obstacle at the initial bend in the hallway. The SEAL's leader raised his fist, halting the team and holding position. They could hear two guards heading in their direction in the adjacent passageway. The leader motioned for everyone to silently take position and await the guards.

As the two guards rounded the corner, all five SEALs pounced. Two attacked from behind, striking the men on the head and knocking them out, while two others caught them to minimize the sound of their fall. Along with Hunter, the fifth man positioned himself to cover them in case other guards were about. Within seconds, the guards were bound and gagged. Neither knew what had hit him.

Two SEALs dragged each of the men aside while the leader marked down their position on the map. They did not want them to be left tied up to die, and also, they might be needed later for questioning.

After finishing with the two guards, Hunter's team continued checking room to room. They were about to enter their last room before they convened to their rendezvous point. This room was not marked on the map Hunter had obtained, so they readied themselves for anything.

As they had done with the other rooms, two men slowly approached the door while the others held position to cover if needed.

They were still moving into position when the door flew open, knocking the man behind it onto his back.

In front of them stood a very confused and very large guard. Everyone paused for a second in shock.

Even though the guard was not expecting a man crouched down in front of him, he wasted no time and grabbed the SEAL, putting him in a bear hug. Hunter instantly recognized him as the same guard that he had tangled with on his first visit to the factory.

In the room, four more guards jumped to their feet. The SEALs did the same and the fight commenced.

Hunter took out his expandable baton and struck the large guard on the head, causing him to release the SEAL. However, this did not send the big man to the floor. It just seemed to just make him mad. He turned to Hunter and let out a loud yell as he swung his massive right arm and struck Hunter in the face.

Hunter, dazed, fought back and landed another blow with his baton on the big fellow. Again it seemed to have very little effect as the guard retaliated and threw yet another hard blow to Hunters' head.

Barely conscious, Hunter stumbled back as the large guard charged, grabbed him and squeezed him into a bear hug.

Having dropped the baton, Hunter continued to send punch after punch to the big guy's head. He was fighting a losing battle as the guard tightened his grip. Hunter's world began to go black and he slowly drifted into unconsciousness, wondering if he would awake from his bad dream.

In the room just behind him, the SEALs were showing their superior fighting skills by quickly overpowering the four guards. By the time Hunter was getting knocked out, they had already had them subdued and were beginning to bind and gag them.

Two of the SEALs turned their attention to Hunter. They could see he was about a moment from death so they didn't hold back. The first SEAL swung the butt of his rifle, hitting the large guard in the temple and stunning him enough so that he released his hold on Hunter.

Not giving up, the big man swung his massive arm toward the

closest SEAL, making contact and knocking him to the ground. The second SEAL attacked, but this guy was no lightweight and he struck the SEAL down with another powerful blow, knocking his weapon free.

The large guard quickly scooped up the weapon and headed toward the downed SEAL. As he lifted the weapon into firing position, he felt cold steel pressing against the back of his neck.

"I wouldn't do that if I were you!" came a voice from behind. The guard, knowing he was not going to be quick enough to take the man behind him, dropped the weapon and put his hands on his head.

The SEAL ordered him to drop to his knees while, from the other room, the rest of the SEALs came out to bind and gag the big man.

They dragged him into the break room with the others and continued to secure him while the lead SEAL left to check on Hunter's status.

While he was examining the swelling on his face and checking to see if there were any broken bones, Hunter began to come to.

"Sir, are you all right?" the chief asked as soon as Hunter opened his eyes. "You took a hell of a hit."

"I'll be fine once the pounding in my head stops," Hunter replied.

"How did we do?" he asked as he gingerly touched swelling on his face.

"We have them all in restraints but need to get to the rendezvous point to meet the others," the Chief replied.

"Even the big guy?" Hunter asked, still in pain from their encounter.

"Even him," replied the Chief.

"All right, Chief, just help me up and we are gone," Hunter said as he extended his hand.

The Chief pulled the dazed Hunter to his feet and leaned him against a wall to steady him as they waited while the rest of the SEAL team finished securing the prisoners.

Hunter would have to work through the pain because they had

no time to wait for him to recover. They were already late to meet the others.

It took them only a couple of more minutes to finish the task. They regrouped in the hallway and made haste toward the others with the chief in the lead.

*   *   *

Hardy's team was the first to finish and subdue the guards on their route. They successfully worked their way through the factory floor and held their position outside the main lab awaiting the other teams.

Spencer's men did the same, going from room to room and restraining the guards on their path. Because it was a Sunday, they only found the guards, some cleaning personnel, and one confused scientist. This played into their hands and was one of the reasons they had moved so quickly to get the plan together. That, and the fact that Hunter and Spencer wanted some payback for being shot out of the sky.

Spencer's team was the next to arrive at the rendezvous point.

"How did it go?" Hardy asked the Lieutenant Junior Grade that was the next in charge to Spencer.

"Everything went as planned, sir. We took down four guards and a janitor. No one made a sound."

"Great. Now we wait for Hunter's team. I wonder what is taking him so long?" Hardy whispered quietly, just low enough for Brad and the lieutenant to hear. "His team had the shortest distance to cover and I thought he would have been the first to arrive."

"Would you like me to try and contact him?" Brad asked, reaching for the radio talk button located on his throat.

"No, I want to maintain radio silence just in case," Hardy said. "If he does not arrive in the next fifteen minutes, I will send a team to investigate."

Brad gave a nod and they both hid in wait for the team's arrival.

Fifteen minutes went by with no sign of the last team. Hardy was about to assemble men to go find them when Hunter and his men arrived.

"What happened?" Hardy asked as they approached.

"We got tied up in a fight with a few of the guards," the chief replied.

"Is everything all right?" asked Hardy.

"Yes we stumbled into the lunchroom where five guards were taking a break and had to fight it out cowboy style. We got a few cuts and bruises but they are all tied up and none of us got seriously hurt," the chief replied.

"Is our cover blown?" asked Hardy.

"No, we got them all. It was not the prettiest situation, but we are still a go," replied the chief.

"How about you? That eye does not look so good," Brad remarked as he approached Hunter.

"Thanks for noticing!" Hunter said. "Remember that big guard from the last time we were here?"

"The one that almost killed you?" Brad asked.

"Yes. He surprised us, so I attacked him. He proceeded to use my face as a punching bag."

"That big fellow knocked your man clean out," interjected the chief.

"Thanks, Chief. I could have done without anyone else knowing that," said Hunter.

The banter could have gone on a while longer but Hardy interjected.

"Enough talk. We need to get our game faces on and get into the laboratory," ordered Hardy.

Hardy gave out hand signals to position the men where he wanted them. He then motioned for his code-breaking specialist to gain entry into the lab.

Without hesitation he went to the door and started to work his magic. Brad could tell this man's skills were better than his, because within a few short moments he broke the code and the door unlocked.

Hardy grabbed the handle and held position while the others filed in behind. He turned the handle slowly, trying not to make a sound. As soon as he heard the latch let go, he pushed the door open.

The room's alarm went off with a sound so loud Hardy almost fell back!

Since they did not know what was in the lab and they still wanted the element of surprise, Hardy ordered the first wave of his men through the door to secure the lab. They charged in with their guns raised high. For some reason there was just one guard. The five SEALs easily overpowered him and made sure the room was clear.

With a gun pointed at his temple, the SEAL team bound and gagged the guard and placed him in a corner of the room.

After they were positive everything was secure, they radioed back to let the others know. Hunter and Brad went to investigate while the remaining SEALs stayed outside to make sure no one came up behind them.

As they entered the room where they had copied the files on their first visit, they noticed that the main computer was gone. The room looked like it had been recently vacated.

"I think they cleared this room out a couple of days ago," Hunter stated.

"They must have known we were on to them and moved their operations elsewhere," agreed Spencer.

"We are all clear in here but can one of your guys turn off the alarm?" asked Hunter over his radio to Hardy.

"As soon as you guys clear out, I will have my men reset the system, which should disable the alarm," Hardy answered.

They did as he said and brought the guard with them. After securing the door, the SEAL team reset the keypad and the annoying sound of the alarm disappeared.

"We need to find out what the guards know," Hunter said. "Are your men schooled in the art of interrogation?"

"You are not suggesting we torture these men are you?" asked Hardy.

"No, that is not what I am saying," responded Hunter. "I just think if we talk to each of them individually, we are bound to find one who is willing to tell us something worthwhile."

"I do have two Spanish speaking gentlemen on my staff. They should be able to ask the right questions," replied Hardy.

"Great. Let's leave enough men behind to accomplish that task. I will need myself, Brad, and about five men to infiltrate the main house and see what we can dig up," Hunter said.

"OK, you can have your men, but I am coming with you," Hardy ordered.

"No problem, but we need to get on this right away. There is no telling what that alarm triggered," replied Hunter.

Lieutenant Hardy instructed his men about what would happen next. He then asked for volunteers for the house mission. As expected, all the men raised their hands. After picking the five he thought he would need, he pulled them aside to discuss the game plan.

The others got busy rounding up the guards for interrogation while Hunter, Brad, Hardy, and the five SEALs gathered their equipment for the hike to Bruner's house. It was approximately five miles from the factory, but with a little hustle, they figured, it would take about forty-five minutes.

Hardy took the lead and they began the journey through the woods to the house. Although Hunter and Spencer were in great shape, they were not used to carrying fifty pounds of gear at full speed over rough terrain. They started to fall behind and for a while did not think they could keep up. Brad shot a look at Hunter and without saying anything they both realized they needed to pick up the pace and keep up no matter what. Neither wanted to look weak in front of their new friends.

With time to spare, the SEALs and the exhausted Hunter and Spencer arrived just outside the house. They were on the edge of the forest and far enough away to keep out of sight of any guards.

"Men, we all know what we have to do, so no mistakes," Hardy announced.

"How many guards do you see?" he asked one of his men, who had been looking through a set of binoculars toward the house.

"I can only see two, sir."

"Very well," Hardy said. "I'm sure there are more of them, so we need to be ready for anything. Let's go. Hunter, I need you and Brad to cover the rear."

The first SEAL approached the compound's side gate and went to work on the security system. He had it disabled and the gate opened in under a minute. After gaining access, the next two entered and held a position that would cover the rest of the team while they entered.

The others went past the first two to a position just below the back patio. Hunter and Brad followed, keeping to the rear and trying not to make a sound.

One of the two guards they had spotted earlier was starting to make his rounds of the back yard when the SEALs got into their position. He did not see them and was soon to have the surprise of a lifetime.

"You have the first guard approaching your position," One of the SEALs from the first position announced to Hardy. "He will be right above you in three, two, one."

As he said "one," Hardy and two other SEALs rose up from behind the wall and grabbed the guard, covering his mouth and subduing him before he could make a sound.

Hunter and Brad watched from behind a bush with amazement. The SEALS had not only abducted the man without him making a sound, but also had him tied up and sleeping like a baby.

Although they were impressed, they did not have long to think about it because Hardy was on the move again. This time, he headed toward the back door. Again his man picked the lock and gained entry without a sound and without the alarm going off.

Hunter and Brad remained outside and watched through binoculars while the rest of them traveled from room to room, checking for other guards. Hunter had hoped they would catch Bruner here and stop him once and for all.

It looked unlikely; because the only two people in the house were the guards they had spotted when they arrived. The SEALs easily took the second guard down and placed him in restraints.

"This all seemed too easy," Hunter said. "Only two guards. It was almost like he wanted to keep the appearance that the place was being guarded to lure us in."

"Let's take a look around and see what we can find out," Brad said, getting up and racing into the house.

Hunter followed and the two headed toward Bruner's office. The SEALs had passed it and announced its position when they were making the room-to-room security sweeps.

They arrived at the office and immediately went to the desk. Hunter tugged on every drawer and was surprised to find that they were all locked. Brad pulled out a knife and handed it to Hunter. "Will this help?" he asked with a big smile.

"I think it just might." Hunter replied.

They went through drawer after drawer with no luck.

"There has got to be something we can use. I just know it," said Hunter.

"If it were a snake it would have bit you," Spencer remarked.

"What are you talking about?" asked Hunter.

Brad did not say a word but just pointed to a cell phone and an envelope sitting on the desk. Hunter had been so focused on the drawers he hadn't seen them.

The envelope had "Mr. Hunter" written on the outside. Hunter grabbed it and opened it slowly, half expecting something to attack him or blow up.

It read, "Open the cell phone push the number 2 to talk."

A little surprised, Hunter did as it instructed and put the phone to his ear.

"Hello Mr. Hunter," the voice said when it answered.

"Who is this?" Hunter asked.

"Do you really have to ask that question?" the voice answered with a question.

"Mr. Bruner I presume," Hunter said. "To what do I owe this pleasure?"

"I just thought we should talk, you and I. I suspect you liked the missile I sent your way." Bruner replied. "My main man said he got you, but I figured you would be a little harder to kill."

"I am not easy to get rid of, if that's what you mean," said Hunter.

"I am beginning to figure that out," Bruner continued. "No matter. Soon it will be of no consequence."

"What do you mean?" Hunter asked.

"You will soon see what happens to those who oppose me," Bruner replied.

Hunter paused a minute to take in what he was hearing.

"I have someone you may be interested in hearing from," Bruner said.

There was a short pause before a soft voice spoke into the phone. "Hunter? Is that you?" The female voice said.

"Amy?" Hunter replied.

Before Amy could respond, the phone was taken away from her mouth.

"I wanted you to hear her voice for the last time," said Bruner.

"If you hurt her, I will make it my life's ambition to find you and bring you down!" Hunter said, trying to contain his emotions.

"Her life is in my hands now. I want you to remember that and keep your nose out of my business. If I even think you are continuing your pursuit, Mr. Hunter, I will end her life." Bruner demanded.

Hunter paused, not saying a word, trying to figure out his next move.

"At this point I don't believe you could stop me if you tried, but let's just say she is my insurance policy. As long as you back off, I will let her live," Bruner said.

"So what is it that not even I could stop," asked Hunter, hoping to finally learn what Bruner was up to.

"I hope you don't take me for a fool with questions like that, Mr. Hunter, because make no mistake, I don't take you for one," Bruner said and then hung up the phone.

"I take it the conversation did not go well?" Brad asked.

"They have Amy again and this time I don't know if we can get to her in time," Hunter said.

Chapter 30

Jack Hardy and his SEALs had just finished securing the house when one of his guys from the factory called.

"Sir, I think we found a man you may want to talk to," the SEAL said.

"What does he know?" asked Hardy.

"I am not sure, sir, but he said he overheard something and will only tell it to the person in charge. I think he wants to discuss a bargain."

"Good job just keep him separated until we get there," ordered Hardy.

Hunter and Brad walked into the room as Hardy was hanging up his cell phone.

"I think we may have something, but we need to get back to the factory," Hardy said.

"What is it?" asked Brad.

"I'm not sure. The man only wants to talk to who ever is in charge and can make a deal. I think that would be the two of you," Hardy said. "You should get a move on. It's a long hike."

"Jack, I think we can get there a lot sooner. Just tell your men to open the front gate in fifteen minutes," Hunter said and walked out of the room.

He and Brad headed to the garage and pushed a button that opened one of the garage doors. The light streaming in from the hot

Puerto Rican sun showered down on a shinny red Ferrari 360 Spider convertible. Hunter looked at Brad and without having to say a word walked over to the car and climbed in the driver's seat.

"Are there keys in it?" Brad asked.

"No," Hunter replied with a disappointed look on his face.

"Maybe the key is in this glass key holder," Brad said, walking to the box on the wall. Inside was a key with the Ferrari symbol hanging on a hook. He attempted to open the box, but it was locked.

"Hunter, what kind of trouble could I get in if I broke into a locked box to get the key?" asked Brad.

"Probably less trouble than I am going to get in for borrowing the car," Hunter replied.

Without taking the time to comment on what Hunter had said, Brad grabbed his M-16 and used the butt to smash through the glass on the box.

Brad grabbed the key and threw it to his friend. He had barely climbed into the passenger seat when Hunter hit the accelerator, launching them into the light of day. They left so fast that Hunter almost hit a wall on the other side of the driveway, but true to his style he kept the car under control and headed at high speed toward the factory.

They arrived at the gate in just a few minutes and were stopped by two SEALs dressed in the guards' uniforms, posing as security.

"Nice set of wheels, sir," said one of the SEALs as they pulled up to the factory.

"Thanks, I just borrowed it," replied Hunter.

"Where did you get those fancy uniforms?" Brad asked.

"They were just lying around," one of the SEALs commented.

They opened the gate to let Hunter and Spencer pass, then quickly shut it behind them.

"SEAL Team One, this is SEAL Team Two. The package has arrived," the guard relayed into his radio as Hunter and Brad pulled away.

"Roger that."

Hunter and Brad pulled up to the warehouse and were greeted

by the chief of the remaining SEALs team. He led the two of them to a small room where one of the guards was waiting.

"Do you speak English?" Hunter asked as he entered the room, wanting to waste no time.

"Yes, senor," replied the guard.

"I am told you have some information but want to talk to the guy in charge," Hunter said.

"That is correct, senor," the guard replied. "I am just a guard at the factory and I don't want to go to jail for what my bosses do."

"If you tell me what you know, I will make sure you will be acquitted of all and any charges. You will be able to go back to work without any worries," promised Hunter.

Hunter had no idea of what he could do for this man, but he did not have time to waste. He needed the information.

"OK senor, I will tell you what I know," the guard said. "I overheard Mr. London talking on his phone to someone about how they were going to kill the President because he stood in the way."

"Stood in the way of what?"

"I don't know, senor. I had to leave because if he found me listening he would have fired me."

"Did he say the President of the United States?" Brad chimed in.

"No senor, I only overheard what I said and nothing else," the guard replied.

"Well, at least it is something," Hunter said under his breath before he continued.

"Get this guy something to drink and eat," he said looking toward one of the SEALs.

"Gracias, senor," the guard said as he was escorted out of the room.

"Get that guy's name, social security number, address, and telephone number. Make sure they are accurate and then let him go," Hunter ordered.

"Sir, are you sure about that?" asked the chief.

"Yes, I am a man of my word. Don't worry, chief, I will take the heat for it," replied Hunter.

"What do you think all this means?" Brad asked.

"I don't know, but I think I know a guy who may be able to figure it out," replied Hunter.

"Do you have a phone that I can use to call back to the States?" Hunter asked one of the SEALs.

"We all carry field cell phones just in case our radios fail. I have only used it to contact headquarters so I don't know if it will call the States, but you are welcome to try, sir," replied the SEAL.

Hunter dialed and got through.

"This is Clyde speaking," said the voice on the other end. "What can I do for you?"

"Clyde this is Hunter. I need a favor."

"Hunter, I don't think you ever call me without needing a favor," said Forman. "What can I do for you?"

"I need you to look up all of Oasis and Bruner's dealings in Washington," said Hunter.

"What are you looking for?" asked Forman.

"I don't know, but I think there maybe an attempt on the President's life."

"That sounds like something I should get on right away. Give me a couple of hours and I will give you all the information I can. Where can I reach you?" Clyde asked.

"I don't have a phone so let me call you back in exactly two hours. I have a feeling we may need to get back to Washington as soon as possible. Brad and I are going to head toward the airport," Hunter continued. "Could you contact Marty and get us on the next flight out of San Juan? We can be at the airport in under three hours."

"Will do, talk to you in a couple of hours," Clyde said and hung up the phone.

"You do realize it takes at least three hours to get home from here," Brad said.

"Not for what I have in mind," Hunter replied.

Brad had a good idea of what that would be and just shook his head.

They gathered up their equipment, stuffed it all in the front seat of the Ferrari, and were on their way. Hunter was determined to test his driving skills to the limit. He took off with a speed and determination that few could muster.

They wove in an out of traffic traveling at speeds and performing maneuvers that could only be accomplished with a well-engineered sport machine. Since Hunter was in control he felt at ease, but Brad was not so comfortable riding shotgun.

"Do you think you could slow down a little?" he screamed over the sound of wind whipping by their ears at over one hundred and twenty miles an hour.

"Sorry, buddy, I am having too much fun. Besides how often can you say we are speeding to save the President?" Hunter yelled.

"We don't know if the President is in grave danger," Brad screamed back.

"My philosophy is, why take the chance," replied Hunter.

"Any excuse to go fast!" Brad said in return.

"That's right!" Hunter yelled as he hit the accelerator and turned up the radio.

A trip that would usually take nearly three hours took slightly less than two. They only slowed down to pay the tolls that cluttered the northern east-west highway of Puerto Rico.

Hunter pulled into the hotel driveway with ten minutes to spare before he was supposed to call back Clyde Forman.

"Next time, I am going to drive. I think my nerves are shot," Brad said as he got out of the car.

As soon as they parked, a hotel worker showed up to get their bags. He stopped suddenly when he noticed they were in combat fatigues and almost fainted in fear when he saw two M-16's sitting between Brad's legs.

"It is OK. We're part of the Department of Homeland Security," Brad said, holding out his badge. "We just left a training exercise. We prefer to get our own bags due to the nature of the contents."

"Yes, senor, but you must register your weapons with the hotel manager so he can verify your credentials," the man said.

"No problem. Brad can you take care of it?" Hunter asked. "I need to call Clyde and see what he found out."

"Oh great. I get to stand in the lobby and look like the idiot," Brad complained.

"Senor, I will send the manager up to your room if you like," the man said.

"That would be great," Hunter replied.

Hunter gave the hotel employee the keys to the Ferrari and took his receipt.

"Nice car, senor," the man remarked.

"Thanks. I just picked it up," replied Hunter with a big smile before he headed toward the elevator.

Because of the way they were dressed and the fact that both had M-16's strapped to their backs, they got stares from the hotel guests they passed.

"I wonder if my hair is out of place," Brad said in jest as they entered the elevator.

"It could be, but I'm willing to bet they're staring at that big gun you carry," Hunter said as they boarded the elevator.

"I thought my pants covered that up," replied Brad.

Hunter ignored the comment because he knew where that line of talk could take them. As soon as they were in their room, Hunter headed straight for the phone to see what Clyde had found out.

"What do you have for me?" he barked into the phone.

"No small talk first?" Clyde said.

"No time. Just give me the good stuff."

"All right. Your guy Bruner has a lot of smaller companies that at first seem to be separate entities. But when you dig deeper, they are all linked to the Oasis mother company."

"Any of them in Washington D.C.?" Asked Hunter.

"He has financial companies in downtown D.C., and an import-export business that ships heavy machine equipment mostly out of the Port of Baltimore. He also has a construction business that does a lot of the city roads in and around D.C., and he has a company that owns and manages commercial properties in the District."

"Go back to the import business and construction company," interrupted Hunter. "Does he have any contracts currently under construction on roadways downtown?"

"Let me check," Clyde said before continuing. "They just completed five small repair jobs."

"Where are they located?" asked Hunter.

"On some random streets around the monuments." Clyde answered. "What are you getting at?"

"I need you to cross reference those roads and roads the president may proceed down when he travels by motorcade," Hunter replied.

"Hunter, the President usually flies in by helicopter," replied Forman.

"Normally you are right, but doesn't he travel by motorcade when he addresses Congress?" asked Hunter.

"Let me check," Clyde said.

It only took him a few moments to pull up the information. He was one of the best in the information world and since he had one of the most advanced computer systems around, most information was just a click away. Besides, he had a little bit of moral flexibility when it came to hacking other government computers.

"You are right he does. Get this -- he is addressing Congress today at five," Clyde reported.

"Have you finished cross checking possible routes he may take to get there against recent Oasis construction?" asked Hunter.

"Oh my God, you are not going to believe this. In the last twenty years the President's motorcade has only taken five different routes to that building and all five routes have streets that have been recently fixed by Empire Construction Company. That is the name the company goes under but when I dug further their paper trail shows strong financial ties to Oasis."

"Could you pull up the manifest of any ships that left cargo in Baltimore and cross reference that with the Oasis ships you found?" asked Hunter.

"I am already ahead of you my friend," replied Clyde.

"It says here that only one of our target ships has arrived in the past three months and it off loaded construction equipment and explosives for mining."

"Are there any truck manifests leaving the docks?" asked Hunter.

"It says that four trucks left carrying the equipment en route to Colorado Springs," replied Forman.

"Do you have any record of their arrival?" Hunter asked.

"Give me a minute while I take a look." Clyde pulled up the database of all the possible weigh stations en route to Colorado Springs.

"There is no sign of the trucks passing through any weigh stations," he said into the phone. "This does not 100% mean they did not arrive at their destination. Some of the weigh stations could have been closed during their transit."

"Would you like me to cross-reference which ones where closed during that time?" he asked.

"If you have time but I would bet my next year's pay that they never made it to their original destination," replied Hunter.

"You are not thinking that they buried the explosives in the roads they fixed, are you?" asked Clyde.

"I am not just thinking that, I am believing that is exactly what they did," replied Hunter.

"I am willing to bet that the President's car is vulnerable to an attack from below," he continued.

"Did you get us on a flight?" Hunter asked.

"Yes, you and Brad are on the 12:30 flight leaving Puerto Rico non-stop into Reagan International."

"Great, I need another big favor," Hunter said.

"Is this going to get me into trouble?" asked Clyde.

"No but you will have to do some politicking to pull this off," Hunter said. "I need you to convince Reinquest to stop the President from traveling to his speech."

"Are you saying you want me to ask our boss to request that the President does not go to a speech that most of the United States and a large part of the world are going to be listening to?" asked Clyde.

"That is exactly what I want you to do," Hunter said in a calm smooth tone.

"All right, but I think you are crazy even to suggest it."

"I need a car and driver standing by when we arrive at the airport and clearance for us to bring our weapons on board the plane as well," Hunter continued.

"The car should be no problem but I don't know if I can pull off getting your weapons on the plane. Handguns are one thing, but in this post 9-11 world I don't know if the President's men could get an M-16 on board. At least do me a favor and put it in a bag big enough so passengers won't know," replied Clyde.

Before Hunter could respond to Clyde, he heard a knock on the door.

"Thanks. I have to go. Just do your best. That's all I can ask," Hunter said as he hung up the phone.

He answered the door to find the hotel's manager with a clipboard in his hand.

"Mr. Hunter?" the manager asked.

"Yes. I presume that is the registration form we need to fill out," Hunter said.

"Yes, senor."

"We are going to be checking out in less than an hour. Is all that necessary?"

"Senor, I have filled out most of the form for you. All I need is your government ID number and a copy of your government credentials," replied the Manager.

Just then Brad was getting out of the restroom cleaned and dressed to go.

"Brad!" Hunter said and then continued. "This nice man needs a copy of our government ID's. Could you go with him so he can get them copied?"

"I always get the glamour assignments," replied Brad as he followed the manager out the door.

"Oh cheer up, old buddy. I will buy you a souvenir at the airport," responded Hunter as Brad walked out and shut the door on him.

Chapter 31

Hunter and Brad approached the ticket counter. Both were curious as to how the next few moments were going to play out because of the weapons they had tucked away in their bags. As they approach they both handed their ID's to the lady at the counter for check in.

She pulled up their itinerary and paused for a moment before speaking.

"Mr. Hunter, Mr. Spencer, we have been expecting you," she said.

She entered their information in the computer and picked up the phone.

"Mr. Hunter and Mr. Spencer are here. Could you send over the escort?" she asked into the phone. After she got the answer she was looking for, she hung up and placed her attention back on them.

"Here are your boarding passes. As you will see, you are both booked non-stop to Reagan International. As your office requested, we have bumped you up to first class," she said as she handed them their envelopes.

"Would you gentleman mind stepping over there to await your escort?" she asked, pointing to the end of the counter.

"No ma'am. But what escort are we awaiting?" asked Brad.

"A man from airport security is going to escort the two of you on the plane as requested," she said and then turned to help the next customer.

They did as they were told and stepped aside to await the rendezvous.

"Clyde never ceases to amaze me," Brad said.

"He got us booked in first class and now has some mystery security officer that will probably wisk us through security."

"Don't get too exited until we are on the plane," replied Hunter. "Remember, we have some heavy fire power in these bags, not the kind of equipment airlines take lightly."

"Are you losing your faith in our friend?" asked Brad.

"No. Just being cautious until we are boarded and sitting in our seats," replied Hunter.

It only took a few moments before a man in plain clothes approached them.

"Mr. Hunter and Mr. Spencer I presume?" he asked.

"Yes sir, my name is Hunter." Hunter replied. "And you are?"

"My name is Air Marshal Tack Adams and I will be escorting you and your weapons to Washington," he replied, showing them his credentials and holding out his hand toward Hunter.

"Just call me Hunter," Hunter said while he shook his hand.

"Sure thing Hunter. And that means you are Mr. Spencer?" he said, again holding his hand out in friendship.

"You can just call me Brad," he replied while shaking his hand.

"Brad it is."

"I am curious," Hunter said. "Are you here to escort us on the plane or through security?"

"I am riding all the way to Washington with you." Tack replied.

Hunter and Spencer picked up their bags and they all headed toward the security checkpoint.

"I am lucky you two showed up. I was not slated to go back until tomorrow," Tack stated as they walked.

"Where is your home base?" asked Brad.

"Washington D.C., just like the two of you I am told," he replied.

As they approached the security checkpoint, a man in a TSA uniform walked over to greet them.

"Tack, I just got word you were escorting some big wigs from D.C. through and figured I would come out to meet you," he said.

"Omar, good to see you again," Tack replied.

"This is Hunter and Brad," Tack said.

"Omar is the head of security around here," he continued.

"Well, one of many," Omar replied, trying to be modest.

"Omar, here is the verification letter I was sent," Tack said, holding out the letter. Omar took a moment and read over the letter before responding.

"Gentlemen right this way, please," he said as soon as he finished. He led them around the normal security lines and into the terminal, waving away the few guards who tried to question his motives. Since he was the person in charge, he did not have to give an immediate explanation as to his intentions.

"Enjoy your flight gentlemen. If you need anything, please ask. Tack, let's do lunch when you're back in town." He said before making his leave.

"What was that all about?" asked Spencer.

"You two must have people in high places because this letter, signed by the head of Homeland Security, says under my escort you two can pass without restriction. I think that when he read this he figured you two were very important and should not be bothered with wasted small talk," Tack replied.

"Clyde works fast," Spencer said to Hunter.

"When this is all over I'm going to have to ask him how he pulled this one off," Hunter said.

Tack approached the counter and told the agent who he was and she informed him they would be the first to board.

After a short wait, the gate attendant motioned to Tack. She waited a few minutes for them to walk down the jet way before starting the rest of the boarding.

The three of them found their seats and stowed their bags in one of the overhead compartments. They quickly shut the door to the storage area and asked the flight attendant to make sure it stayed closed and that no other bags be placed in the bin.

For obvious reasons, they did not want anyone else to access their compartment due to the cargo they were carrying. Hunter and Spencer settled into their seats next to each other, with Tack taking the aisle seat across from them.

"One of us needs to be awake at all times to make sure no one messes with your weapons." Tack said. "You boys look pretty tuckered out, so why don't you get some shut eye and I will keep watch."

"You won't get an argument from me," replied Brad as he reached for his blanket and pillow.

"I think I'll take you up on that also," agreed Hunter.

The day's events had worn them out and they were both happy to get some much-deserved rest. If Hunter's hunch was right, they were going to need all the strength they could muster for what would come next.

Chapter 32

They awoke to the sound of the pilot's voice informing them that they would be landing soon at Reagan National Airport. Hunter stretched and looked at his watch.

"I can't believe I slept so long," he said to a groggy Brad Spencer as he wiped the sleep from his eyes.

"We've only had a couple of hours of sleep in the last thirty six hours," Brad replied. "I can't believe we are still going."

"You two were out cold." Tack said. "The flight attendant tried to wake you twice to see if you needed anything."

"Were there any problems during the flight?" asked Hunter.

"I had to fight off a couple of hijackers about an hour ago but other than that everything was smooth," Tack replied.

"Nice sarcasm," Hunter remarked. "I thought you guys were not supposed to joke about that kind of stuff."

"We're not, but sometimes I like to lighten the mood," Tack replied with a sinister smile.

As soon as the Captain turned off the Fasted Seat Belts sign, Hunter, Brad, and Tack were out of their seats and collecting their belongings. It was four o'clock and they did not have much time before the President was supposed to make the journey to visit Congress.

They proceeded straight out of the terminal since they only had carry on luggage.

"Tack do you have a cell phone I could borrow?" asked Hunter as they were walking off the plane.

"Sure, I have my work phone you could use," he replied, handing Hunter his phone. "They need to give you guys a larger budget if you can't even afford company phones."

"Ours fell to the bottom of the ocean two days ago and we have not had an opportunity to get new ones," Brad said, since Hunter was already making a call.

"Office of Domestic Readiness Adam Reinquest speaking," the voice said on the other end.

"Chief, this is Hunter."

"Mr. Hunter. It's great to hear from you. It sounds like you and Brad have had a crazy couple of days."

"Yes, sir, it has been an adventure, one I will have to tell you about sometime," Hunter replied.

"On a more important note, has Clyde informed you of our situation?" Hunter asked.

"He has."

"And the results were?" asked Hunter.

"You're not going to like them," replied Reinquest. "I contacted the Secret Service and they informed me that they needed more to go on than your hunch and a couple of shipping manifests."

"This could mean the life or death of the President," replied Hunter.

"Eric, listen to me. I know your hunches are good but do you think you could be wrong about this one?" He paused before he continued. "If you are wrong you could hurt our credibility, which in turn could directly influence our future as an organization."

"Sir, if I am wrong we take a couple of hits and then we will have to lick our wounds. But if I am right the President is in grave danger."

"Are you willing to risk your future on it?" asked Reinquest.

"Sir, if it means saving the President's life, the answer is yes."

"That's what I needed to hear. I will back you, but we are not going to get the support of Secret Service. So what is your plan?" he asked.

"I don't have a solid one formed just yet. I am going to try and intercept the President before he reaches any of the newly repaired sections. I will call you back as soon as I know more," Hunter said.

"OK, but Hunter, be careful."

"I always am, sir," Hunter said before he ended the call. Next, he dialed Clyde.

"Clyde, this is Hunter. Have you discovered the route the President will take?"

"No, my searches have come up with nothing. I can gain access to the video cameras along the routes. It will be close but I should be able to guide you to the right area," Clyde said. "You need to get going. According to my estimate, you have fifteen more minutes until they leave."

"Thanks. I'll call you back as soon as we are rolling," Hunter said as he hung up the phone.

Hunter stopped at small magazine stand before leaving the airport and picked up a map of downtown.

"Good thinking, but we need to keep moving," Brad said, trying to hurry things along.

They entered the lower level of the airport to find a driver holding a sign with their names on it.

"Mr. Hunter and Mr. Spencer?" The driver said as they approached.

"Yes, sorry we don't have time to get acquainted we need to leave immediately and I am driving," Hunter ordered as they approached.

"Sir, I am the only one that is allowed to drive," the driver said as they walked outside toward the car.

"You're either getting in or staying here, but I am driving," Hunter said as he approached the driver's side of the Lincoln Town Car in front of him.

The driver could tell by the look in Hunter's eyes that there was no point in arguing, so he reluctantly threw him the keys.

Hunter was happy to see that Clyde had gotten them a town car and not a limo, which would have been twice as hard to maneuver through traffic.

"Tack, I am going to need to borrow your phone. Can I get your business card so I can get it back to you?" he asked.

Tack paused for a brief second to contemplate his next move.

"Forget it. I am coming with you in case you need some help," he replied.

Hunter knew things could get hairy. Extra help couldn't hurt, so he nodded in agreement and the four of them jumped into the car.

As soon as all the doors were shut Hunter stomped on the gas.

"Brad, we need to call Clyde and see if there is any update. Also mark all the places on the map that have had construction done in the last six months," Hunter ordered.

Brad did as he was told and called back Clyde.

"The motorcade is on the move," Brad yelled out.

"Which way should I go?" screamed Hunter.

"Just get on the GW Parkway, cross the Potomac, and then go east on Constitution Ave!" Brad yelled. "Clyde is going to update us as we go."

"What do you have?" Brad screamed into the phone at Clyde.

"He said they are taking the most common route down Pennsylvania Avenue." Brad stated in an exited tone.

"OK. Where is the patch of new constructions on that road?" asked Hunter as he weaved in and out of cars at breakneck speed.

"It is at the junction where Constitution Avenue connects to Pennsylvania, so just stay on Constitution and we can intercept them." Brad replied.

"There is going to be a problem with your plan, gentlemen," the Driver remarked.

"And why is that?" Brad asked in a smart tone.

"Because they close down the roads around the Mall, including Constitution Avenue. You're not going to be able to get close to that area until the President gets to the Capitol," the driver answered.

"How do you know all this?" asked Brad.

"I've have been on the airport route for the last five years and I can tell you the President's schedule better than the Secret Service can," he replied.

"Brad, give him the map and the phone," Ordered Hunter.

"What?" they both said at the same time.

"I need you to find me an alternate route to intercept the President," Hunter replied.

"I don't think I can," said the driver.

"Listen, you just said you know this route better than anyone, and I need an expert if we are going to get through this. There are men right now plotting to assassinate our President, so unless you want to witness our President's death, grow a pair and get to work," Hunter snapped.

The driver took a quick moment to let Hunter's words sink in.

"Give me the phone," he said with new confidence.

"Clyde, I am the driver from the car service and in a few moments I am going to need you to let me know what kind of traffic the cameras are showing on the following roads," he said into the phone.

"Mr. Hunter, turn right on Seventeenth Ave. now!" the driver screamed.

Over the sound of the car engine and screeching tires, Hunter could not hear the conversation between Clyde and the driver. He had to drive as fast as he could and hope the driver could keep up with his directions.

"Follow the one way around onto Independence Ave.," the driver ordered.

Hunter did as instructed and again squealed the tires as he made the turn.

"Clyde says Independence is backed up at Fourteenth Street, so take this first left on Fifteenth and an immediate right onto Jefferson Drive," the driver barked.

Hunter maneuvered the car at speeds in excess of 60 miles an hour. He barely kept the car on the road as the rear end swung around onto Jefferson.

"There is traffic ahead! Now what?" Hunter screamed.

"Turn left on Ninth and then right onto Madison Drive!" the driver replied.

"Aren't they both one way in the wrong direction?" Hunter yelled back.

"Yes they are, but Clyde tells me they are the only roads that are open. Besides, no one can turn down them because they are closed at the other end."

Hunter did as he was told.

"Clyde just informed me that they are almost to the junction point. The only way to cut them off is to take your next left on Fourth and drive on the sidewalk that parallels Pennsylvania," the driver stated.

"What's your plan once we get there?" he asked.

"You better just buckle up," Tack said to him as he tightened his own belt.

Hunter rounded onto Fourth Street without slowing. He let off the accelerator just slightly as he reached the corner of Pennsylvania and Fourth Street, then turned left and hopped the curb onto the sidewalk. He didn't want to hit anyone who may have been standing by.

They only had to travel about 25 yards after they turned to intercept, which would hopefully work to their advantage because they wouldn't have much time before the Secret Service would be on them.

Hunter floored the accelerator as soon as he rounded the corner and was in sight of the President's car.

With a closing speed of 80 miles per hour, the Secret Service had only a few seconds to react to this new threat. Without delay, the lead Secret Service car turned toward them.

Hunter swerved to the left to avoid the collision. But he was a moment too late, and the lead car slammed into the back of his car, knocking the rear end around.

To Hunter's surprise, the impact did not alter their course drastically. He immediately smashed the accelerator and continued on his mission. He got just enough momentum before slamming into the right front side of the President's limo to knock it to the left and out of the danger zone. It eventually came to rest in the middle of the street.

The explosion that was intended for the President went off as Hunter's town car was clearing the danger area. The force was so great it lifted the back end of the car, flipping the entire car twice before it came to a rest upside down about 20 yards from the explosion.

The next car in the motorcade rushed to the President's aid while the remaining two cars headed toward the overturned car.

As soon as they arrived on the scene, five Secret Service agents jumped from each of the two black SUVs and, with weapons drawn headed toward them.

Two agents laid down on the ground in front of the car while two more laid down on each side making sure all four men were covered.

"Secret Service! Let me see your hands!" one of the agents yelled out.

Both Hunter and Brad, even in their shaken state, had their IDs ready and threw them out of the car as they showed their hands.

"What did you just throw at us?" the agent yelled back.

"Our identification. We are with the Office for Domestic Readiness," Brad yelled back.

The agent slowly reached down and grabbed the ID closest to him.

"What the hell is going on?" the agent barked.

"Get us out of here and we will explain it all," Hunter said.

By this time two ambulances had arrived on the scene. The agents ordered one to assist the President and the other to help out with the overturned car.

"Hang in there. We have paramedics on their way," one of the agents yelled to them.

"Is everyone OK?" Hunter asked his amigos.

"I am all right, but I am going to need a drink after this," Tack replied.

"I am fine but I may have to find another job," reported the driver.

Other than a few bruises, I'm fine. Nothing a little R&R couldn't fix," replied Brad.

For the next few moments, they all waited patiently in silence for the paramedics to arrive.

"Is anyone seriously injured?" one of the paramedics asked, breaking the silence as he leaned down to get a look at them.

"We are all fine. We just want to get the hell out of here," replied Brad.

It took the paramedics about twenty minutes to get all four of them out of the car and do an initial assessment of health.

The paramedics told them they were all lucky to have only minor scrapes and bruises. They could thank the big Lincoln Town Car for their fortune. A smaller car would have folded under the pressure and most likely killed them all.

The head paramedic was just finishing Hunter and Spencer's evaluation when they were approached by what looked to be a senior Secret Service agent.

"Are you two Mr. Hunter and Mr. Spencer from the ODR?" he said as he approached.

"Yes, my name is Brad Spencer and this is the notorious Eric Hunter." Brad replied.

"My name is John Ross and I am in charge of the President's detail," the man stated.

"What can we do for you, sir?" Hunter asked.

"I just got off the phone with your boss Adam Reinquest and wanted to be the first to express my gratitude on the behalf of the President for saving his life," he replied, holding out his hand.

"Please let the President know it is our honor," Hunter said as he shook the man's hand.

"How the hell did you put it all together?" Ross said as he continued on and shook Brad's hand.

"It was easy. We just used great detective skill," Brad said with a smile.

"We will have to come up to the White House and tell you all about it sometime," chimed in Hunter.

"I don't think I will have to wait that long," Ross replied.

"This is Special Agent Jenkins and I have assigned him to record your statement," Ross continued.

"Sorry to disappoint you, but we don't have time right now. We still have one more life to save," Hunter said. "Excuse me I need to make a call."

"Does he ever stop?" asked Ross.

"Not until the job is through," Brad replied before taking his leave.

Brad rejoined Hunter as he was finishing a call with Clyde Forman.

"What was that all about?" asked Brad.

"I will have to explain on the way. We need to hitch a ride back to the airport," he replied.

"What?" Brad asked.

"I had Clyde also searching all his sources to find the whereabouts of Bruner." replied Hunter.

"What did he find out?"

"The FBI ran a check and it looks like our friend Mr. Bruner passed through customs in the British Virgin Islands and boarded his yacht the Serpentine earlier today. The FBI has a small team standing by to watch the vessel, but not a large enough team to take action. They are going to monitor the situation until back-up arrives," Hunter said.

"I am assuming we are part of the back-up team?"

"You got it," replied Hunter.

"Can they verify if Amy is on board and still alive?" Brad asked.

"They could not give a definite ID, but they did see a woman board the boat and from what they saw it did not appear to be her will to do so," Hunter said.

"Well what are we waiting for? We need to get down there," Spencer said.

They walked toward the ambulance, where Tack was resting.

"Tack, it was good to meet you, I hope this was not too thrilling of a time," Hunter said as he shook hands good-bye.

"It has been an adventure. Here is my card, please look me up when you get back," he said.

"I will do that," Hunter replied.

"Brad it has been something," Tack said, shaking his hand.

"Yes it has. You take care," replied Brad.

"Where is our new friend?" Brad asked.

"I think the Secret Service is still asking him questions," replied Tack.

"Please give him our thanks and apologize for wrecking his car," Brad said.

"I will, but where are you two going in such a hurry?" asked Tack.

"We still have one more mission to complete," Brad replied as they left.

Chapter 33

Hunter and Brad landed at the Tortola Airport in the British Virgin Islands just as the sun was setting on the water. The peacefulness of the evening was an illusion, nothing like how they expected their night would play out. Neither wanted to expect the worst, but they knew if they did not get to Amy soon, the worst was exactly what would happen.

After a smooth touchdown, they gathered their belongings and exited the plane to find two gentlemen in dark suits awaiting their arrival.

"I am Special Agent John Garmin and this is Special Agent Ronald Eagle. We have been given the privilege of assisting you this evening," Agent Garmin announced displaying his identification as they approached.

"My name is Eric Hunter and this is Brad Spencer," Hunter replied.

"What do you mean privilege?" Brad asked.

"Well sir, a couple of hours ago we got a direct call from the President of the United States informing us that you had saved his life and were on your way here," Garmin replied. "I consider it a privilege to work with anyone who put their lives on the line to protect our great nation and its President."

"We have been told to assist you in any way possible. I think you will be pleased with what we have set up," Special Agent Eagle added.

"Well, what do we have at our disposal?" asked Hunter.

"Mr. Hunter, we have groups standing by to take the ship. We have the Coast Guard Cutter Cushing hiding just north of this island. Lying low and out of sight, we have FBI, DEA, and Coast Guard helicopters. The Coast Guard helicopter has a man with a fifty-caliber sniper rifle and rescue capabilities if needed. The DEA helicopter is equipped with six small missiles on each side, totaling twelve. It is able to stay at a distance but still hit its target up to five miles away. The FBI helicopter is equipped with a fifty-caliber mounted machine gun and can act as our central point of contact in the sky, coordinating the other two so they can act as one during the incursion," Agent Eagle replied.

"That sounds like a lot of assets. Do we have anyone to assist us in boarding the boat?" Hunter asked.

"Yes sir, we have three black ops FBI teams standing by with SEAL style inflatable rafts just a mile from the boat," he replied. "We also have an additional private helicopter waiting to take you to the team when you are ready."

"I guess all we need is a place to change," Brad remarked in his normal jovial manner.

"Yes sir, in the hanger there is a side room that should suit your needs," Agent Garmin replied, keeping his professional tone.

Agent Garmin lead them to a nearby hanger that housed the private helicopter in which they would be traveling. After they entered the hanger Hunter and Brad Spencer excused themselves and headed for the room to change.

"We have a lot of fire power at our disposal," Brad said as they entered the room.

"I know. Kind of makes you feel important or something," Hunter replied.

"Well don't let it get to your head. I am sure we will be back to our normal status soon," Brad replied with a nervous laugh as he thought about what was ahead.

Fifteen minutes later, they emerged dressed all in black, with faces painted so they would blend in with the night. They each donned nine-millimeter side arms with an extra forty-five rounds in their gun belts. Around their shoulders they each strapped an M-16 with an extra long magazine. A knife in each boot completed their outfits.

"Is everything in order gentlemen?" Agent Eagle asked as they approached.

"We're ready!" Brad replied for the both of them.

"Good. If you two would be so kind to hop in the chopper, we will get started."

They boarded in the hanger so nobody would spot them in their special ops gear. No one knew how many spies the Oasis Company had at their disposal. If the wrong person spotted them there cover could be blown, severely limiting their element of surprise and hindering the mission.

Hunter and Brad jumped into the helicopter and secured their doors. The agents gave a final check to make sure everything was in order.

As soon as they were satisfied, they turned out the lights and opened the hanger door. A ground crew member fired up a small machine that pulled the helicopter out and into takeoff position.

The pilot immediately fired the engines and started the takeoff checklist. They knew the longer they lingered on the ground the more likely they could be spotted, so as soon as the pilot received clearance from the tower they took off.

Neither Hunter nor Brad spoke a word as they flew. Less than ten minutes into the flight, the pilot signaled that they had arrived. As planned the helicopter, hovered less than ten feet above the ground over the predetermined spot. Hunter and Brad opened their doors and jumped out, utilizing the tuck and roll as they hit the ground.

Without delay the helicopter took off and headed back toward the airport.

"Brad are you all right?" Hunter asked as he came to his feet.

"I think my M-16 may have gone up my butt, but other than that I am perfect," he replied.

"Good. We have a hike ahead of us and not much time to get there, so we need to get moving," Hunter remarked.

Brad gave a nod and they started walking. They traveled down a small hill for about half a mile before reaching a clearing that was exposed to the sea.

"Do you see anyone?" Hunter asked.

"No. Are you sure we're in the right location?" Brad asked as they continued walking.

Before he could answer, two men dressed all in black jumped from behind a tree with weapons drawn.

"Mr. Hunter and Mr. Spencer?" one of the men asked.

Even though they were expecting to meet the FBI agents, the two men severely startled them. It took Hunter and Brad a couple of seconds to gather their composure before answering.

"Yes my name is Brad Spencer and this is Eric Hunter," Brad replied, his voice cracking a little.

"We have been expecting you. I'm Agent Ryan and this is Agent Thompson. We don't have time to waste. The teams are standing by, hiding just a few yards away. If you will follow me, I will take you there," the FBI officer replied.

They gave a nod and followed the agents toward the boats. As they arrived, the agents motioned for Hunter and Brad to join them in their boat, which they did without hesitation.

The three boats, powered by quiet high-speed electric motors, took off toward their target. Due to the swiftness of their boats and the short distance they traveled, it took only a few minutes to get there.

As they approached, the boats slowed and advanced on Bruner's yacht from astern. Utilizing the darkness of night, they kept their landing in the shadows as to not be detected.

As the first boat touched the back of the yacht, the four agents aboard climbed onto the swim platform of Bruner's boat. Two of the four men positioned themselves behind the transom wall as backup, while the other two climbed over the stern rail.

The agents were just turning around when out of the darkness flashes of light followed by loud bullet sounds rang out. They took repeated shots to the chest and head, which knocked them to the deck, killing them instantly!

All hell broke loose as the other two agents opened fire, shooting blindly into the darkness. One of the agents on Hunter's boat radioed for backup while the driver moved the boat away from the stern.

The third boat ran up onto the swim platform and four more agents jumped out and opened fire. The two men responsible for the other agent's death were no match for all that firepower. The agents sank bullet after bullet into them. Both fell to the deck in puddles of blood.

The victory was short lived as two more men appeared from above and began to open fire. They shot one of the agents in the arm and another in the shoulder before they could take cover.

They were pinned down and the men on the roof appeared to have the upper hand. Hunter and Brad's boat swung around from the side to draw their fire. They were hoping to give the agents on the stern enough time to take cover at another location.

Their plan worked as both men turned their attention toward Hunter's boat, giving the FBI agents time to board and get out of harm's way.

However, they quickly realized they had no place to run. The men on the roof raised their weapons and readied them to fire.

They had to abandon ship. All jumped in and swam down as fast as their bodies would allow. The men on the roof opened fire, sending a spread of bullets onto the boat and into the surrounding water.

The bullets shredded the inflatable boat and continued to penetrate the water, passing just inches away from the men below.

After they had emptied their magazines, the two men on the roof reloaded and halted further firing in order to check for survivors. Their plan was to finish off anyone who surfaced.

Underwater, Hunter motioned for the two agents to swim to the stern as he and Brad headed toward the bow. He figured it would give them an increased chance of survival if they split up.

The agents nodded in agreement and did as instructed. Brad and Hunter made it to the bow and planned to stay down as long as their lungs would allow. Unfortunately this plan did not last long. After a few moments, Brad gave the sign that he could hold his breath no more and the two of them made for the surface as quietly as possible.

They broke the surface, took a breath, and were about to dive down when from above they heard one of the men yell out.

"I see them over here! Open fire!"

Shots rang out! They did the all-too-human thing and put their hands between themselves and the bullets while making a crazy scrunched up face, which of course would accomplish nothing.

To their surprise, the bullet fire was not toward them. They looked up to see both men on the roof take direct hits and fall from their position into the water just a few feet away.

They looked at each other with relief. Before either of them could comment on the situation, the Coast Guard Cutter Cushing rounded the bow of Bruner's boat with its fifty-caliber machine guns blazing. Its bullets pierced the side of the yacht, shattering glass and creating havoc on the vessel.

Three more helicopters appeared on the horizon and assisted the Cutter in the fight, clearing the deck of any one that got in their way.

Hunter and Brad took a few moments to regain their composure before saying a word.

"I can't believe we are still alive," Brad said, breaking the silence.

"I know, buddy, it feels good to still be here!" Hunter replied.

"What's our next step?" Brad asked.

"Do you think you have enough left in you to climb up the anchor line?" Hunter replied.

"I can if you can," Brad responded.

With that, they swam over to the anchor line with a new determination. Adrenaline from their near death experience flowed through their veins and it did not take them long to make the climb. They stayed as low as possible as they pulled themselves over the rail.

"We need to stay low and crawl toward the ladder that leads to the bridge," Hunter whispered.

Brad nodded in agreement, and with Hunter in the lead they made their way toward the bridge ladder. As soon as they arrived, Brad got up and took a cover position with his weapon, while he signaled for Hunter to start the climb.

Hunter reached the top and gave cover while Brad climbed up to join him.

Once they were together, Hunter signaled that he was going to enter first and that Brad should directly follow. Hunter pushed the bridge door open and, his weapon drawn, rushed the bridge with Brad close behind.

"No one move! Get your hands up!" Hunter screamed as they entered.

Two men and a young lady instantly put their hands in the air.

"Who are you and what are you doing aboard?" Hunter screamed at the man he assumed was in charge.

"My name is Jose Gevalia and I am the captain aboard this vessel. The man and woman to my right are part of the ship's crew. There are four other crewmembers locked in a stateroom below where we just came from," he said nervously.

"We have taken out four men with weapons. How many others are aboard?" Hunter asked, only partially believing the captain's story.

"There should be four more men with guns roaming the deck. Mr. Bruner, Kyle London, and a lady I don't know just went below," he replied.

"He still has Amy!" Brad said, looking at Hunter.

Hunter gave a nod of agreement before continuing.

"Where were they headed?" Hunter demanded.

"I am not positive. As I said, we were just pulled out of the locked stateroom. Before he departed, he said he would kill us if we left the bridge. I think he meant for us to slow you down," he replied.

Hunter was about to ask another question when four agents busted through the opposite door, yelling for everyone to put their hands up.

They instantly noticed that the crew had already been subdued. Agent Ryan lowered his weapon and headed over to talk to Hunter and Brad Spencer while the other three agents gave cover.

"It looks like you beat us here. I wasn't sure if you two made it, but I am very glade to see you alive," Agent Ryan announced as he approached.

"How did you get here?" he continued.

"Anchor line," Brad replied, keeping the prisoners covered.

"The crew said that the two main guys are down below, but there are four more men with guns about," Hunter said.

"I wouldn't worry about those other men. Either the Cutter or one of the other assets made Swiss cheese out of them when they did their sweeps with the fifty-caliber," Ryan said.

"We need to go after Amy. Can you guys process these three and get the other four crew that are locked up below?" Hunter asked.

"Sure," Ryan responded.

Since the agents had everything under control, Hunter and Brad went below. They continued down a passageway toward a room where they heard the sound of hydraulic pumps working.

Hunter motioned for Brad to take a cover position. He centered himself, took a deep breath, and kicked in the door. The door swung open and they entered a room where the back was open to the sea.

Hunter peered up and his eyes locked with Bruner's. With London at the helm, Bruner quickly jumped into one of the ship's inflatable boats and prepared to take off.

Hunter launched into motion with Brad close behind! He did not want to fire, fearing he may strike Amy, who was lying on the deck close by.

Seeing this, Kyle London lifted his sidearm and opened fire. For self-preservation, they had no choice but to take cover and shield themselves from the onslaught.

London, knowing the fire would only keep them at bay for a few moments, pushed down the throttle, propelling their vessel out to sea.

Brad and Hunter immediately got up and ran toward them. As

they moved toward the stern, they eyed an inflatable boat from the Coast Guard Cutter coming their way.

"We need to use your boat," Hunter yelled.

At first, the driver approached slowly and did not answer.

"Anything for you two," Chief James yelled back after recognizing who they were.

"Good to see you again, chief," Brad said as he came into sight.

"We need you to follow the boat that just left," he continued.

"I was just about to recall my men and do just that," he replied.

"Let's go!" Hunter screamed as they boarded.

The chief did not hesitate; he hit the gas and turned toward the target. Hunter and Brad held tight as the Coast Guard boat crashed through the small chop of waves. Since the Coast Guard boat was much faster it only took a few minutes for them to close the gap.

When they got within ten yards, Hunter motioned for the chief to pull alongside. Because it was night and the sound of their engine was loud, London and Bruner had not yet noticed they were being pursued.

The Chief gave his vessel full power and pulled alongside, striking into their boat and catching them off guard.

The jolt knocked Bruner off his seat and managed to stun London for a brief second. Hunter took this opportunity and jumped aboard feet first, giving London a blow to the head as he landed.

Brad grabbed Bruner and was about to jump over when Kyle London yanked the wheel hard to the right. The force sent Hunter to his back and threw Bruner and Brad out of the boat.

London, worried more about self-preservation than his boss, gunned the small boat and took off. He pulled out his firearm and lifted it into position. Hunter jumped up and, with his left hand, grabbed the gun. With his right he landed a punch across London's face.

The punch stunned London and caused him to drop his weapon. He quickly recovered and returned a hit, landing it across Hunter's right cheek. A stunned Hunter knew instantly that he was dealing with someone who knew how to fight.

London landed two more punches, knocking Hunter onto his

back and laying him out next to Amy, who was still tied up on the bow of the boat.

Hunter looked over at Amy lying there helpless. The thought of her tied up made his blood boil and gave him new vitality. He jumped up and landed a blow to London's mid section, doubling him over in pain. He then landed two more punches to the back of his head, knocking him to the deck. Still in a rage, he pulled out his sidearm and struck him twice more on the back of the neck, rendering him unconscious.

Hunter quickly grabbed the throttle and pulled it back, slowing the small boat to a crawl. He could not stand the continued sight of Amy tied up and immediately went to her aid.

He cut the ropes that bound her and then slowly pulled away the duct tape that had been placed across her mouth. He gathered her up in his arms and embraced her as tight as he could.

"You are alright now," he whispered in her ear as he held her.

She could not muster the strength to talk but buried her head in Hunter's chest and held on with all her strength.

Hunter would have held her in his arms forever, but he knew that Kyle London could come to at any moment.

"I need to let you go for a moment to tie up our prisoner," Hunter said, looking softly into her eyes.

Even though she did not want to let go, she nodded and released her hold.

As Hunter turned around to deal with his prisoner, he felt a sharp pain shoot down through his spine as London landed a blow to the back of his neck.

Hunter reached for his gun and turned around, only to receive another blow to the face. The hit made him drop his weapon and knocked him back on top of Amy.

London was sick of these games and leaned down to find his sidearm. Finding his weapon, London instantly turned and aimed it toward Hunter.

Hunter was on his knees and about to get up.

"Not so fast, Mr. Hunter," Kyle said.

Hunter stopped cold!

"Any last words before I end your miserable life?" London asked, taunting him.

Hunter did not say a word. He knew he only had a fraction of a second to act before it was too late.

"As you wish," London said as he squeezed the trigger.

Hunter jumped up as the shot rang out. The bullet hit him in the shoulder but did little to slow him down. He buried his boot knife into London's stomach before falling back in pain, holding his left arm.

Although the knife had severely wounded London, he managed to keep possession of his gun. With all his might, he reached down and slowly pulled the knife from his stomach.

Overhead, the Coast Guard helicopter and the FBI helicopter descended, bearing down on them with their spotlights.

"This is the FBI! Drop your weapon!" came from the helicopter.

London was not going to go that easily. He lifted his gun and fired repetitively at the helicopters, knocking out one of their spotlights and causing both to turn away.

He had only a couple of rounds left in his gun and turned his attention toward finishing off what he started.

He raised his arm and two shots rang out!

London immediately grabbed his chest, paused suspended for a second, and with a look of disbelief fell overboard.

Hunter patted his chest to check for wounds before looking up. The Coast Guard's small boat approached with Brad on the front, still pointing his M-16.

"Is everyone all right?" the chief asked as they came alongside.

Hunter nodded as he reached down and grabbed Amy with his good arm. She again buried her head in his chest, determined never to let go.

As he held Amy tight, Hunter looked toward Brad, who stood on the bow of the Coast Guard boat. Next to him was the bound body of David Bruner.

"Is he still alive?" Hunter asked.

"Yes, but I have a feeling when the President gets done with him he will wish he was not," replied Brad.

Hunter nodded as he held Amy tight, guarding her from the ocean spray that shot up from the helicopters

"It's over. The nightmare is over," Hunter whispered into her ear as he held her tight.

Chapter 34

Six months later.

"I'm going for another drink. Who else would like a drink from below?" Brad asked, heading toward the companionway of Hunter's freshly finished sailboat.

"I will take one. Don Q and Coke please," Hunter replied from the helm as he steered.

"How about you, babe?" he asked Amy.

"Sure, why not?" she replied laying back and sunning herself.

"Me too," chimed in Brad's date.

"Four Don Q and Cokes coming up," Brad announced as he headed below.

"Brad tells me you two were responsible for saving the President's life." Brad's date remarked.

"Brad likes to exaggerate things from time to time, but we did have a hand in it," Hunter replied, smiling at Amy.

"It must be exciting having a job like that," she continued.

"I don't know. I think a day like today with the sails up and the wind blowing in our hair is a great way to live," Hunter said, and then turned away distracted by something he heard on the radio.

"Brad, turn up the volume!" he yelled down.

"What is it?" Amy asked.

"I think I heard them say something about the Bruner trial," Hunter replied.

"Just in. David Bruner, the head of the Oasis Company, has been sentenced to four consecutive life sentences in prison without a chance of parole," the radio announced. "Bruner was involved with a plot to assassinate the President of the United States over his stance on stem cell research. Agents from the FBI and the Office of Domestic Readiness, also known as the ODR, apprehended him six months ago on his boat just south of Tortola in the British Virgin Islands. We will have more late breaking news when we come back."

"I think I have heard enough," Hunter said. "How about some music?"

Amy and Brad's date nodded in agreement. Brad went below to turn the station to a cheerier one and returned with a tray of drinks.

They raised their glasses and toasted to their success, sitting back to enjoy their sail as Jimmy Buffet played over the radio.

The End